# When All the Birds Sing

*Also by Suzie Peace Pybus*

The Truth About Irene
Paint the Walls Red

# *When All the Birds Sing*

## SUZIE PEACE PYBUS

Echidna Ink

I acknowledge and pay my respects to
the Moomairremener people of Unghanyenna country
on whose unceded land this book was written.

# Contents

For Joseph and Rose

And for Doug who helps God grow things

the woods would be very silent if no birds sang there
except those that sang best

—Henry Van Dyke

# Prologue

I was nine when I met Harry Fernley and twelve when they took him away. The years between were an Eden of woodsmoke, birdsong and adventure.

Jon's urging me again—get that story written down, Lily love. So I try, but my mind goes straight back to the day he was taken, even though it wasn't the beginning.

I'd heard my mother's end of a phone conversation. The words 'arrest' and 'Harry' swam in my head for a moment before I tore out the back door and grabbed my bicycle. I took off, legs pumping, down the main road and slid around the corner into Murphy's Lane. I came to a halt before Harry's gate with the back tyre skidding in the gravel as the police car appeared between the pine trees on either side of the gate posts. I wobbled and slipped off the seat.

Constable Munnings in the driver's seat glanced at me and looked away—no amiable wave and grin. Instead, he riveted his eyes on the road and turned sharp into the lane. That's when I caught a glimpse of Harry's face through the rear window.

Dad found me later, folded over with grief on Harry's front step, my cheek pressed into the cold concrete.

Perhaps my mind swings back there because it was where my childhood Eden ended and my venture into the hazy world of grown-ups began. I was about to discover that people can appear shiny and good on the outside, but be rotten underneath. If you've ever flipped the glossy-feathered body of a dead bird over with a stick and found a mess of maggots underneath, you'll know what I mean.

So, if I'm to record this story, I must go back to the start so the middle makes sense. Back to 1975, when I'm nine years old, all arms and legs and itching for adventure. The day I pack a pile of tomatoes into an old string bag to take over to Nan's. Getting ready, though I didn't know it yet, to meet Harry.

# 1

# Meeting Harry

My heart flapped like a bird inside my ribcage. I was going out by myself today—all the way to Nan's in Helmut Road.

Mum and I were in the backyard—me squatting on the damp grass picking tomatoes and Mum hanging her whites on the Hills Hoist. Helen Reddy's *Leave Me Alone* played from a transistor radio perched on the kitchen window sill and Mum was swaying her hips to the music.

'It's nearly full,' I said as I plucked another tomato and added it to a string bag Mum had lined with a piece of old sheet.

'There's a nice one.' Mum wandered over to the garden bed and leaned forward to twist a ripe fruit off the vine. 'That'll do. We don't want too many jars of pickles coming back.' She placed the tomato in the bag, stood and wiped her hands on her apron.

I was ready to go! I hoisted the bag up and swung it gently from side to side.

'Can you manage that?' she asked.

'Uh-huh. I've got good muscles.'

Mum jerked her head towards the gate. 'Off you go then. And don't go rushing off from Nan's too soon.'

She didn't need to tell me twice. I skipped to the gate and lifted the latch.

'Stay on the footpath,' Mum said.

'Orright.'

'*Alright.*'

'All. Right.' I slipped through and let the gate click shut.

'Stay at least fifteen minutes and mind your Ps and Qs.'

'Yep.'

'*Yes.*'

'Yesss.'

'Ta-ta, then.' Mum headed towards the back door, waving her hand over her shoulder.

My heart skittered a bit as I left the security of the fence. This was a new thing, me being allowed out without a grown-up. I looked back once, saw that Mum had turned to watch me from the corner of the house, and scooted off.

I was Little Red Riding Hood, taking a bag of goodies to my grandmother. Instead of a red hood, I wore the typical garb of a Tasmanian country girl—a cotton dress (a tad too short and bearing a few neatly sewn patches), long white socks and a pair of gum boots. Mum had tamed my dark, unruly hair into two plaits that swung from the top of my head.

Clutching the string bag, I trudged along the footpath, glancing at each house, eager to see if any neighbours were observing me going past on my important mission. At the first corner, I looked left along the road where old Molly Crouch leaned on her front gate, pushing her false teeth out and in. We waved to each other. Crossing the road, I spied Mrs Hammond, the minister's wife, pulling weeds from the church garden with her head wrapped in a brown scarf. She looked up.

'Good morning, Lily. Lovely day.'

'Morning,' I said breathlessly as I hurried past.

From the corner of my eye, I glimpsed her struggling to her feet as she called, 'Where are you off to?' I pretended not to hear and scurried down the street, my gumboots slapping the backs of my calves. If I stopped, I'd have to hang about for her to pick some flowers for Nan. Or worse, she'd disappear inside for a jar of jam, and come out talking ten-to-the-dozen. I'd have to wait for her to run out of words and hand over the jar before I could continue on my way. I hummed loudly as I clopped up the road so she would think I couldn't hear her over my own voice.

I passed the few weatherboard houses at the edge of town where the footpath ran out, sticking close to the explosion of eucalypts by the roadside. Finally, I reached Murphy's Lane, a narrow gravel road flanked on either side by rows of poplars that ran down to the Murphy's cattle farm. At the end was a public walking track which wound its way past the farmhouse, down an embankment and onto the beach.

Nan lived in Helmut Road, off to the right of Murphy's Lane. I planned to take the tomatoes to Nan's first before heading to the beach. From there, if the tide was out far enough, I could wander back into town along the shore and take the short-cut to my friend, Kylie's house.

But as I turned into Murphy's Lane, I saw a man. He carried a fishing rod and a rucksack and loped along the road ahead of me, his big leather boots crunching on the gravel. His dark hair was wild and curly and lifted in the wind, and he had the longest legs I'd ever seen which put me in mind of the Murphy's horse and almost made me giggle.

I scuttled along behind him, my gumboots clapping against my much shorter legs. His strides were long and purposeful, yet he seemed to glide like a sailboat surrendered into the wind, as if he had all the time in the world to get where he was going.

The man glanced briefly over his shoulder, saw me and slowed his pace. My breath caught in my throat. I'd been so engrossed in watching him, I'd passed the turnoff to Helmut Road and Nan's house where I was supposed to go. The obvious solution was, of course, to turn around and go back, but my nine-year-old pride wouldn't allow it. (How foolish I'd look!) So I kept walking.

The man's pace slowed further still, as if he intended me to catch him up. I looked behind me to see if anyone was about but we were alone. If I kept walking there were only two places I could be going, Murphy's farm or the beach, and I would need to decide which by the time I reached the end of the lane. I slowed down. As I did so, the man stopped and I had no choice but to meet him.

As I drew alongside him he began walking again, slower steps this time to match my childlike pace. The bird in my chest was frantic now, hitting itself up against my ribs. I glanced sideways up into his face and judged him to be roughly my parents' age, though there was an air of something wild about him I couldn't have put into words at the time.

I was surprised when he nodded his head towards me in greeting like the men in those old movies Mum watched on Saturday afternoons. I'm sure he would have tipped his hat if he'd had one.

Then he smiled.

Oh! —*what* a smile the man had! Straight white teeth and a good-natured grin. But his eyes were the thing—they were blue and bright and crinkled up in a kindly way as if I were his dearest friend and he was glad to see me.

'Fine day,' he said. His voice was warm like cocoa.

I no longer cared where I went at the end of the road. He could have been the Pied Piper and led me to a cave and I would have gone in.

'I'm Harry Fernley,' he said, as we approached Murphy's Farm.

I gazed into his face and my lips turned up in a smile of their own accord. 'I'm Lily Craig.'

'Where are you off to, Lily?'

I shrugged, grinned stupidly and almost tripped on a rock.

He glanced at my bag. 'What have you got there?'

I lifted the bag and held it open as I clopped along so he could see the tomatoes inside. 'Me and Mum grew 'em.'

'They're beauties. Do you need to take them somewhere?'

'Nuh, not yet.'

He nodded once and looked ahead. 'Maybe you've got time to come fishing, then?'

You might think the bird in my chest would be doing cartwheels by now but, for some reason, its beating slowed and came to rest. We made our way down the road and passed the farm together, Harry matching his steps to mine despite the length of his legs, so it was no effort to walk beside him.

There was a place where I usually clambered down to the beach, using footholds which had been moulded into the bank over the years. However, we passed it and continued along a narrow track through the bushes until we came to an outcrop of sandstone boulders. We slipped through a gap between them and stepped down onto a platform of rock. Harry took my bag and went first, holding out his hand to help me down the last part. His hand was warm and huge, and my small one disappeared into it. We made our way to the edge of the platform and climbed down into a hollow in the cliff, the floor of which jutted out over the water.

'Tide's about right for fish,' Harry said, and pointed downward.

I peered out over the lip of the shelf where the water lapped and gurgled in and out of crevices in the cliff face.

I knew this place already. It was not only a fishing spot but also a good place for picnicking on sunny days. My friends and I called it the Hollow. From its vantage point, we'd spent many hours munching sandwiches and watching the comings and goings of the folks of Crayfish Cove (population four-hundred, give or take) through Kylie's binoculars. We would take turns looking out over the bay to the jetty and the fishing boats, the tiny figures bent on industry amongst the cray pots or sitting at the end of the pier with fishing rods. At the road end of the jetty, intermittent bushes struggled up a bank to the main road where more tiny townsfolk trickled in and out of the general store and post office.

Beneath the town, a cliff encircled the rocky shore with a face of orange sandstone, the exact colour of honeycomb, cut out in a semi-circle as if a giant had waded in and taken a bite out of it.

Decades later, Jon and I still go down there with bags of picnic food slung on our backs like we did as children (only we've swapped the jam sandwiches for cheese and crackers.) When I lean against the rock with the sun on my face, salt tang in the air and the seagulls skirling overhead, I can close my eyes and slip back in time to that day with Harry. I feel the fishing rod gripped in my small hand and sense Harry leaning towards me, showing me how to hold it just right, how to recognise the tug of the fish and the slow way to reel it in.

I can hear his voice, soft and low so as not to disturb the fish, yarning about the ocean and the tides and how the waves crashing in from the sea had hollowed out the cove which gave the town—Crayfish Cove—its name. And I see those two flapping silver fish we reeled in, the name of which I no longer remember.

I wanted to stay there, to catch more fish, to spend more time with my new friend. But Harry said, 'That'll do for today,' and I helped him pack up his gear.

We made our way back up Murphy's Lane and stopped at Helmut Road.

'Your folks, are they Brian and June Craig?' Harry asked.

'Yep,' I said.

He took a faded tea towel from his rucksack, reached into the bag he'd been carrying the freshly-caught fish in and lifted one out. He wrapped it in the towel and placed it carefully in my string bag, on top of the tomatoes.

'Take this home to your mother. Tell her you caught it yourself, and say Harry Fernley sends his regards.'

'Do you know my mum?'

His sun-browned face crinkled in a grin. 'I went to school with her.'

'Oh,' I said, surprised.

Harry pointed to a gate further up on the other side of the road, mostly hidden by pine trees.

'That's my place through there. You can come over anytime. Follow the gravel drive a-ways and you'll see the house around the corner.'

I couldn't believe my ears. Did he just invite me to his house?

'Some of the kids are coming over tomorrow arvo. You know Jacky Hix?'

I nodded.

'He does a bit of gardening for me. And the Pevensie kids are getting a treehouse up at the back of mine.'

'Orright,' I said, still nodding.

'Well, hooroo.' He turned away.

'Hooroo,' I replied.

I stood at the corner of Murphy's Lane and Helmut Road, gazing after Harry as he ambled back up the road. I didn't move until he turned into his gate and disappeared between the pine trees.

At Nan's, I spent fifteen minutes (I watched the clock) drinking milk and munching Milk Arrowroot biscuits. Nan wrinkled her nose and muttered as she rubbed at the tomatoes in a sink of water, making the point that fish and tomatoes shouldn't go into the same bag together.

'Harry ought to know better. You can tell him that from me.'

I tried to find out more about him from Nan but her answers to my questions were short, sharp and not particularly enlightening. When I left her house, instead of visiting my friend Kylie, I hurried straight home and burst through the back door into the kitchen, shouting, 'Mum!'

Mum stood at the stove, one hand on her hip, the other stirring something in a saucepan. She looked up and frowned. 'Boots off. Come on, boot's *off*.'

I hurriedly kicked off my gumboots and pushed them across the kitchen floor and out the door with my foot.

'You're back early.'

'Look what I caught!' I thrust my hand into the string bag and pulled the towel away from the fish. I held the bag open for her to see inside. 'A fish. Harry Fern-tree helped me catch it. He said to say his regards.'

'Harry Fernley?'

'Yep, Fernley.'

Mum paused her stirring and peered into the bag. Her face visibly softened. 'Now, where did you see Harry?'

'On Murphy's Lane. He took me fishing.' Quickly, I added, 'I went to Nan's like you said and gave her the tomatoes.'

'Fishing? Where?'

'At the Hollow.'

'How about that. Pop it in the fridge then—not like that, on a plate.' She turned back to the stove and continued to stir. 'So, tell me about this fishing.'

I stood next to her and told her all about my afternoon with Harry while she nodded and asked questions in the cunning way she had of pulling information out of you.

'So can I go tomorrow?' I asked, when I got to the part about Harry's invitation.

'Jacky Hix and the Pevensies, you say?'

'Yep.'

'*Yes.*'

'Yesss.'

'We'll see.'

I sighed and slumped into a seat at the table. I could do nothing more but wait, hoping *we'll see* turned into a *yes*. Mum wasn't one to be rushed.

Mum took the pot off the stove and set it on a trivet on the bench. She pulled out the custard-covered spoon and handed it to me. 'Here, lick that. Careful, it's hot.'

I took the spoon and blew on the custard.

'It's only a bit after three, do you want to visit Kylie for a while?'

'Um...nah. I'll see her at church tomorrow.'

Visiting Kylie and playing on her new ping-pong table had seemed an exciting prospect only that morning. Now, it had lost its appeal.

All I could think about was Harry.

2

# A never-ending morning

SUNDAY MORNING DRAGGED ITS feet. I flew out of bed, dressed in a hurry and swallowed my Weet-Bix down so quickly it was a wonder it didn't get stuck. I had the idea that my haste would speed everything else up—church, home again, lunch—so I could head off to Harry's. But being ready before everyone else and having to wait for them had the opposite effect and time seemed to stand still just to provoke me.

Mum had said I could go! She knew Harry from her school days, she said, though he was a few years younger. About thirty, she reckoned. She'd telephoned both Jacky Hix's and the Pevensie children's mothers the night before, after which it was agreed I could go over for an hour after lunch. She even defrosted a cake from the freezer for me to take as thanks for the fish.

Now, what to do with all this *time*. I followed my usual routine of hanging about my parents' bedroom after breakfast, watching Mum brush her hair up into a bouffant. As she sprayed it into place, I slipped up behind her and breathed in the exotic scent of Gossamer Invisible Net.

Mum had hair the colour of lemons and cheeks like peonies, and Dad was always saying he didn't know how he got to marry the most beautiful woman in Crayfish Cove. Mum would tut and say, 'Don't be silly,' but I could tell she was pleased. I took after Dad with my thick, dark hair and eyebrows and brooding look, and I prayed often that God would turn my hair blonde and make me even half as pretty as Mum.

Dad was sick of me moaning, 'Are you ready yet?' and sent me outside to wait with my sister. Maudie, two years older than me, was already spinning on the front lawn—turning her body round and round with her blonde pony-tail swinging out and her skirt floating about her waist. I glanced up and down the street for Wayne Bottle on his dragster, in case I needed to coax her inside before he rode past yelling, 'Spaz!'

Finally, Dad called out, 'Everyone in the Mini,' as he and Mum came out of the house, and we squeezed into the little car in our Sunday best.

In the seventies, the church was the hub of the local community and a popular meeting place for locals, whether they believed in God or not. The building was modern for its time—long, low and brick, resembling a giant shoebox with windows. It had a large shed attached at the road end and at the other, a separate dwelling we called the manse where the minister and his family lived. The carpark was the pride of the town, having been sealed with funds raised by a zillion bake sales.

Kylie was waiting for me in the foyer when we arrived. We headed straight for the auditorium and our favoured seats in the furthest corner of the back pew where we had a good view of everything.

'I have to tell you something,' I said, as we slid onto the wooden seat amidst the smell of old hymn books and furniture polish. 'I met a really nice man yesterday.'

'Who?' Kylie blew her fringe out of her eyes and it flopped back again.

'Harry Fernley. Have you heard of him?'

'Nuh.' She leaned over to pull her wrinkled socks back up to her knees.

'We went to the Hollow together, just me and him, and we caught some fish. I'm going to visit him today. See if your mum will let you come.'

Kylie screwed up her nose. 'I can't, we're going to Pop's. Anyway, why didn't you come to my house yesterday?'

'I was too tired after fishing with Harry.'

Kylie sniffed and turned away. I felt a slight pang of remorse when I realised I had offended her, but not enough to quell my sense of self-importance. I had a new friend and he was a grown-up. Not even Kylie—who had nearly everything a kid could want—had that.

Mum gave me a wave as she and Dad headed towards their seat while Maudie came over to give Kylie and me a hymn book each. Kylie gave my sister such a warm smile, I forgave her disinterest in my fishing expedition.

The room filled with local folk in their Sunday finest, greeting each other and shuffling into seats. Old Molly Crouch stood hunched in the aisle in a stretched cardigan and brown stockings rumpled at her ankles, handing out peppermints to a swarm of children. Eight-year-old Jacky Hix—Molly's favourite—came away with a handful.

'I'll go,' Kylie said, jumping up to join the crowd around Molly. When she came back, she dropped two sweets into my hand and said, 'She called me "dear". I think she forgot my name again.'

Finally, Mr Hammond tapped the microphone and welcomed the congregation. We all stood and opened our hymn books as Mrs Hammond pumped the pedals on the organ, and *How Great Thou Art* echoed around the auditorium.

As we sang, I glanced along the length of the back wall at the other kids who shared the row with us. Still munching his peppermints, Jacky Hix stood about half-way along with his older brother, Maurice. Jacky had a face full of freckles and two large front teeth that put me in mind of a rabbit. As he chewed, he jigged up and down as if he couldn't keep still. I watched him with a new interest. How long had he been gardening for Harry, I wondered? How did he even know Harry? Had Harry seen him walking down the road one day and introduced himself, like he did with me? If Jacky had ever mentioned Harry at school, I didn't remember hearing it. However, Jacky was a boy and a year younger, so not someone I took much notice of.

The Pevensie children stood in a pew further towards the front with their mother, Nora. Harry said those kids were building a treehouse at the back of his place. How did that even happen without me knowing about it?

The music stopped and we sat down. Our Sunday school teacher was away so we were given colouring-in pages and pencils to occupy ourselves. When the minister, Mr Hammond, began to speak, I tuned out and coloured absent-mindedly, disappearing into my daydreams. What would Harry's place look like? How wonderful if the treehouse had rooms and furniture like the one in my favourite book, The Magic Faraway Tree.

I looked up and studied the backs of the heads of the Pevensie children—Bobby, Aileen, Curly, little Sarah and the rest. There were eight of them altogether, sitting up straight and quiet. Did they all go to Harry's, or only some of them? Did he help them with the treehouse? Did he smile at them and ask them questions about themselves like he did with me? I pursed my lips. Well, I went fishing with Harry all by myself. Maybe none of them had done that. I returned to my colouring. By this afternoon, I would be one of those children who'd been to Harry's place and knew what his house looked like.

I was drawing spots on a balloon when Kylie jabbed me in the ribs with her elbow. I looked up to find her sucking in her lips and hunching her shoulders, obviously trying not to laugh. She jerked her head towards the front of the room where the minister was pacing the platform and waving his arms about, his voice steadily rising. Kylie snorted, slapped her hand over her mouth and snorted again. From the seat in front of us, Glenda Hill turned and shooshed her.

One of the boys on our row hissed, 'Here he goes' as Mr Hammond's voice rose to a crescendo. As we watched, he suddenly grabbed the sides of the pulpit with his enormous hands and stared out at the congregation, his face all red like an underdone roast.

'And what about YOU?' His voice thundered across the auditorium.

He closed his mouth and the room grew silent. Even the children held their breath, except Kylie who dropped her head with her shoulders shaking, and hid her face in the front of her jumper.

Now that the minister had the attention of the room, he cast his eyes across his audience, drawing out the pause. Then, in a quiet voice, he said, 'Can *you* count yourself among the righteous?'

The congregation sang with gusto after that, with *Joy is the Flag Flown High* fairly lifting the roof off.

Afterwards, as the adults cut up cream cakes and sipped tea, I hung about my parents, pestering them to leave until Mum grew tired of me and told me to go and find Maudie. We finally made it past Mr Hammond who was pumping hands at the door. I heard Kylie's mother's voice behind us, gushing, 'What a wonderful sermon, Walter!' and I pictured Kylie rolling her eyes.

I couldn't say what we had for lunch that day, except it would have been a roast complete with all the trimmings—typical Sunday fare—and Mum would have put it in the oven at a low heat in the morning so it would be ready when we arrived home from church. I doubt I could have told anyone five minutes later what I'd eaten, my mind was so preoccupied.

At last, I set off for Harry's carrying a basket containing a cream cake set on a paper plate, and wearing my second-best dress. (Mum made me take off my good Sunday one.) I slipped through the gate holding fast to my basket, waved to Mum and hurried down the road.

I was Little Red Riding Hood once more, carrying my goody basket, except this time I wasn't going to my grandmother's. Who could Harry be in the story—the woodcutter? I was taking a cake to the woodcutter to thank him for saving my grandmother from the big, bad wolf. I began to skip, corrected myself and slowed to a walk, in case anyone was watching.

Trotting down Murphy's Lane, I slowed as I approached Harry's gate which was old, rusted and wedged permanently open. Weeds and grass grew through the wire and scraggly pine branches hung over the wooden gate posts.

I peered past the gate and into the gravelly track that served as Harry's driveway. But the trees were so thick, and the way so shadowy and dark, I couldn't see a thing.

# 3

# Billy tea and a hankering for cake

I ventured through Harry's gate and found myself walking into a veritable forest. It was impossible to see where one tree ended and another began. I stood for a moment, breathing in the mingled scents of pine and eucalyptus and gazing up into a canopy of branches. Continuing on, I passed an oak tree which stood at a bend in the track. As I turned the corner, there before me was a large, flat space and what I came to know as Harry's place.

First, a wooden fence enclosed a good-sized garden bursting with tall, lush corn stalks. Next to this, a wooden cottage with a tin roof, chimney and concrete steps leading up to the door. A few old chairs and odds and ends scattered about the front of the house. A ute, a stack of firewood under a lean-to, a couple of young trees protected by wire at their base and some fruit trees. Past the cottage, the trees were thick on one side and on the other was a glimpse of the sea and a view up into the hills.

I jumped as a kookaburra cackled above me. At the same moment, a movement from the garden caught my eye—a flash of brown amongst the corn plants, then gone. I stood motionless, breathing quickly. The plants shuddered, there was another flash and a *whoop*, and Jacky Hix appeared, bare-chested and brown. Harry emerged, flinging his arm around Jacky's neck and gripping him in a throttle-hold. Jacky shrieked and Harry dropped him, both disappearing into the corn stalks. A moment later, they were up again, twisting about like wild animals.

I tightened my grip on the basket handle and watched. I was no stranger to this male-bonding thing called wrestling. I'd seen my cousins and Uncle Bert doing it—rolling on the ground, squirming about and sitting on each other. When my cousins were little, Uncle Bert would lift them up in the air by their feet and let them dangle while they squealed.

Jacky flew at Harry and they gripped each other—big man and wild boy—before disappearing again, hooting.

I glanced down at my second-best dress with the pink tulip pattern and my black buckled shoes and frilly socks. Oh, why hadn't I worn my jeans and boots? And what had possessed me to insist on carrying Mum's cream sponge in a white wicker basket?

'Lily!' Harry had emerged from the corn and stood waving over the fence. 'Come on over.'

As he turned away to say something to Jacky and no one was watching me, I slipped closer to the bushes by the side of the driveway and shoved the embarrassing wicker basket into the middle of them. I gave it a swift kick to ensure it was completely hidden in the foliage and scooted forward with my hands empty.

As I approached, Harry came through the garden gate with Jacky bounding after him. He turned to Jacky and said, 'Mate, put your shirt on when ladies are present.'

Jacky retorted, 'She ain't no lady,' but he yanked a T-shirt off the fence and pulled it over his head.

Harry shook his head at Jacky and smiled at me. I couldn't help grinning back.

'Well, this is my place.' Harry held out his arm, indicating for me to go up the steps into his house, and he and Jacky followed behind. 'Jacky and I were just saying we should put the billy on. Wait here a sec' and I'll get the things.'

As Harry disappeared through a door into another room, Jacky said, 'He's gonna make billy tea on the fire.'

I turned to look at the fireplace at the other end of the room, which I'd spied as we came in.

Jacky said, 'Not there. Outside,' and leapt back out the front door, leaving me to look around.

The house had a damp, smoky smell. The fireplace at the far end of the room, blackened from much use, was swept and piled neatly with fresh logs. It was framed by bookcases either side, set into the wall, the shelves filled with random paraphernalia—a row of small stones, a few ornaments—and set around it was a couch and two armchairs, covered in a faded floral fabric. At the end where I was standing, the kitchen ran along the wall and consisted of a narrow bench, it's laminate peeling up in places, a sink, a stove and a small fridge. Above the sink, a shelf caught my eye for its incongruity. Made from a single piece of curved wood which put me in mind of a wave, it held an orange shell as big as my hand and a framed photograph of an elderly couple.

Harry entered the room carrying a wooden packing box. 'Here we go. Want to have billy tea with us, Lily?'

I nodded. 'I'm allowed to stay for an hour.'

'Perfect.' He waited for me to exit the house and followed behind. He set the box on the ground and asked, 'Have you had billy tea before?'

'Nuh,' I said.

'You're in for a treat, then.'

Jacky trudged over, carrying an armload of logs. After setting them on the ground, he sat on one of the old chairs which I now saw were arranged around a fire pit—a hole dug into the ground and lined with blackened rocks. A metal structure stood over the pit, its legs embedded into the earth. It looked a bit like a tiny swing frame. I sat next to Jacky on a chrome chair with a cracked vinyl seat that made a puffing sound under my weight. Harry took newspaper and sticks from the box and stuffed them into the pit with a few logs.

'I'll get the water.' Jacky leapt from his seat, grabbed a tin can and took it into the house. He came back carrying the dripping can carefully by its thin handle. Harry helped him latch the handle over a hook on top of the metal frame so the can dangled over the logs. Harry lit a match to the newspaper and blew on the flames until they fanned out and the sticks caught fire.

'There, that won't take long,' he said. He jabbed at the logs with a metal poker until sparks shot out with a crackle and the wood began to burn.

We looked up at the sound of children's voices and two of the Pevensie children ran around the corner of Harry's shed. I must have looked surprised because Harry grinned at me and said, 'There's a shortcut through the scrub from the Pevensie's place.'

They skipped over to the fire and slapped themselves down on two of the seats as if they'd been doing it forever. I couldn't help feeling irritated that these children had been coming here without me knowing about it and I hadn't even met Harry until yesterday.

'Do you all know each other?' Harry asked, and we nodded. I knew them from school and church on Sundays, though not well. Curly was Jacky's age and Sarah was a tiny girl of about six. Both were very blonde and Curly's head was entirely covered in soft curls like a cherub. No one used his real name. I don't believe any of us knew it.

'Where are the rest of you?' Harry asked.

'They'll be down soon,' Curly said.

'Have a look in there,' Harry said, jerking his head in the direction of the shed.

'Did you fix it?' Curly asked as he jumped off his seat. Without waiting for an answer, he dashed over to Harry's shed with Jacky following close behind. They yanked the door open and a few seconds later came out wheeling a billy cart.

'Thanks Harry!' Curly called.

'No worries, mate. It just needed a new bolt in the axle. Should be good to go.'

Sarah, glancing up at me from under her fringe, invited me to have a look at the cart and we joined the boys, leaving Harry to tend the fire.

The billy cart was an ingenious invention of nailed together pieces of wood, an apple-box, a rope and four spoked wheels—planned and put together by the Pevensie children. Curly wriggled into the apple-box seat, Jacky pushed him from behind and they trundled away behind the fruit trees. I watched them take turns doing a circuit around the fruit trees until Harry called out that the water was boiled, and we all ran back to the fire pit.

Wearing an oven glove, Harry took down the billy can and poured in some tea leaves while we crowded round and watched.

Harry told us to stand back as he swung the billy can (without a lid) in a big circle using his whole arm. Round and round he swung it, four or five times, and I couldn't believe how the tea didn't spill out. For the second time that afternoon, Harry answered my stunned expression with a grin. 'Science,' he said. 'Ask your teacher about it.'

By the time we helped him bring down cups, spoons, sugar and milk from the house, the tea was ready. He poured us all half a cup and we filled up the rest with milk and added sugar. For the next half hour we sat around the fire on the old chairs, sipping tea and getting covered in smoke from the fire. When Jacky asked Harry if he had any cake left, Harry apologised and said he'd eaten it all.

'Jacky's mum makes the best seed cake,' he explained to me. 'Trouble is I can't resist it.'

I felt my cheeks heat up as I thought of the basket I'd kicked into the bushes near Harry's gate. We could have been eating the cake *my* mum had made.

'Are you alright, Lily?' Harry asked. 'Is the tea too hot?'

'No, it's nice.'

And it *was* nice. Despite my regret over the cream cake, I don't think I've ever tasted a more delicious cup of tea than the one I drank that day.

When we finished, we helped take the tea things back to the kitchen and tidy up. Harry reminded me my hour was nearly up and I'd need to start heading home. Disappointment weighed heavy in my belly and must have shown on my face, as Harry smiled, patted me briefly on the head and said, 'You can come back any time. Come and have a look at the treehouse before you go.'

We circled the fruit trees and came to a large pine with a rope ladder hanging from one of its branches. I watched as Jacky held the ladder and Curly climbed up. Then Harry held it for Jacky. It was probably a good thing my time was up, as there was no way I was going to climb a tree in my second-best dress and buckle shoes.

'You coming up, Lily?' Jacky called.

'Lily has to go home now,' Harry said. 'You can show her next time.'

I reluctantly said my goodbyes and turned to go. Harry offered to walk me to the gate but I said, 'I'm alright,' as I thought about the basket in the bushes.

As I skipped towards the fruit trees, a loud whooping started up as a hoard of Pevensie children crashed through the scrub and headed towards the treehouse. Once more, I felt left out, as if a wonderful adventure had been going on without me. I was determined that from that moment on, I would be part of the adventure too.

I ran up to Harry's driveway, looked behind me to make sure no one was watching and dove into the bushes to retrieve the basket. Once I was around the corner, out of sight of the house, I stopped and took the cake on its paper plate out of the basket. I broke a piece off with my fingers and stuck it in my mouth so I'd be able to tell Mum truthfully what it tasted like (and hope she didn't ask any awkward questions.) I shook the rest of the cake into a tangle of bushes, shoved the plate back into the basket and hurried through the gate.

Turning into Murphy's Lane, I was startled by someone coming towards me. We both stopped momentarily to stare at each other.

'Hello, Lily.' It was twelve-year-old Jonathan Abbot.

I said hello back and we both resumed walking. As we passed each other, I looked over my shoulder to see him going through Harry's gate. So, Jonathan Abbot knew Harry too? As I turned my eyes back to the road, I felt something slip down my chin. Wiping my face with the back of my hand I discovered a big blob of cream. My cheeks burned with embarrassment.

Jon swears he doesn't remember me having cream on my face that day. He just wants to know whether my heart skipped a beat as I passed him, to which I roll my eyes and remind him that I was only nine years old.

I rushed home and took the wicker basket straight into the kitchen. Mum turned to me, but before she could open her mouth, I blurted, 'I had great fun. Harry made us billy tea and showed me the treehouse. The cake was yummy. Can I change my clothes now?'

I scooted into my bedroom before she could utter a word, pulled off my second-best dress and shoved it into a drawer. Next time I visited Harry, I'd be wearing jeans and sandshoes, and I'd show them all the right way to shimmy up a rope ladder into a tree.

# 4

# The story of a long-legged man

THE FOLLOWING WEEK, I unwittingly began writing in the first journal that would later be taken away and read by the police. The journal was in the form of a shiny new exercise book I found on my school desk. Miss Aubrey had left one on the top of every student's desk with *Journal* written on the front in Cord Cursive. I ran my hand across the cover, opened it and dipped my head down to smell the new pages.

'What are you doing?' Kylie said, beside me.

'Nothing.' I snapped my head back up.

Kylie screwed up her nose at her own book and whined, 'She's gonna make us do more writing.'

'Yeah.' I did my best to look disheartened, but inside, my creative spirit was dancing.

At the front of the room, Miss Aubrey leaned back against the edge of her desk, facing the class. She clapped her hands together, clasped them to her chest and smiled as if her spirit was dancing too.

'In front of you is your new journal for creative writing. We'll be doing some more work on characterisation, and writing some stories and poems.'

I sucked in my breath and felt my whole body expand. Kylie groaned.

'It could be fun,' I whispered, but Kylie rolled her eyes and leaned her head in her hand.

'Let's begin with a simple exercise,' the teacher said. 'Think of someone who is significant in your life. You could choose a family member, a friend or neighbour. Write four sentences about your person, each sentence describing something about them.'

On the blackboard, she wrote an example:

**Marion is my friend.**
**She lives next door in a brick house.**
**She has white hair.**
**She likes to cook.**

We listened to her instructions and took up our pencils. I ignored Kylie's huffing and went straight to work.

**Harry is my friend.**
**He lives in a wooden house.**
**He has brown hair.**

Brown hair? Surely I could think of something more interesting about Harry's appearance. His hair is curly?... His hands are big?... I cast my mind back to the first time I'd seen him on Murphy's Lane, taking long strides down towards the farm, and grinned as I wrote:

**He has long legs.**

Now, what does Harry like to do? He makes billy tea, fixes things for kids and helps them make a treehouse in his yard. Again, my mind turned instead to our first meeting, when it was just the two of us, and I finished with:

**He likes fishing.**

I leaned back in my chair and chewed the end of my pencil as I waited for the rest of the class to catch up. Miss Aubrey had squatted down at the front desks where the younger students sat, our class being a combined grade three/four. She tilted her head towards Dot and Minnie-May, smiling and nodding as she explained something, and even from behind I could see how those girls hung on her every word. Our teacher had a smile that made you want to do your best work, just so she'd smile at you again. As Miss Aubrey stood and moved away, Dot and Minnie-May grinned at each other and began scribbling furiously in their journals.

I watched the teacher speak quietly to Jacky Hix next, whose back was bent over and rigid in concentration, like a tight spring longing to snap open. He'd be first out the door to the playground when the bell rang.

Finally, a shuffle sounded through the room as the last of the students finished the exercise and stretched in their seats. By the time Miss Aubrey gave us the next instruction, I had chewed a chunk off the end of my pencil.

'Now, expand on what you've written and make your descriptions more interesting. Read over each sentence and write a new one, adding something extra about the person you've chosen.'

On the blackboard she wrote:

**Marion is my next-door neighbour.**
**She lives in a brick house with a rose garden.**
**Her hair is white like cotton wool.**
**She bakes biscuits and invites me over for tea.**

'See how I've included myself in the last sentence? See if you can include yourself somewhere in your description. Perhaps write about something you do together.'

I was so engrossed in the exercise, I barely noticed Kylie groaning beside me.

**Harry is my new friend.**
**He lives in a white wooden cotage in Murphy's Lane.**

What else could I add to the part about Harry's long legs? Again, I pictured the day we met, and the two of us walking down the road together. I added:

**He has long legs but he walks slowly so I can catch**
**up.**

Miss Aubrey moved around the classroom to check our progress, leaving a lemony scent in her wake. She stopped at my desk and looked down at my book.

'Good work, Lily,' she said.

I glanced up at her and back at my work. 'That bit's silly,' I said as I picked up my eraser and began rubbing out the third sentence.

'No, leave it.' Miss Aubrey placed her finger on the words I had partly rubbed out. 'I like what you've written here— "he walks slowly so I can catch up." It tells me something important about your friend Harry.' She smiled and added, 'Just check the spelling of cottage,' before moving on to the next student.

I consulted my dictionary and fixed my mistake, then rubbed out the third line altogether and rewrote it neatly. I thought some more, chewing on the end of my mangled pencil. Something we do together...?

Then I added the last sentence:

**He taught me how to fish.**

# 5

# Yarning with the ravens

I'm THIRTY YEARS OLD as I write this story. Jon encourages me with mugs of tea, frequent kisses and iced biscuits from the bakery as I sit at the patio table wading through my childhood journals. I search for the significant moments and loop them together like beads in a necklace—jewels, pearls, rocks, shadows—the shape of it leading to tragedy.

My entries reveal that my immersion into Harry's world was as swift as I remember it. One moment I had not heard of him, and the next, I was a regular adventurer at his place on Murphy's Lane. The very week after my first visit, I was invited to an impromptu birthday party for Jacky at Harry's place.

Jacky bounded up to me at church to tell me about it and I begged Mum and Dad to let me go. After consulting Jacky's parents and those of the Pevensie children, they gave me the okay to walk down in the afternoon. Kylie pleaded with her mother to allow her to go too, but her mother wouldn't budge.

'Pop's coming over especially to see you this afternoon,' she said.

'But I can see Pop anytime,' Kylie whined.

Her mother's voice hardened. 'I said no.' Then she peered thoughtfully at me for a moment and said, 'Lily, you could come to our place instead if you like. Kylie hasn't shown you the table-tennis table yet.'

I opened my mouth but couldn't find any words. There was no way I was missing out on Jacky's birthday at Harry's, but I didn't want to hurt anyone's feelings either.

Kylie's mum sighed and said, 'It's alright, I can see you want to go. There'll be other children there, won't there?'

'The Pevensies are going,' I said. I didn't know who else would be there.

'That's good.' She frowned and bit her bottom lip. I waited, thinking she was going to say something more about the party but instead, she said she had to catch up with Mrs Hammond and left us. Before she went, she said, 'Come over after school sometime this week, Lily.'

As her mother disappeared into the crowd, Kylie shrugged her shoulders. 'I knew she wouldn't let me go.'

'Why not?'

'She doesn't like Harry.'

'How do you know?'

'I told her about you going fishing with him and I could just tell.'

Anger fizzled inside me. 'Well, that's stupid. He's nice and anyway, we're building a treehouse in his yard.'

Kylie looked hurt. 'When have you been doing that? You didn't tell me.'

'The other kids started it,' I admitted, 'but I'm going to help. I can tell you all about it at school.'

Already, I had identified myself with the children who held an intimate knowledge of Harry Fernley. I was determined to know him in the same way, or even better. To become his special friend.

That afternoon after lunch, I'd just hung up my Sunday dress and changed into trousers and sandshoes to go to Harry's, when Mum's best friend, Fiona, turned up with her daughter.

Fiona would often drive over from Durrunby (the next town over) on the weekends to visit Mum, and I would be expected to entertain Dot. Normally, I didn't mind, but this day I minded very much! I knew there was no way I could wriggle my way out of spending the afternoon with Dot so I slunk into the kitchen, casting what I hoped was a thunderous expression in my mother's direction.

Mum was setting the kettle on the stove. She looked up, ignored my obvious bad temper and told me Fiona had given permission for Dot to go with me to Harry's.

I turned to the large, smiling woman at the kitchen table who greeted me warmly and my fury dissipated. I couldn't help liking Fiona. Dot stood beside her mother's chair looking at me with a hopeful expression.

I forced a smile and said, 'Come on then, I'm going now.'

We said our goodbyes and headed outside, me leading and Dot trotting after me. I opened the gate for her and we headed down the footpath together. I carried a Tupperware container of Anzac biscuits Mum had made and there was no way these were going to end up in the bushes like the cake.

As we passed the church, Dot slowed down to peer across at the manse. Despite my hurry to get to Harry's, I slowed too and looked for a sign of Dot's friend, Minnie-May who lived at the manse with the Hammonds. Her parents had died the previous year in a road accident and, as Mrs Hammond was her aunt, the Hammonds had taken her in.

At school, we were all intrigued by the orphaned red-head with round, downy cheeks like peaches and a habit of sucking her thumb. We forgave her the thumb-sucking (for the reason of her being an orphan) and treated her with, if not actual kindness, an aloof tolerance. Except Dot, who had become her best friend.

When we saw no sign of Minnie-May, we resumed our hurrying and Dot plied me with questions.

'Where does Harry live?'

'Down near Murphy's farm.' I shook my plastic container rhythmically and marched along to the sound of the Anzacs hitting the lid and falling with a satisfying crunch.

'What's he like?'

'He's nice.'

'What do you do there?'

'Drink billy tea and play and stuff. It's really fun.' I didn't let on I'd only been there once.

'I can't wait to meet him.' She looked back over her shoulder for a moment. 'Maybe we can bring Minnie-May next time.'

I glanced at Dot. Her dark, curly hair was wind-blown and messy, and her T-shirt, which was too small for her, had ridden up so her stomach fat spilled out over her trousers. It jiggled as she walked. I looked away and quickened my pace, hugging the Tupperware container to my chest.

'Wa-ait on,' she puffed.

'Hurry up, then. I don't want to be late. They'll be waiting for me, you know.'

I marched on with Dot breathing heavily behind me, until I reached the end of the footpath at the outcrop of eucalypts. There, I turned and told her again to hurry. 'And pull your shirt down,' I said, before spinning away and going down Murphy's Lane.

To my shame, I left her behind at Harry's gate and took off on my own, embarrassed to be arriving with a child who was younger than me and overweight. As I turned into the clearing at Harry's place, I spied Jacky leaping down the steps from the cottage. He saw me and waved. 'We're down at the treehouse!' he called as he ran past the shed and disappeared behind the fruit trees.

I took off after him, ignoring Dot completely, and sprinted past a bunch of balloons attached to the stair railing. As I rounded the fruit trees, I slowed to a walking pace. Jacky and a few of the Pevensie kids stood around a tyre that hung from the pine tree by thick rope. Harry was helping Sarah onto it.

'Look what Harry made,' Jacky called.

I strode over as if I was there by myself.

Harry looked up and called out, 'G'day, Lily.' His gaze shifted past me and I knew he'd seen Dot coming up behind. He straightened up and said, 'Hello, Lily's brought a friend.'

'It's only Dot,' Jacky said.

Dot puffed towards us with a red face and her T-shirt riding up again. I turned away, embarrassed at how ridiculous she looked.

'Hello Dot,' Harry said. The warmth in Harry's voice drew my gaze back to his face. His eyes were crinkled up in a smile. 'I'm Harry Fernley. Pleased to meet you.'

Dot stopped and gaped at him.

Harry jerked his head towards the pine tree. 'Do you like treehouses?'

Dot's face broke into a grin and she nodded vigorously, moving towards him.

'Who wants to go up first,' Harry said. 'Lily?'

'Nah,' I said as I kicked a clump of grass with my foot.

Jacky and some of the Pevensie children asked to go up and Harry held onto the rope ladder as they climbed. He stayed right behind each child, keeping his hands ready in case anyone slipped. Dot kept looking at Harry and grinning at him every time he turned her way.

I stood next to Sarah on the tyre swing and watched. Would Dot try and heave her body up the rope ladder? I imagined it snapping under her weight.

Harry turned to Dot and I studied his face, watching for a frown or a look of unease. But he smiled at her in the same way he'd smiled at me when we'd walked down Murphy's Lane together, on the day we went fishing. 'How about you, Dot? I'll help you.'

Dot's grin wavered and she took a step back, giving her head a quick shake.

'Yeah, that rope's a bit tricky,' he said. 'I thought it was a good idea at the time but I reckon I'll swap it for a wooden ladder.'

I was about to ask Harry to hold the rope ladder for me when Jacky's brother, Maurice, appeared and told Harry he'd got the fire going. At the same time, more of the Pevensie kids arrived and came galloping around the shed, so Harry called the others to come down from the treehouse for tea.

By the time we scampered up to the cottage, a fire was crackling in the fire pit, its flames licking the bottom of the billy can. Jonathan had arrived and he and Maurice were setting up a card table with crockery and snacks. I set my container of biscuits next to a plate of seed cake and a bowl of potato chips.

I felt nervous being in such close proximity to the two older boys—Jonathan who was two years older than me and Maurice who was already in high school. Maurice was the spitting image of Jacky, with his freckled face, but a lot bigger. He already had broad shoulders and towered above the rest of us.

'Oh, happy birthday,' I said, remembering the small gift in the pocket of my jacket and handing it to Jacky. The children gathered round while he ripped the paper away from a purple yoyo—probably a gift Mum had put away for me or Maudie. I was supposed to say it was from Dot as well, but I didn't. I avoided Dot's eyes and watched Jacky trying to do walk-the-dog until the billy boiled.

We witnessed the billy tea ritual again—Harry scooping in the tealeaves, swinging the billy, waiting for the tea to draw, pouring it into all the cups half-way and filling them up with milk. We added our own sugar and settled ourselves in the chairs or on the ground around the fire, sipping our tea and breathing in the scent of wood smoke.

It was marvellous. No games of Pass-the-parcel or Pin-the-tail-on-the-donkey. Instead, Harry fetched a guitar from the house and sat down next to the fire. With his back curved over the instrument, he tuned the strings one by one and played a few chords.

'Ready?' he said, turning to Jacky. 'We'll start with the birthday boy's favourite.'

Harry played *Old MacDonald* and we sang. We shouted the lyrics and animal sounds and frequently burst into peals of laughter. Next, *Waltzing Matilda* and the national anthem lifted into the air and echoed up into the hills. He knew all our songs—the ones we sang at school and the ones we'd heard on the radio. We sang them off-by-heart—*The Pushbike Song, Tie a Yellow Ribbon round the Ole Oak Tree, Rockin' Robin.*

As he strummed a lullaby, we recognised it and joined our voices to his. 'Go to sleep, go to sleep, sleep tight little baby...'

Harry quietened his strumming so our voices rang out above it. After a while, his eyes shifted from his guitar to Dot sitting next to him. He stopped singing and watched her as he played. Dot was gazing up into the trees and from her mouth came a sound so sweet and clear, it startled me. Like Harry, I stopped singing. Most of the kids kept their voices up, but because we were sitting so close to Dot, we heard her voice above the others.

Harry finished strumming and the song came to an end. Harry was still looking at Dot when she turned and discovered his eyes on her.

Harry smiled and said, 'Dot can sing.' The awe in his voice caused everyone to fall silent and look at Dot, who blushed. Harry winked at her and turned back to his guitar, saying, 'How about one more?'

We sang the kookaburra song, another of Jacky's favourites, and just as we finished, a kookaburra cackled from somewhere overhead. Jacky leapt to his feet, cupped his hands either side of his mouth and started squawking like a kookaburra, his voice echoing up into the hills. He was answered by the 'Aaaah' of a raven which set us all laughing again.

'That raven sounds a bit like me when I try and sing,' Harry said. 'Listen, there's more of them. Don't you reckon they sound like a bunch of old men yarning?' The ravens cawed as if in conversation, replying to each other in drawn-out vowels.

Jacky, ever the entertainer, picked up a long stick from the ground and leaned on it as if it were a walking stick. He shuffled towards Harry, imitating an old man and crowing, 'Aaah, how ahh ya, Harry me maaaate?' He continued his old man impersonation, hobbling about and crowing, 'Hoow's the coorn, maate!'... 'Where's me teef? Aaah!' while we roared with laughter.

It was one of the funniest things I've ever seen. Even Harry hooted and slapped his sides, saying, 'Mate, you should be on stage! Serious, you've got a gift.'

All the kids did raven imitations then—except poor Sarah who was curled up on the ground in stitches—until melodic warbling curled out of the gums and everyone grew quiet.

'That was a magpie,' Harry said. 'Pretty nice, aye? Makes you want to stop and listen.' Then Harry pursed his lips and whistled and it sounded so much like a bird, we couldn't believe it was really Harry.

We sat quietly for a while, enjoying the birdsong, until a kookaburra laughed and broke the spell.

'Must be time for birthday cake,' Harry said.

Maurice ran up the front steps into the cottage and came back holding a cake on a plate, one hand shielding the lit birthday candles from the wind. As Jacky blew out the flames, Harry played *Happy Birthday* on his guitar and we sang along in very loud voices. It's possible all of Crayfish Cove heard us.

It was the best birthday party I'd ever attended in my entire short life. Sitting there watching Jacky cut the cake, his freckled face a picture of joy, I made up my mind that in three months, I would have a birthday party exactly the same as this one. Right here, with all the kids and Harry.

<u>**Jacky's birthday party at Harry's**</u>

It was the best party ever! Harry played his guitar
and we sang songs and he made us billy tea again.
We ate so much food and cake!
Then we climbed up into the treehouse and I was the
fastest up the ladder. Its got a floor made of planks
of wood and the branches around it are really thick
so its like being in a little secret house.
Then we all had a swing on the tyre swing that
Harry made. It was great fun. I felt like a bird flying.
Sarah was too scared to swing by herself so Harry
sat on it and put Sarah on his knee and swang very
high. Sarah couldn't stop giggling.
I want to have my birthday party at Harry's in July
and have billy tea and swing on the swing with
Harry.

# 6

# Digging a hole to China

Kylie and I were sitting on the playground seats, eating our lunch, when Dot hurried up to us, grinning.

'Lily, guess what! Harry came to the school and talked to Mrs Farrell about me.'

'The music teacher?'

'Yes!' Dot wiped her sweaty forehead with the back of her hand. 'He told her I can sing. She took me to the music room and got me to sing while she played the piano, and she said she wants to give me singing lessons.' Dot was panting by this time, in her excitement. 'She's going to talk to Mum.'

I sat dumbly, fiddling with my banana peel.

'That's great, Dot,' Kylie said.

Dot let out a huge sigh, said, 'I'm so happy!' and skipped off to sit with Minnie-May on their usual lunch seat.

'Is she really a good singer?' Kylie asked.

'She's alright.'

'As good as us?' Kylie put her hand on her chest, opened her mouth wide and sang, 'La-la-la-laaaa!' in a mock operatic style.

'Nah, she's not as good as us superstar singers.' I lifted my arms in the air, pulled what I imagined was a funny face and sang a loud, quivering note. 'Laaaaaaaaa!'

Kylie laughed and joined in. We sang louder and sillier notes until the other kids eating their lunch in our area were looking at us. We burst into laughter.

I glanced over at Dot. She was blinking at us with her face flushed, an apple in her hand suspended halfway between her lap and her mouth as if she'd forgotten what to do with it.

'Come on,' I said, jumping up from my seat and shoving my lunch box into my school bag. 'Let's go play.'

I saw them together the following Sunday afternoon—Dot and Harry. I sprinted down Harry's drive, rounded the corner and there they were, sitting on the chairs next to the fire pit. I pulled up short. Harry had a guitar on his knee and Dot sat on her hands, grinning. Her mother, Fiona, stood nearby, laughing at something and shaking her head.

Fiona looked my way. 'Lily! Hello there.'

I arranged my face into a smile and wandered in, my hands in the pockets of my parka. Harry had the fire going and I drew up beside it.

'We came over to show Harry the song Dot's been learning with Mrs Farrell.'

'She's pretty good,' Harry said.

'Would you like to hear it, Lily?' Fiona said. Before I could reply, she said, 'Sing it again, Dot.'

Dot was red-faced by now, but clearly pleased.

Harry strummed a few chords, smiled encouragingly at Dot, and Dot opened her mouth. Her voice rang out with pure, sweet notes like some exotic bird. I was stunned. As she sang, her eyes went else-where—a bit like Mum's when she would day dream—like she was in a trance. I dropped into a seat by the fire, mesmerised by the melody coming from her lips. The music moved something deep inside me. When Dot finished I was embarrassed to find tears in my eyes, for which I blamed the smoke from the fire.

Dot and Fiona left soon after, and Harry and I continued to sit by the fire. Harry leaned forward, his hands outstretched to warm them, and from the corner of my eye I sensed him looking at me.

'Dot's a good singer,' I said, feeling unusually generous about her.

Harry nodded. 'True, and with some training I reckon she'll be top-notch.' He leaned back in his chair, put his hands behind his head with his fingers laced and stretched his long legs out before the fire. 'Everyone's good at something.'

'What are you good at?' I asked.

'Gardening, I guess. I like helping God grow things.'

'Yeah, you are good at that. But what about all the other things too, like making billy tea and treehouses and fixing stuff. Oh, and doing bird whistles.'

Harry chuckled. 'How about yourself, what are your talents? Besides being a leader.'

'Me?'

'You're a natural leader. The other kids look up to you.'

'Do they?' I pulled a face like I couldn't believe him.

He grinned. 'I'm sure you have other talents too, don't you?'

I shrugged. It wasn't cool for kids to admit they were good at anything. It was tantamount to bragging. I didn't feel like I was bragging to Harry though, when I turned to him and said, 'I'm good at writing.'

He lifted his eyebrows. 'That's something I didn't know about you. What do you like to write?'

'Stories about...um...' I pictured the writing in both of my journals that was almost all about Harry and felt my cheeks warm up. 'Oh, I know.' I straightened up. 'I wrote about the fire pit that Dad's building. I told him about yours and he thought it was a good idea.'

'Really?'

'Yeah, he reckons he's gonna cook sausages on it. It's not as big as this one but it's pretty good. It's mostly made of old bricks he had lying about.'

Harry nodded thoughtfully. I waited for him to say something about the fire pit, but instead he said, 'I'd love you to read me something you've written sometime.'

My heart pattered with excitement. Before we could talk more about it, we heard Jacky shouting, 'G'day Harry!'

We turned to see him tearing down the driveway on his bicycle and skidding to a halt. He jumped off, dropped the bike to the ground and thumped himself down on a seat. His brother, Maurice came around the corner next, also on a bike but more sedately. He came to a slow stop, dismounted and leaned his bike against the garden fence.

We greeted each other and Harry asked what they'd been up to.

'Nothin' much.' Jacky said.

Maurice took a seat next to Harry. 'Squirt's been digging a hole in the back yard.'

Harry turned to Jacky. 'Are you doing some gardening at home, then?'

Maurice answered with a smirk. 'No, he ain't. He reckons he's digging a hole to China.'

Harry raised his eyebrows and said to Jacky, 'How far did you get?'

Jacky's shoulders slumped. 'Not far, I hit clay.'

'Ah,' —Harry nodded gravely— 'that clay'll get you every time.'

Maurice frowned. 'Mate, don't encourage him. He thinks he can actually do it.'

Harry turned a serious face to him. 'What makes you think he can't?'

Maurice spluttered. 'Because it's impossible! No one can.'

'How do you know?'

'Everyone knows you can't dig a hole to bloody China!'

Harry frowned. 'Language, mate.'

Maurice blew a blast of air from his lips. 'Alright, I'll play your silly game. The earth's too big to dig through.'

Harry said, 'And how do you know that?'

Maurice clicked his tongue. 'We learnt it at school. No one's ever dug through the whole earth, not even with a super-power drill.'

'So, you know this because a teacher told you. But Jacky here—' (Harry nodded at Jacky) 'knows because he tried for himself.'

Jacky grinned and looked rather pleased with himself. Maurice muttered and picked up a stick to poke the fire.

'Anyway, Jacky. Now you're here, we'd best pull up the rest of those carrots before they go woody.'

Jacky jumped up and headed for the garden gate, pulling his sleeves up to his elbows as he went. He'd become Harry's unofficial gardening apprentice and clearly loved the work. We all pitched in for a while, pulling up the carrots and putting them into grocery bags. Maurice left early to do errands at home and I helped Harry and Jacky finish sorting the carrots. After we'd had a drink of lemonade and a biscuit, it was time for me to walk home. Jacky was ready to head off too, with three bags of carrots to deliver to various families, for which Harry paid him a delivery fee.

'You know the drill,' Harry said. 'If no one answers the door at the manse, leave it just inside the shed and Mrs Hammond will pay me later.'

'Righto.'

Jacky put one foot on a pedal, lifted his bottom off the seat and pushed, pedalling gradually faster until he gained momentum. Then off he went, sailing smoothly up the drive, even with the swinging bags of carrots.

'He does that so well.' Harry leaned back with his hands in his pockets and chuckled, gazing after Jacky until he disappeared around the corner into the trees.

A routine developed around my visits to Harry's place. Maudie would often spend Sunday afternoons at Nan's and I'd go to Harry's, allowing Mum and Dad some rare time to themselves which they called Date Afternoon.

Perhaps the other parents had similar reasons for entrusting their children into Harry's care—a chance to rest, to do something without children in tow—the brief respite on a Sunday being too sweet an opportunity to pass up.

Harry's place was a small Eden where our creative spirits were unleashed. We could be wild and adventurous, or quiet and restful if we wished. Harry had a way of making us feel important. He shared confidences, laughed at our jokes, listened attentively as we told him about ourselves and our families, and told us his own stories.

Harry had been raised in the cottage with his parents and inherited it when they both died some years back. 'Dad was old and Mum got sick,' he explained. 'They were already getting on in age when I came along. I was a surprise.'

'I bet you were a nice surprise,' Dot had said, making me wish I'd thought of saying it.

Whenever I arrived at his home he would, more often than not, be in his garden. Jacky, who had his own dreams of owning a gardening business one day, was usually there too. I was no gardener but I found Harry's ventures fascinating, poking my nose into everything around his property. I found a pile of planks in the shed which he said he was collecting to build a verandah onto the front of the cottage—'Something Dad was going to do before he died.'

'Can I help you build it?' I asked him.

Harry was cleaning up his shed at the time. He sat down on an upturned drum, leaned towards me with his hands on his knees, wild hair falling over his eyes, and grinned. 'I reckon I could do with an extra pair of hands when the time comes.'

I remember feeling taller, a sense of importance expanding my insides as I imagined myself as Harry's helper. I had a sudden urge to run over and hug him but Jacky bowled through the door at that moment holding a rock he'd dug out of a garden bed which he wanted to add to Harry's collection. Harry was on his feet in an instant, holding out his hand for the rock and chuckling as Jacky pointed out the protrusions that made it look like a monster's face.

I followed them into the cottage and watched as Harry set the rock next to his collection on the shelf one side of the fireplace. Wanting to be included in the conversation, I asked him about the other rocks.

He told us how they reminded him of people. 'See this thick, flat one?' he said, lifting it from the shelf. 'It makes me think of Dad. He was a good, strong bloke.' He set it back down and reached for a round, orange one. Holding it up, he winked and said, 'Meet Mum.'

Jacky and I giggled.

I reached for a small, mottled stone with a crumbled side and asked, 'Who's this one?'

'That's me,' Harry said.

'Really?' I turned the stone over in my hand. 'It's a bit—um—'

'Imperfect?' he said. 'It reminds me I've got a lot to learn.'

I collected these stories—these fragments—along with the bigger, wilder adventures. I wrote about them in my journals. Pondered them in my heart.

Over time, I fitted them together and constructed an image of the man I believed Harry Fernley to be.

7

## A secret and a lie

ONE AFTERNOON, I TURNED up to Harry's early and he and I sat outside on the old chairs, enjoying the little bit of cool Autumn sunshine.

'How was church this morning?' Harry asked.

'Good. We had Mr Gilchrist for Sunday school.'

'And what did Arthur teach you today?'

'Um—can't remember.'

Harry chuckled. 'He wasn't very interesting, then?'

'He's alright. Maudie loves him.'

'Does she?'

'It's because he teaches her Maths. She's a Maths whiz! Mum takes her to school on Thursday afternoons so Mr Gilchrist can tutor her.'

'Does she go to school on the other days?'

'Nah. She used to but Mum teaches her at home now.' I shuffled my feet in the dust on the ground. 'Maudie's not like other kids.'

'How's that?'

I shrugged my shoulders. 'She's just different. Mr Hinkley—you know, the headmaster?—he told Mum she should send Maudie to a special school in Hobart. Dad said she tore strips off him.'

Harry put his fist to his mouth and his eyes crinkled up.

I fiddled with the edge of my parka. 'Wayne Bottle calls her Spaz.'

Harry's grin vanished. 'Wayne Bottle has some problems of his own. Tell me some things you like about your sister.'

'Hmm…' I looked up into the trees the way Harry did when he was thinking. 'I like how she's good at Maths because it makes her smile. I like how she's kind—did you know she gives out the hymn books at church? No one told her to, she just does it. And she loves wearing dresses with big skirts and spinning in them. She spins and spins and I can't figure out how she doesn't get dizzy.'

'She sounds happy.'

'She's *so* happy.'

'Would you want to change Maudie?'

'No way. She's perfect, I love her.'

Harry looked down at his lap and rubbed at the back of one hand with the thumb of his other. After a few moments, he looked up and said, 'Do you feel like going for a walk? The other kids won't be here for a while. I'd like to show you something.'

I walked with Harry up the driveway, past the big oak and out through the gate of his property.

'Where are we going?'

'You'll see.'

We crossed Murphy's Lane and went down the road a little way, past a squashed section of wire fencing and some wild hawthorn. Harry slipped in between two poplars and vanished into the bushes behind them. One moment he was there and the next, he wasn't. I stared at the bushes for a moment, until Harry's grinning face appeared amongst the leaves.

'Through here,' he said, pulling the branches aside for me to follow him.

I found myself on a narrow track—barely there and existing only as a trail of flattened leaf litter—completely hidden from the road. Harry indicated for me to follow. We wove our way through the trees and shrubs, squeezing through dense vegetation and ducking beneath a low-hanging eucalypt branch.

Eventually, we came to a small clearing with an old log laying across it. Harry circled the log and sat on top of it, so I followed and climbed up next to him. In this secluded space the air was warm and dense and felt very much removed from the world outside. Grasshoppers leapt about and crickets trilled loudly. A skink slipped across the forest floor as I watched, disappearing beneath the log where we sat.

When Harry spoke, he kept his voice soft and low. 'This is one of the places I used to come and sit when I was a boy.'

'When you learned how to whistle?'

'That's right. I had some magpie friends who would fly down for a chat. I even fell asleep here a couple of times. Mum had to come looking for me.'

'On the log?'

'On the ground. The tree hadn't fallen over then, and the clearing was bigger. A few more trees have sprouted up since then. See those two gums there?' He pointed.

The gums were directly ahead of us—tall trunks of gnarled and twisted bark stretching up into a canopy of leaves.

'They were little ones back then. See how there's a bit of a clearing behind them before it bushes back up?'

I nodded.

'One day, when I was sitting here on the ground listening to the birds—or I might have just woken up from a snooze, I can't remember now—I had a special visitor. I saw it behind those two trees.'

'What?'

Harry turned to me, his face serious. 'A Tassie tiger,' he said.

I opened my mouth wide and gasped. 'You're kidding.'

Harry shook his head. 'I'm not.'

I looked back at the trunks of the eucalypts.

'I saw its face first. It was peering out from one of the trunks, the one on the left. I didn't know what it was at first. I thought, is that a dingo or what? But I knew it couldn't be, because we don't get them here in Tassie. It looked straight at me, but I don't know if it knew what I was.'

'What did you do?'

'I kept as still as possible so I wouldn't frighten it. It looked away and walked towards the other tree. That's when I saw—just for a minute—its whole body.' Harry raised his eyebrows for emphasis when he said, 'It had stripes, so I knew it had to be a Tassie tiger.'

'Wow! What happened then?'

'Something startled it and it vanished into the woods. I don't know where it went.'

'Have you seen any more?'

Harry shook his head. 'I come here every now and then and sit, sometimes for a few hours, hoping I might see another one. It's not likely though. Too many people live around here now. Ours was the only house back then. There was no cattle farm, and no Murphy's Lane to speak of—just a bit of a dirt track as far as our place. The Tassie tigers would have retreated far into the bush when people started coming.'

'I thought they were ex—all dead.'

'Extinct? Maybe they are, maybe they aren't. If they're still out there, they're hiding. And they're smart enough not to let themselves be seen.'

'Wow,' I said again.

'I didn't tell anyone.'

'Not even your mum and dad?'

'Nuh. I kept it a secret.'

'Why?'

'Because of what people would have done to it. Hunted it down, caged it up and gawked at it, most likely. Do you think it would have been happy being locked in a cage?'

'No.'

'Me neither. I reckon it was happier being in its own natural habitat doing whatever Tassie tigers do. It might have had a family out there somewhere and it would have been cruel to take it away from that.'

We sat for a few minutes in silence and I wrapped myself in the moment, in the warm and intimate place of Harry's confidence. My small chest expanded so greatly with feeling that I lay my head on his shoulder.

When I lifted my head and turned to him, he grinned at me, stood and brushed off the seat of his pants. I did the same and we started heading back, Harry leading me through the almost invisible track, while the birds of the forest whistled overhead. As we reached the poplars on the side of the road, Harry stopped and turned to face me.

'Your mum did the right thing,' he said.

'What?'

'Keeping Maudie at home. She wouldn't have been happy in that special school.'

We smiled at each other and continued on our way back to his place.

Maudie and I were doing our homework on the kitchen table as Mum prepared vegetables. Miss Aubrey had given me another exercise book to bring home so I could do extra journal writing, and I was decorating the front of it with coloured pencils. Maudie had progressed to the next level Maths book and was working on algebra problems. I could make no sense of the equations decorating the cover of her book, let alone the problems inside.

Maudie started tapping the table with her fingers which meant she was stuck on a problem.

Mum looked up from top-and-tailing beans and said, 'I'm sorry I can't help you with those, Maudie. They're beyond me.'

Maudie sighed and bent her head to concentrate on her workbook. 'That's okay. I'll work it out, I'm clever.'

'What are you going to write about in your journal, Lily?' Mum asked.

'About Harry, of course.' I giggled.

'Oh? What about him?'

'Did you know, when he was a boy he used to sit in the woods for hours, listening to the birds? That's how he learnt how to whistle like them.'

Mum stopped working on the beans and sat with a faraway look in her eyes, like her brain had gone elsewhere.

'Mum?'

She blinked and smiled. 'I'm listening. I'm imagining Harry as a boy sitting in the woods.'

'Did you really know him at school?'

'Yes.'

'What was he like?'

'He was a couple of grades below me, so I didn't know him very well. But I thought he was nice.'

'Kylie's mum doesn't like him.'

There was a sharp look in Mum's eye when she said, 'Really.'

'Kylie doesn't know why, though.'

Mum picked up a bean and resumed her work. 'Well, I wouldn't worry about that if I were you. Maudie, how are you going with your problem?'

I wanted to ask more about Harry but Maudie started describing her algebra problem to Mum in great detail. I continued to colour the word *Journal* on the front of my book, trying to make it as neat and pretty as Miss Aubrey's writing. My teacher hadn't said I had to bring the book back to school. She had called it my 'home journal.' That meant I could write anything I liked in it and no one would read it but me. I could fill the whole book up with stories about Harry if I wanted to.

After tea, I went into my bedroom, made sure the door was closed properly, and sat on my bed with the new exercise book. I chose one of my best pens, grinned gleefully and began to write.

The recess bell rang as we finished a lesson on acrostic poems. As everyone else was pouring out the door, Miss Aubrey pulled me aside and asked me to sit on a chair next to her desk. She wore a smile that didn't quite work and I fidgeted with the button on my school dress, wondering what I'd done wrong. She sat next to me and placed her hand over an open exercise book on her desk. It was my journal—the one I wrote in at school.

'Lily,' she said, her head bending to the side and her lips trying to maintain the smile that appeared to have been arrested somewhere half-way to its destination. 'I'd like to talk to you about an entry you made in your journal.'

Her voice went up and down like a melody as if she was addressing a two-year-old. I folded my arms over my chest and it's possible I frowned.

'You obviously enjoy spending time with your friend, Harry.' She raised her eyebrows, still smiling, and waited. When I said nothing, she cleared her throat and the smile slipped. 'I'm wondering about what you've written here. Something about a secret.' She slid the journal across the desk towards me, so I could read my words:

**Me and Harry have a secret and I won't tell. Not even if I'm torchered.**

Miss Aubrey inclined her head to me and the smile reappeared. 'Do you think you could trust me with the secret?'

The bird in my chest beat its startled wings. I shook my head.

'May I ask you some questions about it, then? Is the secret something that makes you feel uncomfortable or unsafe?'

I tried without success to understand this new language my teacher was using—the intonation of a mother to a two-year-old and words that made no sense to me in the context of my friendship with Harry.

When I failed to reply, she insisted, 'How about scared? Do you ever feel scared with Harry?'

I felt my face scrunching up tight, my lips pressed together. I shook my head fiercely.

Miss Aubrey pulled the journal back towards herself, and turned a page.

'I like this story, where Harry teaches you how to mimic a golden whistler,' she said, and read the page aloud. '"Harry showed us how to hold our lips together and curl our tongues and whistle like a bird that's called a golden whistler. Jacky can do it so well. Sarah can't whistle yet but she's trying hard. I will keep practising so I can get good like Harry. Harry loves the birds, he listens to them all day while he works in his garden."'

As she read, the breath I was holding eased out of me and my body relaxed. I straightened up in my chair and lifted my chin. When she'd finished and turned to me, I said, 'Harry can whistle like a butcher bird too, you should hear him.'

Miss Aubrey chuckled. 'That's a difficult one. My brother and I used to try and mimic the butcher bird when we were young.'

I was momentarily startled by the incongruous vision of Miss Aubrey in the woods trying to whistle.

Miss Aubrey closed my journal. 'It sounds like Harry is someone who enjoys birds and nature. From what you've written about him, he seems like a nice person. But, because you've written about a secret between you, I will need to show this entry to your parents so they can talk to you about it.'

'But—' I wriggled in my seat. 'But it isn't anything. It's just a—a nice secret.'

Miss Aubrey looked towards the windows and back to me. 'Lily, if you tell me about it, and if it really is a nice secret, I may be able to keep it.'

My fingers worried at the edge of my school dress as I thought quickly. I couldn't tell Miss Aubrey about the Tasmanian tiger because

Harry had kept it secret since he was a boy. That was such a long time. If I told the secret and it got out, how could he ever trust me again? But if I didn't tell Miss Aubrey, she'd go to my parents and tell them what I'd written, and I knew Dad would be able to make me tell.

My imagination took a leap and a story began to weave itself together in my mind.

'Well, see, we found a nest.' My brain raced as it pulled pictures together in its attempt to conjure a believable story.

'Go on.'

'Well, the nest had some eggs in it.'

Miss Aubrey nodded her head. 'Where was the nest?'

I pictured Harry's place—the fruit trees, the pine tree, the surrounding bushes and eucalypts around his property.

'There's a pine tree at the back of his place and we were down there picking up pine cones for the fire. Harry pointed up and said, "Look, there's a nest."'

Before I knew it, the story was spinning itself.

'I looked up and saw it. Harry said he could see some eggs in it. I couldn't see them because I'm too short, but Harry could.'

'It's an odd season for birds to be laying eggs,' Miss Aubrey said.

'I know, that's what Harry said.' —I was on a roll now— 'He said they could be ones that've been abandoned, or maybe the mother bird has been killed or something. So he said we'll keep an eye on it, but we won't tell anyone about it so it won't be disturbed. Because, you know, some of the other kids like climbing and Harry thought they might try and climb up and have a look. Then they might knock it down. Harry's going to check it every day and see if the mother comes back to hatch them.'

Miss Aubrey was nodding her head and her smile had relaxed.

'Does Harry know what kind of eggs they are?'

'He thinks they might be magpie eggs, but he's not sure.'

'Alright, thank you for telling me, Lily. Your friend obviously cares very much about the birds.'

'He cares about all the animals.'

Miss Aubrey stood. 'You may go to recess now.'

I went to grab my lunch box from the cloak room. As I came back out and opened the door to leave the classroom, Miss Aubrey spoke.

'Lily?'

I turned.

'Don't worry,' she said. 'I'll keep your secret.'

I gave her a big smile and left the classroom, astounded at my own ability to lie so smoothly.

**H** appy

**A** dventurous

**R** espectful

**R** elaxed

**Y** oungish

8

# A wild-weathered birthday



July brought wild weather to Crayfish Cove. I was at Harry's when the first bangs of thunder sounded and the air began to crackle. Even from his place we could hear the neighbourhood dogs howling.

Harry scrambled to gather all his firewood—which had been diminished to a small pile of logs—and bring it inside before the impending deluge. 'I meant to cut up that dead tree last weekend! I'm going to run out now,' he lamented.

He told us all to go home before the rain started. I scampered off, disappointed at my visit being cut short, but hanging onto the promise of a birthday party at Harry's the following Sunday. I was turning ten—double numbers! With this happy thought, I flew through my front gate as the first fat raindrops began to fall.

It rained for days and Crayfish Cove filled with water. I heard Murphy's Lane had flooded and I wondered if Harry was able to get out in his ute. Had he been flooded too? I imagined him standing at the top of his steps, looking out at the rising waters swirling around his house like a giant moat.

However, the waters eventually subsided and, despite the continual drizzle and wild winds, Harry threw a birthday party for me the following Sunday, inside his cottage with balloons and a roaring fire. Kylie still wasn't allowed to visit his place, but Dot came over from

Durrunby and we were joined by Jacky, Maurice, Jonathan and some of the Pevensies. We toasted marshmallows on sticks, sang songs to Harry's guitar and ate a layered cream cake Mum had made. We even braved the weather for a short escapade up into the treehouse, helped by the sturdy wooden ladder Harry had nailed to the tree trunk.

'How come you don't go to church?' I asked him, looping my arm in his as we went down to the treehouse together. I wished he would go to church so I could see him Sunday mornings as well. One afternoon a week with Harry was not enough.

Harry gazed up into the trees and answered, 'I reckon I can hear God better out here.'

'Mr Hammond says God talks through his sermons,' I said. 'It's why the grown-ups go to church, to hear Mr Hammond preach.'

Harry's face twisted into something I couldn't read. 'Well, there are those who prefer to sit still with their ears open and their brains switched off.'

'What do you mean?'

'Nothing.' He shook his head. 'Forget I said that.'

I must have looked confused, because he grinned, slipped his arm from mine and put it briefly around my shoulders and squeezed. 'Come on, I'll climb into the treehouse with you.'

It wasn't long before our fingers were numb with the cold, and we escaped back inside for cocoa. In the late afternoon, the balloons popped one by one from the heat of the fire and the guests left until only Dot and I remained. Dot was curled up on the couch and Harry sat on the floor, leaning against a chair with his long legs stretched out. Now that the others had gone, I retrieved my bag from behind one of the armchairs and sat on the carpet next to him. I reached into the bag, carefully brought out a stiff sheet of paper and laid it on his lap.

'What's this?' he asked as he picked it up.

'You said you wanted to read one of my stories, so I wrote this one for you. It's about you when you were a boy. Mum gave me some of her good writing paper for it.'

Harry lifted the scented paper to his nose and sniffed. Mum had taken it from her bedside drawer and it smelt like her perfume. 'Wow, and it's not even *my* birthday. Thanks, Lily.'

'Aren't you going to read it?'

He hesitated, before holding it towards me. 'Would you read it to me?'

I took the sheet of paper from him and read aloud, glancing up intermittently to watch his expression.

'Did you really write that yourself?' Dot asked, when I'd finished.

'Uh-huh,' I said proudly as I laid the story back on Harry's lap.

Harry smiled and ran his hand over it as if he could feel the story through the tips of his fingers. 'I'll have to find a frame for it,' he said. He stood and set it gently on the bookcase, next to his row of stones. I felt the significance of the gesture—placing my story next to the reminders of his parents, and the broken stone that represented himself and his shortcomings. A way of showing me how special he considered it.

I gathered up my small pile of birthday gifts and packed them into my bag. Harry had wrapped up his orange shell from the wave shelf in his kitchen and given it to me. This was my favourite gift, which I placed in the top of the bag to keep it safe.

I curled up on the couch with Dot after that, as we waited for Mum and Dad to come back from their Date Afternoon and pick us both up. Dot fell asleep and Harry, sitting on the floor with his back against the armchair, was also nodding off. I lay back on the cushions, the heat of the open fire warming my face.

It was only as I was drifting off into sated slumber that I noticed an oddness about the fire. With heavy eyelids, I tried to peer into the blaze, and wondered how it was that I saw tiny houses in Harry's fireplace, burning in the flames.

## My friend Harry

My friend Harry is wise like a raven and whistles like a magpie.
When he was a boy he would sit in the woods for hours listening to the birds and learning to whistle.
He got so good at it that he could sit really still and whistle and the birds would come down next to him and sing with him.
He said maybe they couldn't tell he was a human.
Maybe they thought he was a bird like them.
If Harry was a bird he would be the nicest bird of all.

# 9

## The man who draws the large crowd

THE WATTLES FLOWERED, PINK and white blossoms appeared, then the daffodils, the lilac, and Harry's garden produced a glut of broad beans. Spring moved steadily towards summer and by mid-November, we had begun preparations for the end-of-year nativity play.

Every Sunday morning, while the adults sat in mesmerised rows soaking up eternal wisdom from the teachings of Mr Hammond, we were in the church shed with Betty Crouch cutting, gluing and painting. I'd chosen the part of one of the wise men which may or may not have been influenced by Jonathan's decision to be one.

As some of us worked on our props at a trestle table, others sat on a sofa practising their lines. Minnie-May hung about near the door watching, and Betty kept urging her inside, calling 'come in, sweetie' in a sing-song voice. But Minnie-May stayed put, leaning against the doorframe with her thumb in her mouth, and eventually slipped herself down until her bottom was on the floor. In the end, she was left alone and given the part of a sheep. On the day, this only required her to crawl across the stage wearing cardboard ears and a fluffy white blanket over her back.

When the morning of the play came around, we gathered together in our costumes in a small room directly next to the stage, waiting to begin our performance. I peered through the crack of the door into the auditorium and saw Mum, Dad, Maudie and Nan seated together in their usual pew. Maudie sat very still and upright, gazing expectantly at the stage. She'd been excited about seeing me perform.

But where was Harry? He'd promised to come. People were streaming in now and filling up the seats. Just as I despaired of Harry showing, he wandered in through the main door with his hands in his pockets. He looked about and settled himself in a seat at the very back against the wall. My happiness was complete.

Mr Hammond welcomed the congregation, Mrs Hammond played *Hark the Herald Angels Sing* on the organ and the play began.

Jacky was the first onto the stage. We watched him hold up his crook and stride out, thrusting out his chest as if being a shepherd was the most important thing in the world. The other shepherds and a flock of bleating sheep followed him. Jacky turned to point his crook at the sheep and said, 'Come on, get a move on!' causing titters from the audience. 'Nice bit of grass here, look.'

As the sheep pretended to munch on the crepe paper grass, Kylie moved towards the stage door in her angel costume, already in character with her head high. She glided onto the stage and the shepherds recoiled in fright.

'Woah, what is that!' Jacky screeched as he put his hand to his chest and stumbled backward in horror. The audience roared with laughter. He turned his terrified face to the audience, acknowledging their presence, and they laughed again.

I could see Harry at the back wall, his eyes riveted on Jacky and his face crinkled in amusement. Three little angels skipped out to join Kylie on stage, shouting together and bumbling their words—something about glory and heaven and peas. This was Kylie's moment to shine. She stood majestically, waited for the laughter to subside and raised her hands dramatically above her head.

'Don't be scared.' Her voice carried across the auditorium. 'I have wonderful news that will make you very happy. Today in Bethlehem, a king has been born. You will find him wrapped in cloths and laying in a manger.'

'A what?' Jacky said, turning to pull a face at the laughing audience, milking his short moment of fame for all it was worth.

Kylie spoke loud and slow. 'An animal's feed trough.'

'Ahh!' Jacky said, giving the angel a thumbs-up.

Jacky, as ever, was the star of the show and I'm glad to have the memory of his performance to treasure. My recollection of the rest of the play is blurred—Bobby holding a glittered star on a stick, Mary and Joseph and a doll wrapped in a tea-towel. I do recall standing next to Jonathan as we waited to go out on stage with our gifts for the baby—so close I could smell his shampoo. I may have been only ten, but was aware of how handsome he looked in his purple robe and gold crown. I also recall that my performance was terrible. (I bumped into the back of Jonathan on my way across the stage and dropped my golden box of frankincense.)

By the time we changed out of our clothes and put everything away in the shed, the service was over. I hurried into the foyer to look for Harry and found him with a group of adults— Mrs Hammond, Arthur Gilchrist (Maudie's Maths teacher) and some of the parents, including my own. I sidled up to him, on the one hand wanting to ask him if he enjoyed the play, and on the other, embarrassed about my awful acting.

When he saw me, he said, 'Lily, you did a great job out there,' sparing me the angst of asking.

As my parents congratulated me, there was a shout— 'Harry!' —and Jacky bounded through the front door, followed by a band of kids all hustling to be near Harry.

Suddenly, Harry was the centre of attention. I looked around the room to find that people had stopped what they were doing and were smiling over at our group. I inched closer to Harry, a sense of importance washing over me as I stood beside the man who had drawn the large crowd.

I saw that Mr Hammond had stopped at the doorway between the auditorium and the foyer and was watching us. He caught my eye, smiled and walked over.

'Hello. Harry Fernley, isn't it?' he said, holding out his hand. 'Walter Hammond.'

Harry and the minister shook hands.

'It's nice to see you in God's house this morning,' Mr Hammond said.

Harry put his hands in his pockets, leaned back on the heels of his big leather boots and said, 'I'm always in God's house.'

Arthur Gilchrist, next to him, cleared his throat. 'Didn't the children do a marvellous job?'

Mr Hammond shifted his gaze to us and said, 'They certainly did. Well done, children.'

We smiled politely for a moment, then a lot of noise rose up— 'Did you see me...?'— 'Did you like the star, Harry?'— 'Someone trod on my ears!' —and all the children were gazing up at Harry, the little kids tugging at him for his attention, the adults laughing. Harry squatted down on his haunches to talk to the children and Mr Hammond walked away.

Later in the day, we piled into the car to take Nanny Craig home after lunch. On our way back, we came across Harry wandering down Murphy's Lane with his fishing rod. Here we were, crammed into the little Mini, all noise and chatter. And there was Harry going along in his slow, quiet way, all by himself. I wasn't sure what it was I felt at the time—a strange empathy or envy or a tangled mixture of both.

'Now, there's a nice bloke,' Dad said.

I turned my head to watch Harry as we passed him. What was it about this man with the wild, windswept exterior that drew me like a kid to a lolly shop?

<u>25 December</u>

I got a blue bike with gears for Christmas.
Maudie got a measuring wheel. She rolls it along all
the streets in Crayfish Cove recording the distances
in her notebook.
It's 910.5 metres from our house to Nan's.

<u>1 January 1976</u>  HAPPY NEW YEAR!

We had a picnic at the Hollow and watched people
through Kylie's binoculars. We saw:
1.  Mr Foggarty stacking craypots on the jetty.
2.  A person walking a three-legged dog.
3.  Minnie-May going into Lockharts store with Mr
and Mrs Hammond. She came out licking an ice
cream. It made us all feel like ice creams but no one
had any money.

# 10

# Truth, dare or promise

For two more years, I continued my one-eyed obsession with Harry, spending most Sunday afternoons at his place with the other kids.

Any reservations Dad had about it were swallowed up in his work cares. The other local plumber had died and Dad had to juggle all the work of Crayfish Cove and Durrunby while training an apprentice. He worked evenings and weekends and we barely saw him. The only advantage of all this hard work was that the extra money enabled him to buy a new (second-hand) Datsun when the Mini died.

Mum carried on, as mothers do. It's only now as I look back and put certain memories together—Dad coming home to dried-out meals left in the oven, a spontaneous 'holiday' at Nan's for the three of us (without Dad)—that I realise how deeply she felt the strain.

I escaped the tension by fleeing to Harry's, and sometimes, so did Mum. She would drive me there and stay for a cuppa before returning home. She and Harry would sit and talk about their school days while the other kids and I played in the treehouse. Mum began buying vegetables from Harry and bringing him home-made jam and relish, and biscuits to feed all the children. If she ever found out about the cream cake that didn't find its way to his place, she never said.

One Sunday, she brought Maudie and lingered after the other children had left. Maudie trundled her measuring wheel around Harry's property, counting the clicks and recording the distances between objects in her notebook. As she circled the yard, she became fixated on one of Harry's young birch trees whose trunk was bent almost at a right angle. Harry explained to her how it's gradual bowing had been caused by the wind.

'It comes right through here,' he said, waving his arms to indicate the course of the wind from the hills down through his property. 'See how the other tree over there is protected by the shed?'

The other tree stood straight up, tall and graceful.

'This poor devil is exposed to the elements, so it gets knocked about.'

Maudie stared at the bent tree, her face screwed up with worry. 'Will it die?'

Harry smiled at her. 'No, I don't believe so. I reckon it's actually trying to rebalance itself. Which is pretty smart if you think about it. And look at this.' He pointed to the bend. 'There's another branch growing where the trunk should be. It'll be interesting to see what it does.'

Maudie seemed satisfied with this answer and wandered off to pick up leaves and twigs while Harry built a fire in the fire pit. He made Mum and Maudie their first cup of billy tea. Mum said she'd never had one before and how nice it was. She looked so happy sitting by the fire in her woolly coat and scarf with her golden hair in an up-do and her cheeks pink from the heat of the flames. I hadn't seen her so relaxed in a long time.

When the moon came out in the late afternoon, I commented on its sad face. Harry said he thought it looked bewildered and no wonder, with the world in the state it was. Mum laughed and told him he was quite the poet. I remember Maudie shaking her head at the sky and saying she couldn't see a face, which made us all laugh.

Later at home, I looked up the word 'bewildered' in the dictionary and wrote it down in my journal. The word would, thereafter, always remind me of Harry.

Another Christmas came and went. Jonathan began his second year of boarding school in Hobart. He complained about it but he wanted to be a doctor and his dad said he'd receive a better education in the city. My dad said there was nothing wrong with the education at Crayfish Cove school and if I worked hard, I could be just as smart as Jonathan.

In our small school, we continued to have a combined class so Minnie-May, Dot and Jacky were in mine and Kylie's again. Minnie-May stopped talking for a while. Although the new teacher tried, she couldn't get a word out of her. I thought she must be scared of Miss Vance, whose face had lines in places that made her look permanently angry. Dad joked it was because she hadn't found anyone to marry her.

Around this time, I discovered by accident that Harry struggled with reading. Sneaking up the steps of his cottage one day to surprise him, I found him hunched over a book as I tip-toed in. He was reading aloud but the words halted and struggled off his tongue as if they'd snagged there and couldn't find their way out. He caught me watching and something crossed his face, though I couldn't be sure what it was. But he just shrugged one shoulder and said, 'You read much better than I can.' After that, I made a point of reading to him whenever I visited and it seemed to cheer him.

This was also the year Miranda Lockhart started coming to Harry's place. She'd turn up with Maurice in her denim skirts, striped knee socks and desert boots (all of which we younger girls envied). She was fourteen, tall and pretty with long hair that rippled down her back like honey. I was in awe of her.

Miranda and Maurice were 'going together' and I wondered what she saw in that big, freckled boy. She was the sort of girl I imagined marrying a prince when she grew up. One who would drive down from Hobart in an expensive car and whisk her away from her home at the back of the general store to a fancy house in the suburbs where they'd live happily ever after. I never picked her as the kind to settle down in a small town and have four children in quick succession, but there you are.

One afternoon, some of us were at Harry's while he was putting together some new garden beds and digging them up ready for planting. He'd expanded the garden next to the cottage so it went further back behind the house and fenced it all in to keep out the wildlife. He planned to grow more produce to sell. By this time, he was selling wholesale to Miranda's parents for their shop.

Miranda and Sarah sat on the grass making daisy chains. I'd just finished reading a poem to Harry from one of his books. I jumped up from the ground and took up a trowel to help with the garden as Maurice trundled a wheelbarrow of rocks through the garden gate. Perhaps because of having a girlfriend, Maurice had romance on his mind this day.

'Hey Harry,' he said, 'ever thought of getting married?'

I glanced over at Harry, who was raking a garden patch. He looked up. 'I dunno,' he said.

Maurice continued, 'You're getting on a bit. Prob'ly time you got hitched.'

Harry grinned. 'Oh yeah, and who'd have me?'

'I reckon our Aunt Jo would like ya, wouldn't she, squirt?'

Jacky looked up from a patch of dirt, trowel in hand. 'Yeah! You'd like her, she's really funny. She eats onion sandwiches.'

Maurice clicked his tongue. 'You twerp! What did you tell him that for?'

''cos she does! Why not, what's wrong with it?'

'Crikey mate.' Maurice shook his head.

Jacky giggled. 'She ate a witchetty grub once.'

Maurice set the wheelbarrow down with a thump and scowled at Jacky. 'You idiot.'

Harry burst out laughing. 'A witchetty grub?'

'She was just a kid then,' Maurice said. 'She told us about it.'

'Where does she live?' Harry asked.

'In Hobart. She used to live down here. She's a librarian at the town library.'

Harry raised his eyebrows. 'Wow.'

'Yeah, she's smart. I've got her phone number if you want it.'

Harry chuckled. 'That's alright.'

I watched Harry working. He had a faint smile on his face and I wondered if he was imagining being married. But who could he marry? Whoever she was, she'd have to like living out here in the bush. And fishing. And listening to the birds. What if he married some toff who made him live in a fancy house? I couldn't imagine him living in a fancy house. In fact, I couldn't imagine him living anywhere but in this old cottage with his garden, the fire pit, the treehouse and the birds.

Harry looked up and met my eye. 'You alright, Lily?'

I guessed I must be frowning. 'Do you think you'd want to get married?'

Harry tilted his head to the side and looked thoughtful. 'Maybe. I guess so.'

'Then I'll keep an eye out for a nice lady at church for you.' Everyone laughed and I felt my cheeks heat up. 'Well, we can't have you marrying just anyone, can we?' I said.

'No,' said Harry, gravely. 'We certainly can't. Thanks, Lily.'

I nodded and went back to work.

Keep going, Jon says to me now. Write the rest of the story. But the next bit is difficult because I have to admit my own part in what followed.

December arrived. The window of Lockharts General Store filled with tinsel and toys. Father Christmas appeared in a horse-drawn cart, riding down the main street of Crayfish Cove and throwing lollies to the children. Mum played Christmas carols on the tape deck and our house smelled like plum pudding and shortbread.

One weekend, nearing Christmas, Mr Hammond went away to a ministers' conference. While he was gone, Mrs Hammond took ill and had to be taken to hospital in Hobart. The medical issue was minor, and she was back within a couple of days.

Meanwhile, Dot's mother took Minnie-May in and arranged to have Kylie and me stay over. It was fun. We played cricket in one of their sheep paddocks, explored the farm, ate homemade pizzas and slept on camp beds in Dot's room. I was surprised at what good company Dot and Minnie-May were.

On the final night, after lights-out, we were all snuggled down in our sleeping bags when Kylie said, 'Let's play Truth, Dare or Promise.'

Dot's voice wobbled out of the dark. 'I don't like that game.'

'Come on, somebody play with me,' Kylie said.

'Fine,' I said. 'I'll go first if you want.' I was ready for sleep but I knew Kylie wouldn't give up until we'd at least played a round.

Kylie giggled. 'Alright, Miss Lily. What'll it be?'

'Truth,' I said.

In a silly, lilting voice, she said, 'Do you have a crush on Jonathan?'

I was glad it was dark because I felt myself blushing. I clicked my tongue and said, 'I shouldn't have picked truth.'

'I knew it!'

'Only a little one. But you have to keep it a secret.'

'We never tell secrets,' Kylie said. 'It's one of the rules. Who wants to go next? Minnie-May?'

Minnie-May turned over in her sleeping bag to face our beds. The sun had long since set and the moon shone dimly through the one window. Her face, hidden in the shadow of her bedding, was impossible to read but I sensed her looking at me.

'Yoohoo!' Kylie called. When Minnie-May didn't answer, she said, 'Alright, what about you, Dot?'

'I don't know,' Dot murmured.

Kylie huffed. 'Really, you two are boring. I choose dare.'

Dot sighed. 'I dare you to go to sleep.'

'Ugh. Have some fun, what's wrong with you?' Kylie tossed in her bed.

We lay quietly for a while. I wriggled down and secretly watched Minnie-May over the top of my sleeping bag. After a few minutes she repositioned herself, set her head on the edge of her mattress and looked at Kylie.

'Should you really never tell a secret?' she asked.

Kylie lifted her head. I peered into the darkness, trying to see her expression.

'I guess it depends,' Kylie answered.

'On what?' Minnie-May asked.

'On what it's about. What do you reckon, Dot?'

'I don't know.'

'Lily?'

A shaft of moonlight filtered in through the window and lay across Minnie-May's bed. She had turned to face me.

I thought about Harry and the Tasmanian tiger, how he hadn't told anyone because of what they would have done to the animal. He'd shared his secret with me in confidence and trusted me with it. There was no way I would ever tell anyone.

'No,' I said, decidedly. 'You should never, ever tell a secret.'

'Are you sure?' Dot said in a quiet voice.

'Yes,' I said.

When Kylie replied next, I had the sense she'd been trying to decide on the correct answer, and had settled on mine. 'Lily's right,' she said. 'You should never tell secrets. It's one of the rules.'

No one was keen to keep playing the game after that, so we settled down to sleep. But before I closed my eyes, I watched Minnie-May turn onto her back and lay her head on the pillow. She let out a long drawn-out breath as if everything inside her was seeping out into the air of Dot's bedroom.

I was oblivious, at the time, of the significance of the moment. Its in-betweenness. When I look back now, I see myself as a girl who has run up one side of a seesaw—a happy, innocent child—and who now stands balanced in the centre with one foot on one side and one on the other. The seesaw is about to tip. And on the other side, I will find a world where life is more complicated than I could imagine and people are not always as they seem.

<u>1978</u>

**Dear Diary,**
**Finally!!! We are high school students. All the grade sixes look so small! Were we really that little?**

**Dear Diary,**
**Kylie lent me her magazine with Leif Garrett's picture in it so I can drool over him on the weekend.**

**Dear Diary,**
**If Mum won't buy me a peasant dress like Miranda's, I'll simply die!!**

# 11

# Missing

Was there a warning in the chill of the wind that morning? A harbinger of tragedy? It seems now there should have been something, but I suppose there was nothing. I remember pulling up short at the beginning of Murphy's Lane to admire the rows of poplars either side of the road. Their leaves were changing colour from green to gold and orange with such potency, they appeared to alter the colour of the air around them.

I was twelve-going-on-thirteen and caught in the scratchy place between childhood and adolescence—somewhere between balloons and lipstick where you're longing for the lipstick but still wanting the balloons. I'd grown my hair to halfway down my back and discovered if I brushed the front just right, I could make it flutter back either side of my head when I walked, like Miranda's. I even started wearing dresses again, much to my mother's delight.

My time at Harry's was spent less in gardening and tree-climbing and more in lying on the grass with my journal and chatting to Harry while he worked. Jacky's interest in gardening had not wavered and he spent every minute he could with Harry. 'Your thumbs are way greener than mine, mate,' Harry would say, and Jacky's chest would puff out.

This day, we were helping harvest the fruit from the heavily laden apple trees. By the time I arrived, Jonathan was already up a ladder and Curly, Bobby and Sarah Pevensie picking from the lower branches. Jacky turned up on foot shortly afterwards, announcing his bike tyre had a puncture. Harry reassured him that there were only three deliveries he wanted done, and they were light ones—silverbeet and lettuce—so Jacky could walk. Jacky agreed. He'd been building a nest egg with the pocket money he earned from doing small deliveries for Harry.

We stacked the apples in wooden boxes and placed them in the cool spare room inside the house. Some were bound for Lockhart's General Store and the rest for a local market stall.

Harry found some shopping bags and let us fill them with as many apples as we could carry, to take home with us. Then he lit a fire in the living room, poured us glasses of lemonade and we flopped down for a rest. Sarah and I squished ourselves into the armchair on one side of the fireplace and Jacky sat on the arm of the chair opposite. The other three boys sat on the couch facing the fire. We lay back, munching the juicy, sweet apples and seeing who could crunch the loudest. Once the fire was going strong, Harry set about making a pile of cheese sandwiches.

I looked up at Harry's bookshelf where my story sat in its new picture frame. I thought about the day I'd given it to him, how he'd held it out to me and asked me to read it aloud. I hadn't understood the anxiety I'd ruffled in him, this man who appeared as strong and sturdy as the great oak tree at the end of his drive. I'd begun to understand the depth of the bond he shared with Jacky, who also had a learning disability.

I remembered our teacher, Miss Vance, tutting at Jacky in front of the class when he couldn't distinguish between the letters she held up to him—the way his freckles disappeared into the redness of his face in his humiliation. And the day he'd messed up the scoring at the sports carnival—Wayne Bottle yelling, 'Dumb-head!' across the oval and Jacky slinking away, his chin on his chest. In Harry's garden, Jacky was a king of sorts. He could tell you the names of every plant, shrub, tree and flower, even if he couldn't spell them. I watched the two of them now, sharing a smile as Harry set a plate of sandwiches on the coffee table.

We demolished the sandwiches, which Harry had made tasty with some of my mother's tomato relish. Jacky eventually stood up to leave and Harry handed him three bags of vegetables, indicating one in particular.

'If you wouldn't mind, Mrs Hoffman wants these this arvo.'

'I ain't going up there.' Jacky took a step backward and turned an irritated face to Harry.

Harry looked surprised. 'But it's on your way.'

Jacky shook his head. 'I don't want to.'

'Wayne's not there today, if that's what you're worried about.'

'What if he is?'

Gerda Hoffman was Wayne Bottle's foster mother, so Jacky tried to avoid the place.

'How about you just knock on the door, hand over the bag and go?'

Jacky dropped the third bag onto the armchair, shoved one hand in his pocket and said, 'No.'

Harry sighed. 'Could you leave it outside the door, then? Come on, mate, we had a deal.'

'I don't care about the deal.' Jacky's voice had an edge to it. He turned away and headed for the door, his shoulders pulled in tight.

Curly and Bobby twisted around on the couch to watch and Jonathan stood up.

Harry moved towards Jacky. 'Mate—'

'You can't make me,' Jacky muttered, reaching for the door handle.

'I wouldn't make you, of course not.' Harry threw his hands up. 'It would save me taking the ute out, that's all.' Harry put his hand out to Jacky. 'Look—'

Jacky's face flushed with anger and he let out an expletive that made Sarah gasp beside me. 'I ain't going!" he added as he yanked the front door open.

Harry put up his hands in surrender. 'Alright, mate. It's alright.'

With one hand holding the handle of the open door, Jacky stopped. He looked at us at the end of the room, then back at Harry. 'You know why,' he said, and vanished through the door. We heard his feet thumping down the front steps.

Harry stood motionless for a moment, his face twisting with emotion. Then, without a word, he took off after Jacky.

Sarah's face screwed up like she was about to cry. The rest of us hurried to the open door and watched Harry sprinting around the corner of the driveway. I returned to the armchair and put my arm around Sarah's shoulders. The others returned and Curly and Bobby sat on the edge of the couch.

Jonathan stood with his back to the fire and rubbed the tops of his arms with his hands. 'I guess we should wait for Harry to come back,' he said, uncertainly. He looked towards the door, his eyebrows pulled into an intense frown, and shook his head. 'Jacky hates Wayne Bottle.'

'Wayne's a turd,' Bobby said.

'Tell you what,' said Jonathan, 'how about I go and see what's going on.'

The rest of us waited silently by the fire until Jonathan returned a few minutes later, shaking his head and saying he couldn't find them. We waited a bit longer before deciding to leave. Jonathan tore a piece off the edge of a newspaper, found a pen on Harry's bookshelf and scribbled a note. He picked up the bag of vegetables to take to Gerda Hoffman's while I set up the screen around the fireplace.

We grabbed our bags of apples and walked the Pevensies back to their place, through the bush behind Harry's where the track led up to their back garden. Jonathan and I continued through their property to the main road and walked along the street together, silent in our shared discomfort. Jonathan said something about the situation seeming 'weird' and I agreed. We parted company when we came to Gerda Hoffman's house and Jonathan went up the drive to deliver the bag of vegetables.

I kept heading towards home. As I neared the church I looked out for Jacky but there was no sign of him and his bags of silverbeet. Molly Crouch leaned on her fence opposite the church, watching a group of teenagers crossing the road at the corner. When she saw me, she smiled and waved.

I arrived home and discovered Kylie had phoned, so I called her back and we spent the afternoon playing table tennis in her rumpus room. We'd just flopped down with a glass of Fanta when Kylie's mum put her head around the door.

'Lily, your mum's on the phone. She wants to speak to you.'

I followed her out to the hall and took up the handset. Mum sounded anxious. 'Lily, have you seen Jacky since you left Harry's place?'

'No, he left before we did.'

'So you haven't seen him since?'

'No.'

'Alright. I'll see you when you get home.'

I went back to Kylie, who said, 'What's up?'

'Nothing much,' I said, not wanting to mention Harry. 'Want another game?'

We played for a while longer until Kylie's mum came back in, clutching a tea towel and telling me Mum wanted me at home straight away. Mum was at the doorstep ushering me in as soon as I arrived, an urgency in her manner.

'Come and sit down,' she said. She plonked herself next to me on the edge of the couch and leaned towards me with her knees pressed together. 'I need to ask you some questions about this afternoon, when you were at Harry's.'

So that was it—someone had already spread the story about Harry and Jacky and the vegetables. I rolled my eyes.

'It wasn't Harry's fault. Jacky said a bad word.'

Mum's eyebrows pulled together in puzzlement. 'Did something happen?'

Too late, I realised my mistake. She hadn't heard about the altercation. 'Not really. Just that Jacky wouldn't deliver Mrs Hoffman's vegetables because he hates Wayne Bottle. He swore at Harry and ran away and Harry chased him.'

Mum's shoulders stiffened. 'Chased him where?'

'I dunno. Down the drive. Jonathan went after them but he couldn't find them.'

'What happened after that?'

'Nothing. Jonathan came back but Harry didn't. Why?'

'What did you do when Jonathan came back?'

I shrugged my shoulders. 'We all left.'

'Who's we?'

'Curly, Bobby and Sarah. And me and Jonathan.'

Mum nodded thoughtfully. 'Wait here.' She disappeared into the hall and I heard her dialling the telephone, her voice saying, 'Hello, this is June.' Her voice became softer and I couldn't hear what she said, so I assumed she'd pulled the handset by its cord into her bedroom.

After a couple of minutes she returned, sat down and said, 'Jacky's missing.'

I sat dumbly, trying to absorb this piece of information.

'After Jacky and Harry went, how long was it before you all left Harry's place?'

'Not long. A few minutes?'

I think I must have looked scared because Mum took my hand and squeezed it. She smiled and said, 'Don't worry, he'll turn up.'

But Jacky didn't turn up. The Hix family and some of their neighbours searched for a couple of hours to no avail. Later in the afternoon, thanks to the efficiency of the Crayfish Cove bush telegraph, a search party was quickly formed, led by Senior Constable Dave Munnings with help from the police officer from Durrunby. Groups were sent out from the central hub of the local church building.

Dad joined the search. Mum had to be home with Maudie so a group of younger local kids converged at our place which enabled their parents to join the search. Mum and some other housebound residents became part of the quickly organised telephone chain system. They manned the phones and passed on information while everyone else was instructed to keep the lines free to avoid congestion.

Maudie was excited about having so many children to play Snakes and Ladders with. I had a half-hearted game with them before curling into a chair in the corner of the room with a book—*Folklore and Fairytales*—that Nan had given me for Christmas.

The phone kept ringing and Mum would call the next person in the chain. She came into the lounge periodically to check on the kids and shake her head at me with a forlorn expression. At one point, she called me out to the hallway. With her hand over the mouthpiece, she said, 'Lily, is there anywhere you think that Jacky might have gone?'

'Um ...' A picture of Jacky flashed into my mind—peering through Kylie's binoculars and laughing at a three-legged dog. I took in a quick breath. 'What about the Hollow?' If he wanted to be somewhere by himself, it was the perfect place.

Mum spoke into the phone again. 'There's a place the kids call the Hollow... oh, you know the one?... Yes, that's right, have them check there.'

I tried to read some more but found myself rereading the same sentences over and over. It would be dark soon and I worried Jacky wouldn't be found before the light disappeared completely. I kept seeing images of him in my head—leaning on a stick and cawing like a raven, shoving a trowel into a garden bed with his face screwed up in concentration, pushing his feet down on the pedals of his bike and looking back with his rabbit-toothed grin. Despite him being younger than me, and a boy, I'd become quite fond of him.

The phone kept ringing and Mum kept passing information along the chain. My heart fell when she told me Jacky wasn't at the Hollow. I'd been so sure.

Maudie brought out a stack of jigsaw puzzles and the children became immersed in those. I watched them for a while until I had another thought, and slipped into the kitchen where Mum was standing at the sink, gazing out the window.

'Mum?'

She turned and smiled weakly. 'How are they all going in there?'

'Alright. Mum, I just thought of something.'

Her body stiffened in alert. 'Yes?'

'There's a place Harry took me once. I thought, maybe...' I shrugged.

'Tell me.'

'Well, it's too hard to explain. You can't see it from the road. I'd have to show you.'

'Right.' Mum strode out to the hall and I followed behind. As soon as she picked up the telephone handset, we heard voices. She put the handset to her ear, tutted and replaced it on the cradle. 'Crossed wires.'

'You could listen in.'

Mum grinned wryly. 'It's tempting.'

I returned to my book of *Folklore and Fairytales* but the words swam into each other. Someone bawled and I looked up to find a bowl of potato chips turned over on the carpet and little eyes looking about nervously. I scooped the crisps back into the bowl before returning to my book. Still, my mind wandered back to Jacky and Harry and the events of the afternoon. After Jacky had rushed out the door, I'd looked at Harry's face. What I saw there had shocked me. I didn't understand it. I held my book closer to my face, trying to forget about it and concentrate on the story about the villagers who swapped their bags of troubles with each other.

A few minutes later, Mum came in and squatted next to my chair. In a low voice, she said, 'I've sent word out to Constable Munnings via Betty. She'll let the next group checking in at the church know. I'll need to stay here with the children, but would you go with the policeman and show him the place you told me about?'

I nodded and bit my lip. It was scary but I was glad to be doing something important.

Constable Munnings turned up soon after. I was relieved to be out of the house, as the children were becoming ratty. Mum had put a couple of them down to sleep in our bedrooms and was feeding the others sandwiches and milk.

As we drove away, I thought how it should have been an exciting event, riding in a real police car with a kind policeman, but I just felt anxious.

Constable Munnings turned into Murphy's Lane and asked, 'How far down?'

I sat up straighter, peered through the windscreen and pointed. 'There somewhere.'

He pulled over and we exited the car. I crossed the road and studied the poplars. They all looked the same and I couldn't be sure where Harry had disappeared into the bushes. I looked back at Harry's gate and towards the trees again, trying to remember how far down it was.

'Harry knows where it is,' I said. 'We could ask him.'

Constable Munnings said in an overly cheerful voice, 'That's alright. I reckon you and I can find it.'

We poked about in the bushes near the poplars, pulling branches apart and trying to see behind them. My arms were getting scratched but I barely felt the stings. I was determined to find Jacky so everything could go back to normal.

Then I saw it—the section of wire fence almost flattened, next to a wild hawthorn bush. 'Over here,' I said as I recognised the two poplars Harry had disappeared behind. I gingerly parted the branches of the bushes behind them and found the place, looking back at Constable Munnings with a grin. 'You wouldn't even know it was here.'

We squeezed through the bushes and found ourselves on the same track Harry and I had followed. The police officer looked around. 'Well, how about that. Good hiding place, I would think.'

I started walking confidently along the flattened track. It wasn't as difficult as I thought it would be to follow it, now that I was in the lead. But Constable Munnings said, 'Wait, Lily.'

I stopped and looked back.

'Try and keep to the sides, away from the middle, and step gently.'

'Why?'

'If Jacky's been here, there might be clues.'

Of course! My mind swung back to my Enid Blyton *Famous Five* books. To stories of Julian, Anne and the other children, solving mysteries by following tyre tracks and footprints. I edged as far to the side of the track as I could and crept forward with the policeman behind me.

When I came to the small clearing with the hollow log, I turned and pointed. Constable Munnings said, 'Stay here,' and approached the log. He edged carefully around it and stood on the other side. His eyes roamed the area—the ground of the clearing, the surrounding trees and bushes—and came to rest on the log itself. He stood for some time, looking about, before squatting down and bending his head to peer closely at a section of the ground I couldn't see. He looked over the top of the log, directly at me. 'Harry brought you here, did he?'

I nodded. 'We sat there, on that side,' I pointed again. He kept looking at me and it made me feel like I should keep talking. 'He told me how he used to come here to listen to the birds when he was a boy.'

Constable Munnings stood up, looked back at the ground by the log, up into the trees and scanned the area once more. 'Thanks, Lily. You've been very helpful.' He smiled and indicated with his hand for me to go back through the track while he followed behind. When we emerged from the bushes, he stepped onto the road, turned around and scanned the line of poplars. His eyes settled on the squashed wire fence and I presumed he was making a mental note of where the entrance to the track was.

When we were back in the police car, he switched on his police radio and told someone to meet him in Murphy's Lane. A voice spoke back but I didn't understand the words through the crackle of the radio. He drove me home, thanked me again and waited until I'd gone inside before driving away.

Mum met me in the hall as I came in. 'How did you go?'

'I showed him the place. Jacky wasn't there, though.'

'Even if he hasn't been there, the police need to know that too. So you've done a good thing.' She put her arm around my shoulders.

I tried to feel good about showing Constable Munnings where Harry had taken me—Jacky *might* have been there after all—but I couldn't help the feeling I'd betrayed Harry by showing someone else his secret place. Constable Munnings was probably going to show it to the Durrunby policeman. What if lots of people trampled through there and messed it up? It wouldn't be private anymore and the Tassie tiger would never come back.

I didn't feel good. I didn't feel helpful or hopeful, or important. I just felt weary and sad.

When dark descended, there was not much anyone could do until morning. All the little children went back to their various homes. Dad came home with a helpless expression and not much of an appetite. Maudie was the only one of us who appeared cheerful and no one begrudged her that. In fact, she helped me keep my spirits up and for that, and many other things, I loved her beyond measure.

That night, I lay huddled in my bed. Even through my closed window, I heard the sounds of people who, possibly because they couldn't sleep, had chosen to continue the search—Jacky's name echoing hollowly in the street, a rattle of metal bins as someone searched the dark recesses behind them, cars creeping slowly along the road.

Eventually, the sounds stopped, or I slept. Morning trailed in through the chink in my curtains and I woke with a sense of dread in the pit of my belly. When I went out to the kitchen, Mum told me Dad had gone out at first light to rejoin the search. Maudie sat at the table in her pyjamas and Mum stirred a pot of porridge on the stove in her dressing gown. She hadn't brushed her hair.

'Nan's going to meet us at church,' Mum said. 'I don't know if there'll be a service. We'll walk down anyway, and see what happens. I think we need to get out of the house.'

She poured porridge into our bowls and sat with us.

'Poor Jacky,' said Maudie as she stirred honey into her porridge. 'He would be cold.'

'Yes, he would be cold,' Mum said. 'When they find him, they'll warm him up.'

After we'd had breakfast and dressed, I followed Maudie out to the front yard where she began to spin in her new green dress. I stood at the fence and looked down the length of the empty street. I wondered where the searchers were now. On the beach? Up in the hills? As far as Durrunby?

I was sitting on the front step waiting for Mum when Dad pulled up on the road beside the house in the Datsun. He came through the gate, his back stooped and face strained. He shot an irritated look at Maudie, who was still spinning, and said, 'Do that in the back yard,

Maudie. You don't need to show your underpants to the whole town.' He leapt up the front steps and into the house.

Maudie stopped and her bottom lip came out. I reached out my hand towards her and said, 'Come on. We'll both go out the back.'

We went through the kitchen, where Dad was already scoffing a bowl of porridge. Mum slouched in the chair opposite with her head leaning on one hand, watching him. Outside, I sat on the back step and watched Maudie spin and spin without getting dizzy, her face a concentrated frown.

Where was Jacky? How could they not have found him by now? Crayfish Cove wasn't very big and there were only so many places a kid could hide. Harry might have a better idea where he could be. I was about to go inside to ask Dad if they'd asked Harry, when I heard the Datsun start up and the rattle of its engine as it took off along the main road. I sat back down, elbows on my knees and chin in my hands.

We were meant to be squeezing into the car now, heading off to pick up Nan for church. Mum should have been smiling this morning and making herself pretty while Dad kissed her cheek and told her how beautiful she was. Instead, it was as if the air had shifted and brought with it something odious and invisible.

Wherever Jacky was, he'd been there all night. Maudie was right, he would be cold. Had he run away? Was he hiding in the bushes somewhere, still angry with Harry?

I watched Maudie spin, her green dress swirling around her waist like a green mist. Her frown had vanished, an expression of calm now filling her features. Where did her mind go when she spun? My big sister who walked her own quiet and secret path. Did she feel this sinister shift in the atmosphere like I did? I think it was that day, as I watched Maudie in the back yard, when I began to understand why she spun. Why she turned and turned until the angst inside her gathered itself together and spun out of her, leaving her centre calmed.

Mum appeared at the back door and ushered us in. She said Dad had gone to join a search heading towards the woods around Madding Hill, further out of town.

'Why would Jacky go to the woods?' I asked.

She turned her eyes to me for a moment, though they seemed to look through me. She wasn't wearing lipstick. 'I don't know,' she said.

And I wished with everything in my heart that she would go to the mirror and put on some lipstick, spray her hair with Gossamer Invisible Net, spin around and smile and say, 'Chop, chop. Off we go.'

# 12

## A siren in the night

AT THE CHURCH, MOST of the men were missing, having joined the search party. Betty Crouch was stationed at the serving hatch with a boiled urn, a tin of pound cake and a plate of Iced VoVo biscuits. Mrs Hammond bustled about, giving directions, dressed in her usual nondescript colours but sporting a smart spotted scarf.

'Those joining the search,' she called, 'gather in the auditorium with Arthur. Everyone else, grab yourself a cuppa—prayer meeting in the tea-room.'

Betty drew up beside us. 'June, good to see you. This is terrible isn't it? Would Maudie and Lily like to—' A wail rose up in the background. 'Oh dear, that's Molly. Excuse me.'

Mum brushed Maudie's shoulder with her hand and said, 'Maudie, come to the door. We can wait for Nan outside where it's quieter.'

We escaped into the carpark as Nan was striding across it towards us. Betty reappeared with her wailing mother-in-law beside her. 'Sorry, I had to get Molly. She didn't want to come out this morning. There, there, it's alright Mol.'

Nan drew up beside us with a grim expression. 'Terrible business,' she said to Mum in a low voice. 'They're searching up near Madding Hill now. It rained some in the night so it's a bit hard going, apparently.'

Maudie began to rock from her waist and Nan put her hand firmly on her shoulder. 'Maudie love, would you like to come to Nan's? We don't need to stay.'

Maudie nodded and calmed immediately while Molly continued to whimper.

Mum leaned towards Betty and murmured, 'I can take Molly over to your place and sit with her a while, if that'd be helpful.'

Betty clasped her hands together. 'Oh, would you? It's just, with Amos on the search and all the children...' Her voice trailed off.

Nan and Maudie headed off together and I decided to go with Mum. She took Molly's arm and helped her across the road to her house and we let ourselves in through the unlocked front door. Molly kicked off her shoes and shuffled into the lounge room where she dropped into an armchair.

The lounge room windows faced the street and the church on the other side. We could hear cars going in and out of the carpark and the intermittent rise and fall of voices. While Mum went into the kitchen to make a pot of tea, I distracted myself by picking up a *Woman's Weekly* from the coffee table and flicking through it. Nothing of interest there for a twelve-year-old girl—advertisements for cigarettes and Playtex panty girdles, how to crochet a rug from discarded stockings. I contented myself with reading the Marmaduke cartoon until Mum clicked on the television and we escaped the bedlam by watching an old Fred Astaire and Ginger Rogers movie. Molly fell asleep in her chair and was quietly snoring when the front door opened. Mum turned off the telly as Betty came in. From her face, we could see there was no news.

As we were leaving, Molly woke with a start, looked up at Betty hopefully and said, 'Jacky?'

Betty shook her head. 'Not yet, Mol. Won't be long. How about you and me go for a walk?'

Molly shook her head. 'Never come out!' she wailed.

'It's alright, Mol. We'll stay here.'

Betty walked us to the door and we said our goodbyes as Molly wailed piteously from the lounge. Betty glanced behind her and back at us. 'She's terribly upset about it. She keeps insisting she won't come out.'

As we walked down the path to their front gate, Molly's cries came louder and more insistent. 'Never come out...never come out!'

The afternoon was frantic. Dad came home to quickly eat lunch and head back out. Mum and I entertained more children in the afternoon and I started to wish I'd gone to Nan's with Maudie. By early evening I was exhausted and fell asleep on the couch. Mum helped me to bed at some point and I fell into a deep sleep, but woke in the night to the sound of a siren blaring past the house and down the street.

I lay there for a moment, listening, but heard nothing else but the tick of the clock by my bedside. I couldn't make out the time from its glow-in-the-dark hands. Stumbling out of bed, foggy and disoriented, I shuffled to my bedroom door and looked out. The outside light was still on, burning through the glass in the front door and casting golden squares across the hallway floor. A chink of light shone around the door of the lounge. Mum would be waiting up for Dad. I wandered sleepily to the hall window, moved the curtain aside and peered out.

The Datsun sat in the driveway so I assumed Dad must be home already. I squinted my eyes and pressed my nose to the glass. That was strange—I could see Dad still in the car, sitting up like a statue in the front seat. The way he kept sitting there, staring straight ahead, made my breath catch in my body. I backed away from the window, tiptoed through the hall into my bedroom and crawled under the covers. The world felt unsafe, like it was about to crack open and I didn't know what it would look like when it did.

In the morning, I wandered groggily into the kitchen, the remnants of dark dreams swirling in my head. I found Mum seated at the table, surrounded by breakfast things and staring into space. There was something not right about her face, her hair, the way her shoulders curled. I shuffled into a seat and reached for the cereal box and Mum straightened up in her chair. She watched me as I ruffled about in the cellophane and pulled out two Weet-Bix.

'You had a long sleep,' she said. 'Dad's gone to work already. We wanted to—' She blinked rapidly and looked away.

The bird in my chest began to beat its wings so rapidly, I felt dizzy. What was wrong with Mum? And where was Maudie?

Mum slid her hand across the table towards me. 'I need to tell you something, Lily.'

I couldn't seem to catch my breath. There it was—the terrible dream, flapping in my head. Maudie was lost. We searched and searched—all the streets, the lanes and the dark woods—but we couldn't find her. So we hunted through all the metal bins, pulling off the lids, making them rattle and fall over and roll down the road, tumbling, tumbling.

'Lily, are you alright?'

I nodded rapidly, reached for the milk carton and poured milk into my bowl. It was only a dream. But why wasn't Maudie here? My eyes darted left and right. Where was my sister?

'Lily? You haven't woken up properly yet, have you?' Mum smiled, but her smile was watery and sad.

I dug my spoon into my cereal. As I ate, I hoped she wouldn't say anything else. Her face—white as if all the joy had leached out of it—was too much. I didn't want to know what she had to tell me.

'Lily, sweetheart. I'm so sorry.'

Then she said it. She broke the news about Jacky. 'They found him late last night. Your friend, Jacky, has died.'

It didn't hit me for a moment. I remember spooning more Weet-Bix into my mouth. Gulping. Gulping again, forcing the food down my throat. Then it all coming back out, not only that mouthful but everything I'd already eaten, over the table, down the front of me and into my lap.

Mum rushed to my side of the table, pushed herself into the seat beside me and put her arms around me. My breath was coming in rasps. Jacky was dead.

But Maudie was alright. She was at Nan's, of course she was. I should be feeling sad. I tried to conjure Jackie's face in my head but it wouldn't come. So I grabbed at the thought of Maudie—my beautiful sister with her golden hair and her strange ways who wasn't lost, or dead, but was safe at Nan's—and I began to giggle. I couldn't stop. I was horrified with myself, hating myself, while my body shook with laughter.

Mum held me close and kissed my hair. 'It's alright,' she whispered.

Maudie stayed at Nan's all day and Mum kept me home from school. I was desperate to talk to Kylie so I pleaded to go, but Mum wouldn't budge.

'I *need* to talk to her.'

'Kylie's not going to school today either.'

'How do you know?'

'I talked to her mother.'

'But—'

'You can go tomorrow.'

I stomped into the lounge and sat on the floor, my back against the couch and my knees pulled up. Mum came in and knelt on the floor facing me. She cupped my cheeks with her hands and tilted my head up to look into her eyes.

'Lily, when you go to school, you'll hear things about Jacky. Dad and I think it's best you hear those things from us first.'

'What things?'

Mum turned herself around and sat beside me on the floor. She took my hand and held it. 'They found Jacky in the bushes at the bottom of Madding Hill. He'd been strangled.'

I turned to her and shook my head. 'How?'

Mum spoke matter-of-factly. 'Someone put their hands around his neck and squeezed until he ran out of breath. He wouldn't have suffered long.'

'Would it have hurt?' I said in a small voice.

'A bit, but it would have been over very quickly.'

'But who would do that?'

Mum shook her head. 'I don't know.'

The tears came then. A few silent ones dripping down my cheeks and onto my blouse. Mum put her arm around me and said a prayer for Jacky and his family, and we sat for a while, saying nothing.

After that, the phone started ringing and didn't stop. I tried to amuse myself with books and TV, even wishing Maudie was there for a game of Snakes and Ladders. Occasionally, I'd go into the hall and find the telephone sitting on the hall floor instead of on its stand, with the cord of the handset stretched tight and disappearing into Mum and Dad's bedroom. I longed to talk to Kylie. Was she, also, wandering around her house distracted?

I ventured out into the front yard in the afternoon and stood at the gate, looking up and down the street. In the distance, I saw a few people getting in and out of cars in the general store carpark, but there wasn't much else going on. One of the neighbours was mowing his nature strip. Another went by on the other side of the street, being pulled along by a Great Dane straining on its lead.

'Lily!' Mum shot out of the front door. 'What are you doing?'

I turned. 'Nothing.'

'Come inside.'

'Why?' I followed her in, puzzled.

As she closed the door, she said, 'I need you to stay inside.'

'Why?'

She reached out and rubbed my arm. 'Because of what happened to Jacky. The police are out looking for who did it. But, until they find that person...' Her voice trailed off.

The reality sunk in deeper. Jacky was murdered. The terrible word jarred in my head. 'I want to see Harry.'

Mum's mouth turned down and she blinked. 'I'm sorry pet, you can't.'

'But why?'

'Not yet.' She sighed as the phone rang again. 'Let's not answer it.'

'Really?'

'I'm sick of it. Dad's picking Maudie up from Nan's after work. How about we bake them a treat? We could use a distraction.'

'Cupcakes?'

'Cupcakes it is.'

She took the phone off the hook and we baked all afternoon. We coloured the icing in the brightest, most garish colours possible—bold green, blue, yellow and pink—as if the colours could brighten the darkness closing in around us.

# 13

## One more thing...

MUM INSISTED ON WALKING me to school the next day. Beside us, Maudie pushed her measuring wheel along. She counted the clicks as she went, stopping periodically to write down the measurements.

A heaviness blanketed the town. No hellos or cheery waves greeted us. Our neighbours nodded to Mum with grim faces as we passed, in silent acknowledgement of the tragedy that had gutted the town. Within the school grounds, parents mingled in small groups here and there, talking in hushed voices.

We were met outside my classroom by some of the teachers. Miss Vance, who never smiled, greeted us with her face twisted into something that could have been an attempt at one, though I wasn't sure. There would be an assembly first thing, she said, and parents were invited to stay.

We made our way to the assembly hall, along with a gaggle of students and parents pushing along in the same direction. I parted company with Mum and Maudie at the door and made my way to my class area. Lines of chairs filled the hall, adult-sized ones at the back and diminishing in size to the tiny wooden ones at the front where the infant classes sat. I sat on a hard, plastic seat, pulled off my jumper and set it on the seat beside me to save it for Kylie. The room was buzzing with chatter. Anxious faces looked about. On the stage the headmaster, Mr Hinkley, was talking in a huddle with two men in suits.

Kylie turned up a few minutes later, out of breath. 'What's this about?' she asked.

'Look,' I nodded my head in the direction of the stage.

'Huh, who do you reckon they are?'

'I think I can guess. Think *Cop Shop.*'

Kylie's eyes widened. 'Cops!'

Mr Hinkley moved to the microphone and shushed the hall. The babble diminished to a few coughs echoing off the walls and some scuffling of feet. He began by voicing his regret at the tragic death of 'one of our valued students,' assuring everyone that the students were in a safe place at Crayfish Cove District School. He announced that he had some guests, two police officers, who would like to address the school.

'Told you,' I whispered.

Silence descended as the two men in dark suits and ties stepped forward to the front of the stage. Mr Hinkley handed the microphone to the larger, grey-haired man and stepped aside.

The police officer thanked the headmaster and turned to face the audience. 'Good morning boys and girls, parents and teachers. I'm Detective Sergeant Bullard and this is Detective Constable Scott.' The younger man nodded to the audience. 'Firstly, I'd like to say how sorry we are that one of your fellow students, Jacky Hix, has died in such tragic circumstances.'

A rustle echoed through the hall as children shifted in their seats.

'I assure you that we—myself, Detective Constable Scott and your Senior Constable Munnings—will work together to find the person responsible so your community can go back to being a safe place in which to live.'

Someone in the back row where the parents sat, clapped briefly.

'We've set up a room here at the school to work in—Mr Hinkley will tell you about that in a moment—and today, and over the next few days, we'll be talking to some of you and asking questions. It's nothing to be worried about. That's what policemen do, we ask questions. It's so we can find out if you know anything which could help us find this person and bring them to justice. If any of you believes you do know something which could help us, anything at all, please come and speak to us.'

I don't think much work was done in school that day. We sat over our exercise books, chewing on the ends of our pens, whispering and staring into space. The teachers tutted and raised their voices more than usual in an effort to coax some work out of us.

At lunch time, Kylie and I ventured outside, despite the cold, and found a private spot under a tree by the oval.

'Who do you think did it?' Kylie asked as she lifted a curried egg sandwich from her lunch box.

I shrugged my shoulders. 'Who knows? It could be anyone.'

'Someone who hates Jacky, I guess.' Kylie took a bite of her sandwich.

'Everyone likes Jacky. *Liked.*'—I corrected myself— 'He was nice. And funny. He was so funny sometimes.' I took a sandwich from my own lunch box and looked at it. I had no appetite.

'I know, remember the Christmas play?' Kylie began to giggle, stopped herself and grimaced as if horrified she'd let herself smile. 'It's so *tragic!*'

'I hope they catch him quickly.'

'I reckon it was Old Man Skinner from the top of Madding Hill. Was it a full moon on Saturday night?'

'I don't think so.'

'Probably not him then, he only comes out on a full moon.'

'Where did you hear that?'

'Mum.'

I pulled my bread slices apart to inspect the contents of my sandwich. Tuna and lettuce. I thought of the cheese ones Harry had made us on Saturday, smeared with Mum's tomato relish. I wanted to talk about that afternoon with Kylie, but Kylie had absorbed her mother's dislike of Harry and closed up whenever his name was mentioned. So, I was surprised when she lifted her chin with a challenge in her eyes, and said, 'Mum says Harry was the last person to see Jacky alive.'

Thanks to Dad frequently quoting from his favourite police shows, my retort slipped from my tongue almost sooner than I knew it was there. 'No, he wasn't.'

'How do you know?'

'Because,' I said, lifting my own chin at Kylie, 'the last person to see Jacky alive was the person who killed him.'

After lunch, our class was squeezed into the library with the grade sixes while some of the teachers helped the police set up an interview room. Dot and Minnie-May sat at one end of a table together with their bodies squished up so close together they appeared to be joined. Dot saw me and waved. I pretended not to see her.

About half an hour into the lesson, the young detective knocked on the library door and poked his head in.

'Excuse me.' He smiled at the librarian, who started smoothing her hair with her fingers. 'May I please borrow Lily Craig?'

I was horrified. Every face turned towards me and, as I exited the library, I felt all their eyes crawling over my back.

'I'm Detective Constable Scott,' he said, as we walked down the corridor together. His shoes made sharp clicks on the lino floor. 'This won't take long. We're just going to ask you a few questions.'

He took me into the classroom that had been set up for the police officers. Constable Munnings was there, writing on a blackboard. I was led behind a carpet-covered partition that held a ragged times-table poster hanging by a single drawing pin. There was a desk and some plastic school chairs, one of which was occupied by Miss Aubrey, my former teacher. She whispered, 'Hello, Lily,' and smiled encouragingly at me. Constable Scott indicated a chair next to Miss Aubrey for me to sit on, then perched himself on the edge of another and crossed his ankles.

Behind the desk sat the burly detective with the grey hair. He had his shirt-sleeves rolled up and leaned on his elbows, reading something on the desk in front of him, his brow furrowed. As I sat down he looked up.

'Ah, Laura is it?'

I stared blankly at him.

'It's Lily Craig, sir.' Constable Scott leaned forward with his hands pressed together on his knees and winked at me.

'Ah yes, Lily. I'm Detective Sergeant Bullard. I understand Jacky Hix was a friend of yours. I'm sorry for your loss. We're talking to everyone who saw Jacky on Saturday so we can put together a picture of what happened.'

I started jigging my feet on the floor, feeling an urgent need to use the bathroom.

'You saw Jacky at the home of Harry Fernley on Saturday. Is that correct?'

'Yes.'

The detective smiled. 'Good, good. And who else was there?'

'Jonathan and—'

'Jonathan Abbott?'

I nodded. 'And some of the Pevensie kids—Curly, Bobby and Sarah.'

'Anyone else?'

'No.'

'And what were you doing there?'

'Helping Harry pick apples.'

'I see. What time did you leave?'

I shrugged my shoulders.

'Can you tell me why Jacky left Harry's home before the rest of you?'

So, the detectives had already talked to at least one other of us. I wondered who. 'He was going off to deliver some vegetables.'

'Was there an argument between Jacky and Harry Fernley before Jacky left?'

I hesitated. Why was he asking about that?

'Think carefully.'

'No.'

'No, there was no argument?'

'No.'

Sergeant Bullard watched me. Was he waiting for me to say something else? I sucked my lips in and stared back.

'Alright Laura, what can you remember about the conversation between Jacky and Harry before Jacky left the house?'

My fists clenched in my lap as he called me by the wrong name for the second time. 'Jacky didn't want to take vegetables to Mrs Hoffman's because of Wayne Bottle. He doesn't like Wayne because he's mean to him.' A horrifying thought crashed into my consciousness and I blurted, 'Maybe Wayne killed him!'

'We'll be interviewing everyone. What did Harry say when Jacky didn't want to take the vegetables?'

I looked to the ceiling as I thought. 'Something like, it won't hurt you, and something about they had a deal.'

'Yes?' The sergeant nodded encouragingly.

'Jacky said a bad word. Then he said Harry couldn't make him go. And Harry said he wouldn't make him go.'

'Then what happened?'

'Jacky left.'

'What did Harry do then?'

The scene was there in my head. Jacky holding the door handle, looking at us, looking back at Harry. He said something—what was it? *You know why.* But what did he mean? I'd looked at Harry's face and saw... I mustn't have seen right, because it didn't make sense.

'Do you remember what Harry did then?' Sergeant Bullard prompted, pulling me back into the tiny corner of the classroom.

'He went out after him.'

'Why do you think Harry went after him?'

I shrugged my shoulders. 'To make sure he was alright?'

'Did you see either of them after that?'

I shook my head.

'Do you have any idea where they may have gone?'

'No.'

The detective looked across at Miss Aubrey and nodded.

'Lily?' Miss Aubrey smiled at me. 'Remember the journals you had, back when you were in my class? You wrote about all those adventures you had with your friends at Harry's place.'

I frowned. She was speaking in a sing-song, almost childlike voice as if I were a two-year-old instead of twelve.

'The policemen would like to have a look at those journals. You may have written something in there that could help them find the person who hurt Jacky.'

'But I didn't—' I shook my head, confused.

'I know you were just writing about things you all did together. But there may be something that will help them. I've called your mother and asked her if the police can have them for a while. I'm telling you so you know and won't be surprised. When they've finished with them, you will receive them back, I promise.'

I wanted to cry. My journals were private. There were things in there I'd never shown anyone. Like where I'd gushed about my crush on Jonathan. Oh, the mortification! I knew my cheeks had reddened—I could feel them flaming. Constable Scott looked away and picked at a fingernail.

'Thank you, you've been very helpful,' Sergeant Bullard said, in a tone that indicated the interview was over.

Miss Aubrey walked me back to class—my need for the bathroom had vanished—but her smiles and chatter did nothing to dispel the growing tightness in my abdomen. All eyes turned to me again as I re-entered the classroom so I lifted my head, sat back in my chair and said to anyone who asked, 'The police said I was very helpful.'

It wasn't long before the young detective came back to the library and asked for Minnie-May. The poor girl gasped and nearly fell out of her seat.

After school, Mum and Maudie came to collect me. Maudie came into my classroom holding a pile of library books, clearly excited. 'Look, Lily. I'm learning all about police work.'

I ignored her and asked Mum if she'd given my journals to the detectives. She admitted she had so I glared at her, spun around and stomped down the corridor with my arms crossed, leaving her to pick up my bag. I refused to speak all the way home.

Maudie tutted at me as we went inside, and said, 'You're being naughty.'

I made a growling sound, ran to my bedroom and threw myself on the bed. Mum followed me in and sat on the edge of the bed. She stroked the back of my head, so I pulled a pillow over it.

I felt Mum lift one end of the pillow. 'Lily, I'm sorry I had to give the policemen your journals. But I promise you, they're not interested in anything that doesn't directly relate to the case. They have a lot of information to sort through, so they won't even remember any of the other things you wrote.'

I growled again so Mum left me alone. When she'd gone, I slipped off the bed and quietly closed the door. I went to my bedside table and pulled out the bottom drawer. There was a space between the bottom of the drawer and the floor where I kept whichever journal I was presently writing in. There it was, my current journal, safe from the eyes of the policemen. That was something, at any rate. They wouldn't be reading about our secret girls' game of Truth, Dare or Promise on the oval.

The detectives did not keep usual work hours. Over the coming days, the families of Crayfish Cove were visited at all hours, including the evenings and sometimes late in the night. We knew who had been questioned, of course, via the ever functioning bush telegraph. One evening right in the middle of tea, we were not surprised at the knock on the door and the presence in the doorway of two men dressed in dark suits.

Mum had worded me up beforehand, that they may want to discuss the contents of my journals. 'There's nothing to worry about, Lily. Whatever they ask you, all you need to do is tell the truth.'

I heard the detectives introduce themselves to Dad in the hallway. The rest of us were sitting at the tea table. Mum looked at me, nodded a silent reminder, and we waited for them to enter the kitchen.

Sergeant Bullard came first, saying, 'We're sorry for interrupting your dinner, but we'd like a word with Lily, if we may.'

Constable Scott followed, carrying an armload of my journals. He smiled at me and said, 'You can have these back. Thank you for letting us read them.' As if I had a choice! Mum took them and thanked him while I turned away and shoved a forkful of food into my mouth.

Maudie said, 'Are you policemen?'

'Yes, we are,' the sergeant replied.

'Why aren't you wearing uniforms?'

Mum said, 'I'll explain later, Maudie,' and invited the detectives into the lounge room.

Maudie pushed her chair out and stood up. 'I can help the policemen, too.'

'Thank you, Maudie,' the constable said. 'We'll interview you if we need to.'

'I know lots of things. I'm very good at Maths.'

Dad urged her to sit while Mum and I went into the other room, and I heard Maudie say, 'Why won't they let me help?' I was irritated because I hadn't finished my lamb chop and I was looking forward to apple pie.

'We'd like you to stay, Mrs Craig,' the sergeant said.

Mum sat close to me on the couch and the men took the armchairs. Constable Scott opened a briefcase and took out some papers, which he handed to Sergeant Bullard. In horror, I saw they were copies of pages from my journals.

'Lily,' said the sergeant, 'I have a couple of questions about what you've written in your books. By the way, you're a good writer.'

Mum squeezed my hand.

'You wrote here about an older boy, Wayne Bottle, teasing Jacky on the school oval. Can you tell me about that?'

I sat up straight. Did they think Wayne Bottle had killed Jacky? I could tell them lots about him. 'It was at the sports carnival. Jacky was taking his turn recording the race scores and Wayne came second but Jacky wrote him down on the wrong list. Jacky has trouble with reading and makes—made—mistakes sometimes. It wasn't his fault.'

'Of course not,' the detective said kindly. 'What happened next?'

'Wayne yelled at him. He called him a dumb-head in front of everyone.'

'I see. There's something from a few years ago that interests me also. Here, you've written about you and Harry Fernley having a secret.'

I saw the quick turn of Mum's head from the corner of my eye. I turned to find her peering intently at me. 'What's this?' she said.

I thought about the day Miss Aubrey pushed the journal over to me and asked me about the entry. How she wanted to know the secret. The elaborate lie I'd made up on the spot about finding a bird's nest with eggs in it and keeping it a secret with Harry. But I couldn't lie to the policemen. Mum had said it was important to tell the truth.

'Lily?' Mum said.

I sighed. 'Don't tell anyone,' I said, and turned back to the detectives. 'When Harry was a boy he saw a Tasmanian tiger in the bushes. He kept it a secret because if he'd told people, they would've caught it and put it in a cage and it would have been scared and maybe died. He told me about it and that's the secret.'

The sergeant nodded. 'I see. Has Harry asked you to keep any other secrets?'

'He didn't ask me to keep it secret.'

'I thought you said it was a secret between you.'

'*He* kept it a secret. He said—' It was so long ago, I couldn't remember what Harry had said. Had he even used the word 'secret'? I shook my head. 'I can't remember.'

'That's alright. Try to remember if there have been any other secrets you've kept for Harry. Anything you can think of.'

I shook my head. The question left me baffled.

'One more question, then. On the last day you saw Jacky at Harry Fernley's, just before Jacky left the house and Harry followed him, what would you say Harry's mood was? Did he seem upset, angry perhaps?'

My shoulders tensed and I chewed my lip. I thought of the scene, Harry holding out his hand to Jacky, Jacky flying through the door. I'd watched Harry's face at the moment Jacky vanished and had been shocked at what I saw there. He *was* angry. I glanced at the detective and quickly looked away. Could detectives read people's minds?

'What do you think he was feeling, Lily?' Constable Scott asked, smiling encouragingly. 'Was he angry?'

I knew I had to tell the truth. I looked at the constable and nodded.

'How angry?' he asked.

'He was—' I pictured Harry's face again, contorted in an expression of fury. It was only for a moment, but it was there.

'Yes?' Constable Scott leaned towards me.

I squeezed my hands together in my lap. 'Really angry.'

Maudie's voice rang out from the doorway. 'Why are you asking Lily about Harry?'

Mum stood up. 'Maudie, where's Dad?'

'In the bathroom.' Maudie walked up to the sergeant and stood by his chair. 'I thought you were trying to find the killer. Why are you asking about Harry?'

'We're asking about lots of people,' Sergeant Bullard said.

'For the process of elimination?'

Mum and both policemen appeared surprised.

'I've been reading about it in my library books. If you need assistance, I know lots about police procedure.'

'Thank you, Maudie,' Constable Scott said. 'We'll certainly ask if we need your help.'

Maudie nodded. She left the room as Dad appeared, looking for her.

'That'll do for now,' Sergeant Bullard said, rising from his chair. 'We may have more questions so—' (and he grinned at me as he said this) '—don't leave the country.'

I wasn't amused.

'And Lily,' he added, 'I know you like this fellow, Harry, but he hasn't been truthful with you. The Tasmanian tiger has been extinct for over forty years. He could not possibly have seen one.'

I squeezed both hands into fists. That was the end of any trust I had in Detective Sergeant Bullard. I vowed that whatever he asked me next, I wouldn't tell. I would keep all the secrets I wanted.

Mum walked the police officers to the door while I hovered behind, impatient to slip by them into the kitchen and get back to my tea.

As Sergeant Bullard reached the door, he turned and said, 'One more thing,' as if impersonating the detective in the police drama, *Columbo*. He looked directly at me and asked, 'Do you have a recent journal? One you've been writing in lately?'

I looked straight at him, folded my arms across my chest, and said, 'No.'

# 14

## A funeral and rumours

THE SKY WAS A deep, calm blue on the day of the funeral. The sun shone down with stubborn cheerfulness, as if intent on evaporating the heavy veil of sorrow pervading the town like a fog.

Three of us were silent as we stepped outside the house and walked towards the gate. Maudie stopped on the lawn, laughed and began to spin.

'Maudie, not now,' Dad said.

Mum gave her arm a quick touch and said, 'Let's go.' She opened the gate and gestured for Maudie to follow.

We walked to the church in our most demure Sunday clothes, except for Maudie who wore a bright yellow dress. She'd thrown the dark blue one across the room and nothing would induce her to put it on.

We approached Amos and Betty Crouch's house, opposite the church, and were about to cross the road when we heard Molly wailing. 'Nooo, never come out!' Amos came through the open doorway, holding onto his mother's arm and trying to coax her out.

Mum went to the fence and said, 'Would you like some help?'

Betty appeared at the door and waved. 'Thank you, it's alright.' She turned to Amos, said something, and walked Molly back inside.

Amos came through the gate and drew up beside us, his head bent and hands in his pockets. We crossed the road to the church building together.

There was a different smell in the auditorium, likely from the large vase of lilies on the stage. It was quiet. No one seemed to know what to say or how to hold their faces. Bodies appeared in unnatural poses. Jacky's family sat in the front row—Mr Hix with his arm around his wife's shoulders, Maurice's shoulders stiff beside him, some other people I didn't know. I caught a glimpse of Mrs Hix's ashen face and my stomach knotted.

Dad inclined his head towards the stage where Mr Hammond had taken his place behind the pulpit. 'Look. Poor chap,' he murmured. 'I don't think he's had to do a funeral for a child before.'

Mr Hammond was hunched and grey-faced, as if all his charisma had departed him. He held onto the sides of the lectern, not in his usual strong pose, but as if he needed it to keep himself up. I thought I saw his hand shaking.

He raised the microphone to his lips. 'On beha—' He rubbed his nose and cleared his throat. 'On behalf of the Hix family—Gary, Imogen and Maurice—I welcome you all here today. It's always difficult to say goodbye to someone but it's even harder when it's someone so young.'

The room was silent except for the sound of Mrs Hix sobbing into her husband's shoulder.

'I'll hand over to the family. Maurice Hix has some words he'd like to say.'

Maurice stood and took the place behind the pulpit. He was dressed in a dark suit and stood slightly bowed as if a weight rested on his shoulders. I thought I saw a glimpse of the man he would become—perhaps that was the day he left his childhood behind.

Mr Hammond handed Maurice the microphone, lowered his head and backed away with his hands behind his back. Maurice stared across the heads of the congregation for some seconds before beginning.

'Jacky was my little brother. He was the best little squirt—' He hung his head and his shoulders quivered. He took a breath, lifted his head and continued. 'I don't know why he's gone. I don't know how to say goodbye. Anyway—'

Maurice drew a piece of paper from his pocket and tried to unfold it. The microphone made popping noises against the pulpit and Mr Hammond moved forward to hold it while Maurice sat his notes down. He took the microphone once more and cleared his throat.

'Jacky was a kid who made everyone laugh. He never could sit still. He weren't much good at spelling and Maths and that, but he loved getting out in the garden and growing stuff. He wanted to have his own nursery when he grew up. He had it all planned. But he only lived eleven years of his life, so he never got to do that.'

A wail erupted from the front and Mrs Hix's shoulders shook. Mum gripped my hand.

'Still,' Maurice continued, 'he packed a lot into eleven years. Most of you won't know this, but he loved learning the names of plants. Not just the ones he grew, like the veggies, but the trees and bushes and flowers and stuff—you name it, he knew what it was called. Another thing he could do was bird whistles that sounded like real birds. You should have heard him do a raven, gosh he was funny.

'And if you came to any of the Christmas plays you'd know what a good actor he was. In fact, he was such a good actor, he had us believing one day that a bull had gotten into Dad's pond and was chasing the ducks. He came in jumping about looking all frightened like, and holding his face like this, and we all rushed out to see what was going on. Nothing—just Jacky cacking himself.'

A titter erupted through the room.

'Jacky was the best brother I could have wished for. We were good mates. We shouldn't have had to say goodbye because it's too soon. But at least no one can take our memories. We'll always have our memories of Jacky.'

It was my first funeral and it was horrible. As I stood up at the end of the service and turned around, I glimpsed Harry on the back seat. But, by the time we'd wriggled out of the pew and made our way to the back of the room and the door, he'd gone. I looked for him in the foyer, the tea-room and stuck my head out the door to scan the carpark, but he was nowhere. I thought of taking off and running down the road after him, but I knew I'd be in a bucket-load of trouble if I did. Instead, I mingled with everyone else in the tea-room where food was laid out. Soon, everyone moved to the foyer, and eventually ended up in the carpark, edging towards their cars but not wanting to appear rude. Mr Hix thanked people and shook hands while beside him, curled in on herself with a hankie pressed to her face, Mrs Hix sobbed.

In the middle of the carpark, Maudie began to spin. Out flew her yellow dress, her arms, her long ponytail. She closed her eyes and became one with the movement of her body, her expression gradually changing from agitation to relief to calm. A joyous dance at the centre of a wake.

Dad sighed, said, 'Maudie—' and moved towards her.

But Mum took his arm, pulled him gently back and said, 'Let her spin.'

So, there we all were, standing awkwardly in the carpark, feet shuffling, eyes shifting, men holding their hats in their hands—while Mrs Hix sobbed and Maudie spun.

I wasn't allowed to visit Harry. Though I begged and pleaded and bribed my parents with promises of good deeds, they stood firm in their refusal. I stomped and wailed and slammed doors until Dad threatened to call Constable Munnings and have me arrested for disturbing the peace.

'You could come with me,' I pleaded with Mum. 'Have a cup of tea with him.'

'No, I don't want to go there,' she said, which puzzled me. If only Harry was on the phone, I could have sneakily called him while Mum was busy.

At school, rumours ran riot, some of which had truth and some that fell far from it. Jacky was strangled with rope, a scarf, big hands. He was chased and squashed by an unidentified animal. A stranger was seen running away from the body when the searchers found it. Someone saw him arguing with a man in the bush.

One day, I heard Mum talking to Kylie's mother on the phone— 'Hello Lyn...you don't say...you're kidding!' —and she pulled the phone cord into her room and closed the door on it. I crept to the door and tried to listen through the crack but she was half-whispering. I thought she said Harry's name, but it may have been 'hurry.' There was a long murmuring of words I couldn't make out and, 'No, how awful.'

'Who was that?' I asked when she came out.

She pursed her lips and frowned at me.

'It was Kylie's mum, wasn't it? What did she say?'

'Don't be a nosy parker.'

'Ugh.' I stomped to my room.

At school, Kylie was more forthcoming with information. She, too, had been hanging about outside doors listening in on her parents' conversations. Of particular interest was a visit by Mrs Hammond.

'I'd just got home from school and her and Mum were in the lounge,' she said. She glanced behind her before she went on. We were sitting outside on a bench seat facing the oval. 'I couldn't hear everything.'

'That's alright.' I dropped my empty lunch box into my school bag, shoved it aside with my foot and leaned towards her. "Tell me."

Kylie lowered her voice. 'Minnie-May's been helping the police.'

'What!' I pulled a face.

'Yeah, that's what I thought. Well, turns out she saw something suspicious.'

'Like what?'

'Dunno. I think Mum realised I was there and they hushed up. Mrs Hammond left then. Mum won't tell me anything.'

'Nor will mine. Parents are so frustrating!' I folded my arms across my chest and huffed.

'Tell me about it. It's not like we're little kids anymore.'

'I'm not even allowed out by myself.'

'Me either.'

'I hope they hurry up and catch this murderer. I'm sick of being a prisoner in my own house.'

Kylie sighed. 'If they don't catch him soon, we'll have to figure it out ourselves.'

A group of kids walked past us and we waited silently until they were out of earshot.

I half-whispered, 'Do you still think it was Old Man Skinner?'

She nodded. 'He's my chief suspect. We know he fires his shot gun at anyone who goes near his pathetic excuse of a house.'

'Jacky was strangled, though.' My throat closed a little as I said those words. The thought of it still produced a physical reaction in my body.

'Old Man Skinner has hands, doesn't he?'

'Yeah, but what's his motive?'

'Maybe he just felt like strangling someone. He is the meanest person in Crayfish Cove.'

I shook my head. 'I dunno.'

'Alright, who's your chief suspect? Who do you think killed Jacky?'

I gazed out across the oval to the far boundary where, past a smattering of bushes, it merged with an adjoining field. The field ran alongside the main road, directly opposite the turnoff into Murphy's Lane where my friend lived. Was he pottering in his garden now? Was he thinking about Jacky? I was sure of one thing—Harry had nothing to do with Jacky's death.

'My money's on Wayne Bottle,' I said.

'Really?'

I nodded. 'Yep. Mark my words. Wayne Bottle did it.'

Kylie brought dribs and drabs of information to school, surreptitiously gathered by concealing herself in corners and pressing her ear to closed doors.

'The police have been to Harry's,' she whispered close to my ear one morning, as we walked with the class down the corridor to the art room.

'Of course they have,' I said. 'They're questioning everyone.'

'I know, but I wonder what they asked him.'

'Probably the same questions—' I stopped short, realising I was about to reveal my intimate knowledge of the final scene at Harry's.

Kylie huffed. 'I know you were at his house that day. Mum said.'

'Okay.'

'And I know you don't know anything. Mum said that, too.'

There didn't seem to be much Kylie's mother didn't know. We entered the art room and I slumped into my seat.

'She still doesn't like him, you know,' Kylie said.

'Who?'

'Mum. She doesn't like Harry.'

'Do you know why?'

Kylie shook her head. 'I get the feeling she's gonna spit it out soon, though. Whenever anyone mentions his name, she gets this look like she's about to say something awful. I'm just waiting for it.'

Our teacher hushed the class and instructed us to continue the paintings we'd begun the week before—using acrylic paints on paper to express an emotion or abstract thought. We set about retrieving our artworks and gathering paints, brushes and mixing trays.

'How do you do that?' I said, gazing at Kylie's painting as she spread it out on the work table.

'Huh? I dunno.'

She had painted the bottom third of her paper with murky, twisting colours appearing as waves with dark scribbles amongst them. Out of the waves, pastel coloured bubbles rose up towards the top of the paper. She'd described it as, 'bubbles of sense popping up out of confusion.' When I started my painting, I'd been thinking about Maudie, and it was all rainbow colours and hearts.

'I wish I could paint like you,' I said. 'Mine's rubbish.'

'It is not. Anyway, you're a good writer. I hate writing. Everyone's good at something, right?'

'That's what Harry said.'

'When?'

'One day when it was just me and him. He said everyone's good at something and I asked him what he was good at. He said he guessed he was good at gardening. It was like he couldn't see all those other things he was amazing at.'

'What other things?'

'So many things. *Good* things.'

A thought popped up in my head like one of the bubbles in Kylie's painting—Harry's face when Jacky took off out the door. It wasn't a good thought. I scrubbed it from my mind and turned my thoughts to Maudie, and painted happy swirls across the paper in yellow, orange and pink.

By lunchtime the sky had cracked open and rain was pouring down in sheets. We ate our lunch in the classroom before being ushered into the library which was set up with wet weather activities. Though I tried to resist, Kylie dragged me to a corner mat where Dot and Minnie-May sat, doing a jigsaw puzzle. Dot's face lit up when she saw us.

'I haven't seen you for ages,' she said. 'What's it like in high school?'

'Better than primary,' I replied. 'No more Miss Vance.'

'She's alright,' Dot said, before asking us to help her and Minnie-May with the 100-piece puzzle. We plopped down beside them and inspected the pieces. As we worked, our conversation slipped into familiar school-girl gossip—who was going with who, the best and worst of teachers, who had headlice—while Jacky's name hung silent in the air like the proverbial elephant. None of us seemed eager to mention him.

Minnie-May kept putting her thumb in her mouth and pulling it out again. I tried not to look at the angry red lump that had formed from all her sucking.

'That doesn't go there,' I said as she tried to squeeze a jigsaw piece into the wrong hole. The piece was red and obviously not part of the sky. I couldn't understand how she could be so stupid.

'Good try,' Kylie said good-naturedly. 'It's a hard puzzle.'

Dot grabbed a piece and fit it into the middle of the image of a green tin roof. 'Got it!' she said, turning to her friend. Minnie-May pulled her thumb out of her mouth and gave Dot a smile.

Gradually, the puzzle picture took shape—a barn in the midst of a field, the field surrounded by trees, birds wheeling in a blue sky.

'It reminds me of Harry's cottage,' I said.

There was silence for a moment and I was sure I heard Minnie-May take a quick intake of breath.

'Oh, it does!' Dot's face lit up. 'I love it at Harry's place.'

The air lightened between us, but only for a moment, thickening again as Kylie thumped a puzzle piece into place with a closed fist and said, 'What's so good about it?'

'Harry's so nice.' Dot said.

'You don't even know him very well.' Kylie's voice had an edge to it.

'Yes, I do.' Dot bit her lower lip and lowered her eyes.

'I thought you only visited him every now and then.'

Dot's face flushed. 'I do, but—'

'So how do you know he's nice?'

Dot's hand clenched in her lap as she looked up at Kylie. 'Well, sometimes you just know.' Her eyes shifted back to the carpet.

'You're wrong, anyway,' Kylie said. 'He's not nice. I think he does terrible things. And I'm sick of this puzzle.' She leapt to her feet, glared down at me and said, 'Are you coming?'

When I hesitated, she tossed her head and took off across the library without me.

Dot turned a worried face to me. 'Do you want to keep doing it?'

I repositioned myself to lean against the wall. 'I'll watch for a while,' I said. I would give Kylie time to cool down before going to talk to her.

Minnie-May continued to press the puzzle pieces into the wrong holes, but whenever she turned away to select another piece, Dot would quickly remove them and place them into their correct positions. When they'd finished the puzzle, Dot said, 'We did it!' and they grinned happily at each other.

I wondered at Dot's generosity. The way she protected her friend. I thought of my own bad tempered snap at Minnie-May's efforts and had an urge to say something encouraging to her. After all, as Harry said, everyone was good at something. Minnie-May's 'something' just didn't happen to be jigsaw puzzles.

I looked across the room to where Kylie had slumped into an armchair with her nose in a book. She still wore a frown. Why did she think Harry did terrible things? And what terrible things could they possibly be? No matter how I tried, I could not imagine them.

# 15

# Face of a bewildered moon

THE WORST DAY OF my short life happened early the following week. The bush telegraph was never more efficient than it was that afternoon. I was just home from school with Mum and Maudie when the phone rang. I was in the kitchen and heard Mum answer it in the hallway.

'What!' she said, with alarm in her voice.

I crept to the kitchen door and peeked into the hallway in time to see Mum disappearing into her room with the cord of the handset pulled tight. I snuck over to her door and put my ear to the crack. She'd hung up on whoever it was. I heard the whirr of the rotary dial as she made another call. I don't know who she phoned, but I heard what she said.

'It's June. Dave's gone to arrest Harry.'

I couldn't move for a moment. My head spun and I had to put my hand to the wall to regain my balance. As soon as the sensation passed, I sprinted through the kitchen and out the back door. I pulled on my boots, grabbed my bike and took off through the gate and down the footpath, my legs pumping the pedals as hard as I could make them.

'Hello there, Lily. Hold on a minute, I have something—'

I kept pedalling and Mrs Hammond's voice trailed away as I whipped down the street. I turned into Murphy's Lane and swung tight into Harry's drive, squeezing the hand brakes and skidding just as Constable Munnings' police car came through the gate. My bike wobbled and I slipped from the seat, nearly falling off. I edged to the side of the drive to make room for the car.

Constable Munnings turned and looked at me. I waited for a wave, a grin, something to indicate he was there on routine business. But he turned away and stared at the road ahead.

As the police car passed slowly by me, I saw Harry in the back seat, looking out through the glass. His face was as pale as the moon, his eyes like craters, deep and bewildered. I cried out and our eyes locked, and stayed locked, our heads turning in unison, until the car turned sharp into Murphy's Lane. I threw my bike down and ran after it, but it sped off up the lane and round the corner onto the main road.

I stared at the place where it had disappeared. Harry! What should I do? I went back to my bike, began to lift it from the ground, but dropped it again. Instead, I ran away through Harry's gate and down his driveway. A flock of cockatoos startled out of a gum tree as I crashed towards Harry's home—his dear cottage with the garden, a pile of firewood stacked neatly under the lean-to, the fire pit, the frame for the billy can and the circle of old chairs where we'd all laughed, and sung to Harry's guitar and drank cups of milky tea. And there was the birch tree, by the house, bent over like a giant with a great load on its back, trying to find its balance.

I buckled over on the front step and pressed my cheek into the concrete. The sudden chill was a slap, shocking me for a moment. Then it was a comfort, its unpleasantness drawing some of the grief from my bones, from this great shuddering of feeling that was too big.

I sobbed onto the concrete.

Eventually, Dad found me there and took me home.

I pulled the blankets tightly around my body. Mum had tried to rouse me several times but I couldn't face getting out of bed. I couldn't face anything.

The mattress moved as Mum sat on the edge of my bed. 'Sweetheart, come on.'

'I can't,' I croaked, my throat scratchy from crying. I turned to face her with just my eyes and the top of my head poking from the bed clothes. 'How can he be arrested?'

'It doesn't mean he's been charged.'

'Has he gone to jail?'

'No, just to the police station. He'll be asked some questions and then they might let him go. We need to be patient and wait.'

'So he won't go to jail?'

'I don't know.'

Tears slipped down my cheeks. 'You only get bread and water in jail. He'd hate that!'

'Where did you hear that? It's not true.'

I sobbed and Mum stroked my hair. She relented and said I could stay home for the day which turned into two. I kept to my bed and refused to move. The world was a desolate place and I wanted no part of it. Every time I woke from sleep, the reality hit me afresh. I was devastated, I was angry, I was scared. I raged at my mother because she hadn't let me go and see Harry. I hadn't seen him for *ages* and it wasn't *fair*.

Maudie came in at one point and put her arm over me. 'There, there,' she said, and rubbed my back. She'd never done such a thing before; she didn't like hugs or physical contact. I lay as still as I could, willing her to keep doing it, to stay close. But she stopped and left the room and I cried some more.

On the second day, Kylie's mum brought her round to visit me in the afternoon, probably at the request of my mother. When Kylie came into my room, I was sitting up in bed in my pyjamas, trying to read a book.

'Have you been playing sick?' She wriggled up on the end of my bed and sat there, cross-legged.

I slammed my book down on the bed. 'They arrested Harry.'

'I know.'

'But no one will tell me why! He didn't do it so why was he arrested?'

Kylie's eyes shifted around my room as she bit her bottom lip.

'What?' I asked.

She peered at me uneasily. 'You need to come back to school. I've got a lot to tell you.'

'Tell me now.'

She glanced behind her at my bedroom door. 'Hang on,' she said, slipping off my bed. 'Mum's here, I have to be careful.'

She went to my door which was slightly ajar, and quietly closed it. 'I've heard things,' she said, climbing back up onto my bed. 'Remember when I said Minnie-May was helping the police? Well, she saw something. It's all round the school.'

'What did she see?'

'Harry and Jacky arguing in the woods on the day Jacky died. She said Harry grabbed him. Are you alright? You've gone a funny colour.'

I lay back on the pillow and closed my eyes.

'Do you want me to get your mum?'

I shook my head on the pillow. 'What else did you hear?'

'Open your eyes, you're scaring me.'

I complied and wriggled back up into a sitting position.

'Well, they found evidence pointing to Harry.'

I took a deep breath and blew it noisily from my mouth. 'What evidence?'

'I don't know all of it, but I did hear the person who strangled him had big hands.'

I squeezed my own hands into fists and scowled. 'Well, that could be anyone.'

Kylie shrugged her shoulders. 'I know. I'm just saying what I heard. Look, can you come back to school? Pleeease?'

I thought of Minnie-May and her fuzzy face and deformed thumb and a ball of anger grew in the pit of my belly. It made me want to jump up and bang the walls.

'Alright,' I said. 'I'll come back tomorrow. Harry wouldn't grab someone like that. He wouldn't even argue with anyone, and I'm going to prove it.'

'How?'

'I dunno, but I'll think of something.'

I walked to school the following morning, accompanied as usual by Mum and Maudie. The air held a bitter chill and frost sparkled on the surface of the oval. Our feet made wet, green tracks across the grass and our breath poured out in clouds. I put two fingers to my lips, sucked in my breath and blew into the air, pretending I was smoking a cigarette, which made Maudie laugh. It was so good to hear my sister laugh, I kept doing it and Mum didn't stop me. We said goodbye as we approached the playground area, the point from which Mum had decided I was safe from any lurking murderers. (Inwardly, I rolled my eyes.)

Passing the primary block, I spied a line of kids already waiting at the door of their classroom for the teacher to let them in. They were wrapped in coats and rubbing their hands together. Like me, some were pretending to smoke. How awful to be a primary school kid and not allowed inside the classroom without a teacher present. It felt like an age since I was one of them, though it had only been six months.

I scanned the line and saw Minnie-May's wispy orange hair lifting in the wind. She stood with her hands in the pockets of her pink parka, staring into the distance. She was surrounded by kids chattering and jigging about, pushing each other and laughing, but she appeared as someone alone. What was she thinking about as she stood there, oblivious to the ruckus around her? Was she thinking of the day Jacky died and what she supposedly saw in the woods? She must have been lying. Minnie-May never went anywhere, let alone into the woods. I narrowed my eyes at her and willed her to look at me as I walked past. But she didn't.

As I passed, I felt a tightening in my belly—a rising anger. I slowed down and looked back at the line of kids. How dare Minnie-May say such a terrible thing? She didn't even know Harry. I spun back around and faced the line of grade sixes, some of whom had begun a game of Paper, Scissors, Rock. I walked slowly towards them, honing in on the one with the strawberry-blonde hair who stood there staring at nothing.

As I approached, my breath began to shake and any good feeling I had about Minnie-May dissipated. No one noticed me until I was centimetres from her. She looked up and startled as I bent down with my nose almost touching hers.

'Liar!' I hissed.

In a sudden boiling rage, I pulled my foot back and swung it as hard as I could into Minnie-May's shins. She sank into the line, swallowed up by the puffy jackets and beanies and bags. The sound she made as she stumbled was a grunt, like a small animal. She righted herself and hung her head. I waited briefly for a retaliation but it didn't come. Even the kids who saw the kick chose to shift away and find something else to look at, so I spun around and strode off.

As I reached my own classroom, a wave of remorse welled up in me so fiercely, it churned my belly and I thought I would vomit. But straight away, I pushed it back down. I had to. There was no way Minnie-May's story could be true. She *must* be a liar.

There was no longer a police presence at the school. The room designated for interviewing students had returned to its former state as a Mathematics classroom. Kylie and I went sniffing about there at lunch time to see if anything had been left behind.

'What are we looking for?' Kylie said, opening the lower cupboards and poking about inside.

'Notes I guess. Anything that reads like official police business. I'll check the desks in case anything was put inside. You look in the bins for screwed up paper.'

'The cleaners have been. There's nothing in the bins.'

'We'll have to check around the incinerators, then.'

Kylie screwed up her nose. 'Really?'

I lifted a pile of laminated charts that lay on the bench against the wall. 'Hey, what's this?' I pulled a sheet of drawing paper from underneath and held it up. Kylie laughed. Someone had drawn a rather good caricature of Arthur Gilchrist wearing a pink polka dot bow tie, a purple suit and ribbons tied to his long moustache.

'Can I have it?' Kylie asked.

'Why?'

'It's a pretty good likeness. You know, out of all the teachers, I reckon Mr Gilchrist is the nicest.'

'I don't know who's nice anymore.' I handed the picture to Kylie and turned back to the bench, shifting some wooden tubs and an abacus to look behind them.

'Are you sure it wasn't Harry? The police must think he did it, or they wouldn't have arrested him.'

'I know he didn't do it. But someone did, didn't they? And they're still around here somewhere.'

Kylie pulled a face. 'That's a horrible thought.'

'Yeah, so we need to keep looking for clues.'

'All the same,' Kylie said, looking at the caricature of the Maths teacher, 'I can't believe Mr Gilchrist would do anything bad. He's too nice.'

I turned to her and shook my head. 'Kylie.'

'What?'

'Until they find the real murderer, we can't trust anyone.'

Dad walked in earlier than usual that evening. I looked up from peeling carrots at the kitchen table and opened my mouth to say hello, but closed it again and froze with a carrot in one hand and the peeler in the other. I stared at the storm cloud that was my father's face. Mum turned round from the bench where she was tipping peas into a pot. She took one look at him and froze in the same manner.

'What?' Mum said. It was a far cry from her usual greeting.

Dad glanced at me, and back at Mum. 'Harry Fernley's been charged with Jacky's murder.'

Mum's face went white and she stumbled into a chair.

At first I didn't feel anything, then something crashed inside me. 'No,' I whimpered.

Dad's face softened. 'I'm afraid so, Lily. I'm sorry.'

'But he didn't do it!' I dropped the carrot and the peeler and slapped my hands against my head.

Dad's face hardened again as he looked at my mother. 'Actually, he's done it before. Hasn't he, June?'

Mum shook her head. 'Brian—'

'You knew, didn't you?' Dad was speaking quietly but his voice had hard edges which I'd never heard before. 'You knew, and you let our daughter go there and spend countless hours with him.'

Mum's lips quivered.

'What if it'd been Lily?'

Mum moved towards him. 'Brian—'

Dad turned and walked out of the room.

'What's he talking about, Mum?' I waited for a smile and an explanation but instead, Mum hurried out of the room after Dad. I heard Maudie asking what was wrong and Mum soothing her. Then the front door opened and closed and the Datsun started up and roared away.

I looked at the peeled carrots on the chopping board in front of me and felt sick. The world was crashing in on us in a way I didn't understand.

The sun rose the next day and the next. How did it dare? Why wasn't it shut up in mourning and refusing to rise? Our lives had altered, no longer following the predictable course I'd learned to trust. The adults around us were harbouring secrets with burrs which hurt and confused us. I asked Mum what Harry had done before but she said it wasn't her story to tell and that I should forget it. How could I do that? I needed to know the truth, to understand who Harry was.

The tension at our place was like the air being pulled tight almost to the point of snapping. Conversations were stilted. Mum appeared less polished. She stopped painting her fingernails and styling her hair. She looked patched together in the mornings as if dressing herself was an effort. I no longer caught her craning her neck at the window to check if Glenda Hill from two doors down had hung her washing out first.

More and more, Maudie and I asked to spend time at Nan's where everything stayed the same—Nan's no-nonsense manner, the smell of fruit and old crockery, bottles of ginger beer brewing on the shelf by the back door.

I bawled to Nan at the unfairness of everything and begged her to help me make sense of it. She listened and stroked my hair as I lay on the couch with my head in her lap, but she had no real answers.

'Dad said Harry strangled someone before. Did he, Nan?'

'I don't know anything about that, love.'

I sobbed into her lap. 'He seemed so nice,' I said, my voice choking.

Nan sighed. 'Sometimes you can't know a person from the outside. They might be hiding things inside,' she said. And I thought of the dead bird I'd once turned over with a stick, and the maggots underneath.

Kylie and I listened at doors in an attempt to find out more. At her place, there were two telephones and when someone was on one phone, you could quietly pick up the handset on the other and listen in on the conversation. At school, she would share snippets of information she'd gleaned from this method and we tried to patch the pieces together.

The town was abuzz with gossip. We'd go into the general store or the chip shop and find people talking, no longer in semi-secret huddles but across the shop to each other— 'I knew there was something off about that bloke'... 'all those kids at his place, it weren't natural'... 'never had a girlfriend, what does that tell you?'... 'I heard he had a temper'... 'kept too much to himself, you can't trust people like that' —and again my mind would fill with the image of Harry wrapping his hands around Jacky Hix's neck.

The church minister, Mr Hammond enjoyed an influx of new congregants—seeking solace, or the meaning of life or gossip, who could tell? The Hix family, however, stopped going to services altogether. I navigated each day as best I could—go to school, go home, play with Maudie, visit Kylie, spend time with Nan—attempting to retrieve something of my old life and return to a semblance of 'normal.'

As the months passed, Crayfish Cove awaited the result of Harry's trial.

One afternoon, after Kylie's mum dropped me home after school, I went into the house and flung my bag on the hall floor as usual. Mum emerged from the kitchen, her face solemn. After greeting me, she came up to me, held my shoulders with both hands and looked into my eyes.

'Honey,' she said, and I felt my knees weaken. 'Harry's been found guilty.'

'Okay.'

She stroked my hair. 'He's going to prison, sweetheart.'

'Okay,' I said again.

'How do you feel?'

I shrugged my shoulders. 'I have homework.'

I went into my room and shut the door. I sat on the edge of my bed for a while, my hands squeezed together. A whirlwind of emotion began at the back of my head and crashed through me. As it hit my chest, I breathed deeply and pushed it back.

I knelt on the floor and pulled out the bottom drawer of my bedside table. I retrieved the journal hidden underneath, opened it to the latest page, sat on my bed and wrote:

**Dear Diary,**

**Harry is guilty. He is going to prison.**

**I'm glad he is being punished for what he did to Jacky.**

But I didn't feel glad. My pen dug into the pages so deeply, the paper tore.

# 16

# Vile words

At school, we heard Harry's house had been vandalised and that the ringleader was Maurice. As soon as the final bell rang, now that we were spared the humiliation of having our mothers collect us from school, Kylie and I took off as fast as we could to look at Harry's place before we went home.

We half walked, half ran down the main road and into Murphy's Lane. At the sight of Harry's gate, my heart drummed against my chest. I hadn't been to Harry's place since the day he was arrested.

'Come on,' Kylie said, hurrying ahead.

Down the drive, past the oak tree at the corner, and there it was. Mayhem.

'Oh my gosh!' Kylie said. Her first ever view of Harry's place was one of devastation.

My heart sank. Someone had gone wild, venting a raging anger. We crept forward, taking in the destruction. All the front windows of the cottage had been smashed. Jagged bits of glass clung to the window frames and glinted like icicles. Brown paint was slashed across the front weatherboards, formed into vile words that made me blush. The garden fence was flattened and the garden itself ripped out. Bricks, rocks and planks of wood were strewn everywhere. Plants pulled up by their roots littered the ground and hung from the fence, torn out in fury. The lean-to had been pulled down and the firewood had vanished.

'Wow, Maurice really went ballistic,' Kylie said as she strode down to the cottage.

I wandered down after her. Could gentle Maurice really have done this?

Kylie traipsed about, inspecting the garden, the graffiti, the kicked-over frame for the billy can. 'Look at that... well, that's ruined... brutal!... look at this place!'

The light-hearted way she ambled through the ruins unhinged me. I saw not simply a devastated place, but everything that had gone before. Ghosts rose up around me. Little voices singing into the air as Harry played his guitar. Childish faces lifted towards the trees with pursed lips, trying to whistle like the birds. A billycart trundling around the fruit trees. Milky tea and sweet apples.

Years of my childhood were punctuated with these memories, these sparkling gems that had been Sunday afternoons at Harry's. Were they to be cancelled out altogether? Was I meant to regret them now? If a person who had done so many good things did one terrible deed, did it make them a bad person?

Kylie leapt up the front steps of the cottage, dropping her school bag on the ground as she went.

'What are you doing?' I asked.

'Come on.' She turned and grinned before disappearing inside.

I left my bag next to hers and took the steps slowly.

'You should see in here,' she called.

The front door hung precariously from its hinges. Inside, pots and pans and broken crockery littered the floor. I ventured through the mess to the far end of the living room. The lounge and armchairs looked like they'd been slashed with a knife. Everything from the shelves either side of the fireplace had been swept onto the floor. I found the frame containing the story I'd given Harry. The glass was cracked so I carefully opened the back of the frame and took the paper out.

'What's that?' Kylie asked.

'Something I gave Harry. I'm going to take it home.'

'Yeah, don't leave anything here that's yours. Let's look over the rest of the place.' Kylie went to head out of the kitchen to the back of the house where the other rooms were.

'We shouldn't go in there,' I said.

'Why not?'

'He might be in jail but it's still his house.'

Kylie shrugged and turned to the front door instead. 'See you out there,' she said.

I cast my eyes over the kitchen. The wave-shaped shelf above the sink had been pulled off and lay in two pieces on the bench, along with the photo frame that had sat upon it. I picked up the frame which was still intact. Harry's parents smiled out from it. At least they never had to know what their son had done. I held the frame to myself as I exited the cottage. At the bottom of the steps, I took up my school bag and slipped the frame and my story inside.

'Yoohoo!' Kylie's call came from behind the fruit trees. 'Is this the treehouse?'

I followed her voice and saw her staring up into the pine tree we'd spent so many hours playing in. The vandals had even attacked the treehouse. A few planks of broken wood lay on the ground at the base of the tree and the ladder had vanished. It was Harry's best ladder so I supposed someone had stolen it.

'I want to go,' I said, and turned away.

'Alright. I think we've seen everything,' Kylie said, tossing her head. 'It serves him right.' I flinched at the sneer in her voice.

We headed back—past the shed, the birch trees, the cottage, the garden, the old oak. If I'd been on my own I may have stopped for a moment and said goodbye, whispered a prayer perhaps. But instead, I marched out through the gate and away, vowing I would never return.

The tragedy moulded Crayfish Cove in substantial ways, not unlike how the pounding of the waves over thousands of years had hollowed out the cove itself. Each family, every person, felt the loss and found their own ways of dealing with it. Some found strength in each other, others stumbled. Trust never quite returned to its former level, with doors remaining locked that had previously been left unlocked. Maurice left school two months early. I heard from Miranda he'd taken to drinking heavily.

Kylie's mother finally spilled the reason for her dislike of Harry. Once she'd opened her mouth, she blabbed the story all over Crayfish Cove to anyone who would listen. Her poor brother, she said—back when he was at school—had been grabbed around the neck by Harry Fernley and almost strangled to death! Mum told me quietly in my room one night that her 'poor brother' was a bully who had relentlessly teased Harry about having a learning disability.

'So he didn't kill someone else?' I said.

Mum looked surprised. 'Oh honey, did you think that? I'm sorry.'

So, Harry hadn't committed murder before. Even so, he *had* killed Jacky. When I asked Mum why he would do such a thing she shook her head and looked out the window. 'I don't know. Maybe we'll never know.'

On Sundays at church, an awkwardness had grown up between me and the Pevensie children. Bobby, Curly and Sarah would say hello with shifting feet as if they were in a hurry to escape. They no longer knew how to talk to me, nor I to them. It was as if the bond, like glue, that held us together had melted. Which it had—the glue being Harry. After all, what else had we in common but Harry? And now it was no longer okay to talk about him. Harry's name had become taboo. However, I did hear him occasionally referred to as *that man,* or other names I'd rather not repeat.

So, I attempted to deny a significant part of my childhood and bury memories once sweet, now tainted. While everywhere I went, I was reminded of him.

It was difficult to imagine moving on and laughing again, but the days eventually flowed into a routine and I began to feel normal. My body's natural healing mechanisms kicked in and the angst in the pit of my belly eased.

I took my hungry soul and open ears to church and listened for guidance in the Sunday sermons. Perhaps I could fathom the mystery of the world and evil and death if I concentrated hard enough. I sat in the auditorium with the adults and scribbled down notes, wrestling with concepts that appeared to bear little relation to the life of a thirteen-year-old.

Kylie said I was mad. She'd rather colour silly pictures with Betty Crouch in Sunday School. However, I enjoyed listening to Mr Hammond with his melodious magpie voice that made you want to stop and listen, even if you didn't really know what he was saying. He would read from a large black Bible and embellish the passage with stories, throwing his arms about and pacing the platform. Afterwards, he'd have his hand shaken vigorously by folk on their way out, gushing their thanks— 'Wonderful preaching'... 'Most encouraging'... 'That city church must be missing you'... and nodding solemnly at his reply— 'The quiet country life was what Minnette-May needed after the tragedy.'

So I searched for connections between paths of righteousness and bush paths and footpaths, and wondered why a sermon on the lilies of the valley seemed to bear no correlation to actual flowers. And exactly where was hell anyway when it wasn't possible to live at the centre of the earth? And heaven for that matter?

And why did Mr Hammond call the church building the house of God when I'd seen him with my own eyes turning the key in the lock of the front door once everyone was safely out of the building? If the house of God was in there, where were people to meet God on the other days of the week?

So many questions I would once have taken to Harry. Instead, I wrote them all down in my journal and pondered them on my own.

One Sunday morning, Dad said, 'Let's go over to Durrunby for lunch today.'

After that, Sunday afternoon jaunts became a ritual—a way for our family to work through the aftermath of Jacky's death—and we drew closer to each other. Us and Nan—walking in the park, eating at the bakery, visiting historic sites, wandering along the river bank.

Dad and Mum started going out on special dates on Saturday evenings, leaving me and Maudie with videos and hot chips. I'd hang about outside their bedroom, waiting for Mum to appear in her blonde wig and pretty dress. Her scent was lipstick and nylon panty-hose and took my imagination to hazy places I'd only yet seen in movies—candlelit dinners, jazz bands, dancing under stars. Mum and Dad, however, were usually just eating at the local pub.

For my friends and I, life returned to something recognisably normal. We rode our bikes, ate our way through all the Paddle Pop flavours from the chip shop, dive-bombed off the jetty, went to the local dances at the school hall. I'd walk or ride my bike to Nan's on Saturday's, forcing my eyes straight ahead as I turned into Murphy's Lane and refusing myself even a glance at Harry's gate. Nan would be waiting with tea and biscuits and her unflappable manner that grounded me and made me feel safe.

One morning, as Nan and I sat at her little table munching Iced VoVo biscuits, a fog descended on Crayfish Cove. We watched it roll in from the window in the kitchen. Nan tutted and said, 'What will this one blow in, I wonder?'

I waited until the fog began to lift before I set off for home. As I walked up Murphy's Lane, averting my eyes from Harry's gate as I passed, my heart jumped into my throat as I spied a figure standing under the poplars. The fog had caught amidst the trees so the figure melted into it and appeared to be part of the mist itself, almost transparent.

I moved closer to the middle of the lane and tried to pass by silently. I peered sideways at the person, who stood there unmoving and staring ahead. As the fog curled eerily about their face, I caught a faint sparkle of strawberry-blonde hair.

Minnie-May! What on earth was she doing standing all alone like a ghost in the mist? I almost said hello, but something about the way she stood motionless and slightly bent, and was so subsumed by the fog, caused me to quicken my pace and half-run up the road.

I hurried home, wondering if Minnie-May wasn't the reclusive creature we had assumed her to be after all. Maybe she really did like to go wandering by herself in the woods.

## 17

# Vision of a mer-king

JONATHAN PEERED OVER THE rock floor of the Hollow at the clear water below. 'I came here a couple of times with him too,' he said. 'When he was fishing.'

He shifted on his bottom back towards me and leaned against the sandstone wall. We were sitting so close I felt his elbow lightly brushing mine.

Jonathan was the one person with whom I could still talk about Harry. We often met up when he came home from boarding school on the weekends, and our conversation would invariably turn to Harry.

At first, we entertained the idea that Harry may be innocent. It gave us an excuse to talk fondly of him. We tried to ignore the ugly stories circulating around town. Tried to dismiss the fact that he had been tried by a jury and found guilty because of overwhelming evidence against him.

'How did Jacky end up at Madding Hill anyway?' I said.

'Huh?' Jonathan turned his body to face me, his side against the rock.

'Sorry,' I said. 'My mind drifted. I was thinking about the murder again.'

Jonathan's voice was gentle. 'They say Harry must have driven him—his body—there in his ute.'

'How would they know that?'

'They would have found bits of fabric from Jacky's clothing, or something like that.'

'But you've seen Jacky in Harry's ute, going off on his shop rounds with him. Of course there'd be things of Jacky's in the ute.'

'I know.'

'And why would Harry do that to Jacky anyway?'

'They say he lost his temper.'

I took a deep breath and closed my eyes. I felt Jonathan shift beside me and knew he'd turned back to face the bay. I half opened my eyes and peered out through my eyelashes at the water, its surface glinting like so many stars.

Harry loved the water. He could swim all the way across the bay from the jetty to the point on the other side. I watched him do it one summer—a hot January day in the middle of the school holidays. A bunch of us had waited for the fishing boats to leave the cove for the day so we could dive-bomb off the end of the jetty. I don't recall us ever wearing life jackets. We knew not to paddle out too far, to come back in frequently to rest and to look out for each other. Jon and I shake our heads about it now. What were our parents thinking?

The day Harry took off into the deep, I was treading water with Miranda and Maurice while Bobby Pevensie and Jacky mucked about on rubber tyre tubes. I watched Harry swim right over to the point. I was a strong swimmer and imagined racing him one day when I was older. On his way back he stopped swimming, rolled headfirst into the water and plunged down with his legs sticking up, then disappeared. I trod water while I waited for him to emerge.

Behind me, Jacky yelped and there was a lot of splashing and gig-gling. But I kept my eyes trained on the spot where Harry had disap-peared and ignored the ruckus behind me.

Finally, up rose Harry from the depths. He must have pushed him-self up from the bottom with his feet because he shot out with water pouring down his head, his wild long hair, his shoulders and chest. In one hand he held a spear, pointing upwards. It was only a discarded fishing spear which had somehow found its way into the bay, but in that moment, it was as if a mer-king had risen from the sea. Like the picture in my *Folklore and Fairytales* book of King Neptune holding his trident.

The vision photographed itself onto my memory and I have never been able to shake it.

Harry sank back down into the water of the bay and the spell was broken. He leaned forward and swam slowly back to the jetty while holding onto the spear.

I remember turning to the others, my head filled with the vision of Harry, brown and wild and majestic.

'Did you see that? Did you see Harry?'

But the others were still mucking about, slapping the water and spraying each other. No one had seen him. I looked back to where Harry was holding onto the side of the jetty and lifting the spear to set it safely on the wharf. Just an ordinary man and an ordinary fishing tool. But from that moment, for me, he became wrapped in an invisible royal robe and I would thereafter envision him as a sort of king. Even after Jacky died, I could not shake it.

'There's someone sitting on the end of the jetty,' Jonathan said, pulling me out of my reverie.

I looked out at the jetty, its construction of bleached wood swathed in sunlight. All the fishing boats had gone out for the day and it appeared deserted. Except for a small figure, hunched on the end of the pier.

'Hey you two!'

We turned to see Kylie slipping down onto the flat floor of the Hollow.

'How did you both get here so fast? I brought food.' She dropped her backpack and sat beside us.

'Did you bring your binoculars?' I asked.

'Of course.' She opened her bag, pulled them out and handed them to me.

I uncapped the lens covers and put the binoculars to my eyes.

'Who is it?' Jonathan asked.

'Who's what?' said Kylie.

'Hold on.' I adjusted the focus and moved the binoculars so my vision followed the length of the almost empty jetty.

At the very end, the figure sat huddled and unmoving, legs dangling over the edge. A tilted blue cap on its head that I recognised. Staring out at the sea.

'It's Maurice,' I said.

And he cut the most lonely and desolate figure I think I've ever seen.

You can't refute cold, hard evidence. So they say. In the end we had to accept it.

Harry had a temper. He may not have meant to strangle Jacky, but he did do it. We might never know why he did it. Jacky was dead and Harry was a murderer.

I accepted Harry's guilt. He had been tried by a jury. I had to hold onto that truth and move on, my childhood forever blighted by the man who had beguiled me.

# 18

# The thread of the story

I FLICK THROUGH MY journals seventeen years after Harry's arrest, searching for the thread of the story. Harry isn't mentioned again for three years. Instead, the gems embellishing my writings are friends and family, school days and holidays.

Dad taught me to drive out on the unsealed backroads of Crayfish Cove out of sight of Constable Munnings. The day I received my learners' licence, we went out for an à la carte meal at the pub to celebrate.

Mum commenced a job at the school, assisting kids with learning challenges, and loved it so much she decided to train to be a teacher. When she told Dad, he swung her round the lounge and said he always knew he was married to the smartest woman in Crayfish Cove.

Maudie completed an accounting course by correspondence. When she turned eighteen she commenced work with Amos Crouch, doing the books for his auto-repair business and keeping the office in order. She kept bringing work home, hardly believing she was being paid actual money for doing something she loved.

I lost touch with Dot when her parents sent her to boarding school in Hobart, but we heard she'd been having singing lessons and had joined a prestigious city choir.

My favourite primary teacher, Miss Aubrey, became Mrs Rippingale and invited all her former students to her wedding at Durrunby Park.

There were weddings, funerals, baptisms and bake sales. Crayfish Cove moved on and found a way of existing without Jacky Hix and Harry Fernley.

Until 1981.

It was our final year of high school. Kylie and I were wearing big hair and rolled-up jeans, singing *Kids in America* and still obsessed with doing the Time Warp. We were happy.

Until, just after my sixteenth birthday, the world went topsy-turvy again. It began with a simple walk down to the beach to clear my head, that started a snowball rolling.

19

# Scattered stones

ONE FRIDAY AFTERNOON, NEARING the end of the winter school term, I came home from school to find Mum had begun her spring clean early. I offered to help.

'You can start with your room,' she said, indicating some large cardboard boxes she'd set in the hallway for give-aways and rubbish.

Besides my clothes cupboards and drawers, I had a cupboard for other things such as books and keepsakes. Some of the shelves held boxes filled with stuff that hadn't been touched for years. I took everything out, cleaned the shelves and dusted all the containers. Some of the boxes held piles of journals and diaries I'd written in and kept over the years. I picked up the oldest cardboard box, set it on my bed and flopped down cross-legged next to it.

When I opened the flaps, the smell of primary school seeped out and my head was filled with pencil shavings, floor polish and chalk dust. A rush of girlish memories. On top of the contents sat the large, orange shell that had been a birthday gift from Harry. I'd treasured it for years before later tossing it into the box, not wanting to look at it any longer, yet unable to throw it away. I lifted it out and ran my fingers over its smooth curve, its bumps and ridges, before setting it on the floor.

The rest of the box was filled with journals. All my first stories were contained between the covers of those school exercise books. First written in pencil and a young child's irregular printing, later in ink and cursive. Prose, poems, a few pictures here and there. Hundreds of adventures—recorded, documented. So many stories about Harry.

I lifted several piles of books from the box. At the bottom were the journals I'd written in as a young child in the first excitement of meeting and getting to know Harry. Here was the very first one Miss Aubrey had placed on my desk just days after I met him. I set it on my knee and passed my hand across the cardboard cover which was worn and soft, the corners feathered. Pieces of fine paper dust broke away from them and stuck to my fingers.

Opening the book to the first page, I read:

> **Harry is my friend.**
> **He lives in a wooden house.**
> **He has long legs.**
> **He likes fishing.**
>
> **Harry is my new friend.**
> **He lives in a white wooden cottage in Murphy's**
> **Lane.**
> **He has long legs but he walks slowly so I can catch**
> **up.**
> **He taught me how to fish.**

How many times had I relived that first meeting when I sat with him in the Hollow, looking out over the bay and holding onto his fishing rod? His deep, soft voice spinning a story about the sea and the tide and how the waves had hollowed out the cove. The warm, woodsmoke smell of him. The first tug on the line and my excitement as his hand covered mine on the rod and we reeled in the first flapping silver fish.

I snapped the book shut. The man who smiled at me with kind, blue eyes was in prison and my head told me everything was as it should be. I'd been young and naïve. Unable to discern badness in a person. Nine years old—still a baby.

I took hold of the next journal. This was the one Miss Aubrey had given me to take home to keep practising my writing in. I'd poured my heart into this one, hunched over the kitchen table after school and in my bedroom. All my childish thoughts and worries and excitements. Even the thought that Miss Aubrey might ask to see it didn't curtail my pourings-out.

But as it happened, it was the police—the burly, brusque detective and his constable—who read my innocent writings and I'd shrunk with the humiliation of that knowledge. Even now, I felt myself blushing.

I flicked through the pages until I came to the entries about my tenth birthday party at Harry's. Oh, the excitement! I could still feel it.

It had rained for days and I'd despaired of being able to have the party. However, he had come good on his promise and thrown it for me, complete with a roaring fire and toasted marshmallows. Even though he'd run out of firewood.

**When the others left, me and Dot fell asleep on the couch. I remember that the firewood looked weird like the pieces were square instead of round like logs. They looked like little houses burning in the fire.**

And the entry a few days later ...

**I found out Harry burned his verandah wood so the house would be warm for my birthday. He opened his shed and I saw there was only a few pieces left and bits of broken wood near the axe. I asked him where they were.**

**He said he'd run out of firewood and used them instead. I asked him if he burnt them because of me and he looked at me for a minute then he said "Lily your more important than a few bits of wood."**

**I feel bad now. How is he going to build his verandah without his wood? Theres a yucky feeling in my chest like its filled with something heavy.**

I closed the journal and shoved it, with all the others, back into the box and replaced the shell on top. How could one man be so good and so violent at the same time? Jacky's freckled face appeared in my head—leaning on a stick and cawing like the ravens, pulling his silly face, pretending to be an old man—*Aaah, how ahh ya, Harry me maate.* Harry laughing and clutching his sides, his eyes watering. And the first day I visited Harry at his house and saw the two of them amongst the corn stalks, wrestling, Harry with his arm around Jacky's neck. What did it mean?

Harry's words rang out from the past:

*Lily, you're more important than a few bits of wood.*

*Dot can sing.*

*Jacky knows because he tried for himself.*

I found Mum in rubber gloves and an apron, tackling the laundry shelves.

'Is it alright if I go for a walk?' I said. 'I'll come back and do the rest later.'

'Where are you off to?' she asked as she lifted a bucket of dirty water from the floor and tipped it down the sink.

'Maybe down to the beach. Want me to take anything to Nan's?'

Mum turned and considered me. 'No, that's alright. You enjoy yourself.'

I put on a coat and set off. As I passed the corner where the Crouch family lived, I waved to Molly who stood in her usual position, leaning on the fence outside her house. She put her hand up and fluttered it uncertainly. Maybe she recognised me today, maybe she didn't.

I crossed the road at the church where Mrs Hammond stood in the garden staring at a patch of rhododendrons. I called hello but she said nothing, just kept staring as if she could see something through the flowers.

As I turned into Murphy's Lane, I looked to the right, away from Harry's gate, and studied the poplars and the thin sunshine glinting through their still-bare branches. I continued down to the farm, rounded the fence near the house and clicked my tongue to the Murphys' horse. As I neared the beach, the briny salt smell enticed me and I clambered down the well-trodden footholds onto the shore.

The tide was out so I wandered along, creeping gingerly over the slippery seaweed that clung to the flat stone and climbing over rocks that, sometime in the past, had tumbled down from the cliff face. I stopped and squatted down to peer into rock pools where the red tentacles of anemones burst out like exotic flowers. One pool contained a pile of rounded stones glinting under the water, shimmering in a mixture of salt water and sunshine. As I put my hand into the water, a tiny crab scuttled away and hid itself in a crevice. I picked up a smooth stone and placed it in the palm of my other hand, reached for another, and another. One by one, I took the stones from the pool until I had a small pile in my hand. Their various colours glinted together in the sunshine like a cache of jewels.

I thought of Harry's stone collection. The two that reminded him of his parents. The one with the mottled texture and the broken edge—*that's me,* he'd said. Each of these stones in my hand was different in some way. This one had spots and speckles, like Jacky with his face full of freckles. The round, smooth one with the golden flecks could be Miranda with the honey-hair. Which one was me? Maybe the weirdly shaped one with the dent where something had worn it down. Some had jagged bits sticking out. All of them were beautiful.

I thought of Harry who was now in prison, and gripped the stones hard in my fist. The jagged edges pressed into my skin but I squeezed harder and harder until it hurt. When I could stand the pain no longer I lifted my hand and threw the stones with force onto the stone face of a boulder. They made a cracking sound and bounced away from each other. The Miranda stone, the Jacky stone, me, Maurice, the Pevensies, Dot—scattered.

That's what we were like now. Ever since the day they took Harry away, we had been scattered. Mr Hammond had talked one morning about Jesus' disciples scattering when trouble came. We'd done the same, hadn't we? Trouble came, Harry was taken, and afterwards we hardly saw each other. The thread that had held us all together had been Harry, and the thread had snapped.

On the ground near my foot I saw another stone. This one had dried out in the sun and lost its sparkle. I picked it up. It was warped and broken, a bit like Harry's stone back at his house, on his shelf.

Tears welled in my eyes and I wiped them with the back of my hand. No matter how many times I turned my eyes from his gate, I couldn't forget him. No matter what people said about him, or what he'd done, I couldn't bring myself to hate him. I hadn't been free to admit that to anyone. It was the big, deep secret I kept hidden. The thing that weighed like a boulder and wore me down.

I ran my thumb over the rough surface of the stone and was filled with longing.

'Do you still have him?' I whispered. Was God even listening?

'I'm sorry I can't hate him. Maybe he can be good again. Maybe you can help him.'

## 20

# It don't make sense

I PUT THE MOTTLED stone I'd been clutching into my jacket pocket and left the beach. Something had changed in my heart, though I couldn't have said what it was. Perhaps the beginning of forgiveness. I didn't know if I could fully forgive a man who had strangled a child but I knew that not forgiving was twisting me up inside.

On the way up Murphy's Lane, for the first time in years, I made myself look at Harry's gate. I couldn't actually see the gate as it had been completely overgrown with weeds. The pine trees either side had grown wild and hung over the gateposts and grass had grown up through the gravel of the drive.

I crossed the road and stood at the gate. A breeze blew up and the smell of pine and eucalyptus wafted out from Harry's place and enveloped me. My knees almost buckled with the familiarity of it. I took a deep breath and ventured through the gate.

A currawong chortled from somewhere in the trees and a raven cawed as if in answer. I heard Jacky's voice, '*How's the coorn, maate?*'

I wrapped my arms around myself and kept going. As I turned the corner and Harry's cottage came into view, I let out the breath I hadn't realised I'd been holding. I didn't stop, but forced my legs forward.

The cottage was no longer as white as I remembered, but grey and grimy. The foul words that had been painted across the front remained but had faded over the years. The windows were gaping holes with glass still clinging to their frames. The garden next to the house was a ruin, the fence pushed in and the whole space overcome with weeds. It was a picture of sadness.

I stopped short at the sound of someone clearing their throat and a movement near the door of the cottage. Peering closer, I realised there was a man sitting on the front steps. He was hunched over with his elbows on his knees and head leaning on one hand. As he looked up and caught my eye, I saw it was Maurice Hix. I hadn't seen Maurice for a long time. Here he was, bigger and broader with a hint of stubble and looking very much like a man who had left his childhood behind.

Maurice straightened himself from his hunched position, sniffed and nodded, his expression grave. 'G'day Lily,' he said.

'G'day Maurice.'

'Haven't seen you for a while.'

'No.'

'So, you come here too?' he asked.

Overcome with shyness, I didn't know how to answer. I nodded, though I hadn't been there since the day Kylie and I had gone there to see the vandalism. I slowly walked closer with my hands in my pockets, trying to think of something to say.

Maurice stood, threw a cigarette butt on the ground and scuffed it with his foot. He hesitated before bending down to pick it up. I was surprised to see him put it in his pocket.

'How have you been?' he asked.

'Alright. What about you?'

He took a deep breath, turned away and looked up into the hills. I had the feeling he was trying to pull himself together. When he turned back his face was twisted into an expression of pain and his eyes had misted.

He shook his head. 'I dunno.'

I moved up near the fire pit and stood looking at him, sensing there was something else he wanted to say.

'You know it don't make sense?' He said it like a question.

'What doesn't?'

'You know—what happened.' He scuffed his feet on the ground. 'That's what Miranda's been saying. She found a photo of Jacky and Harry and she's been looking at it. She reckons she can't get them out of her head.'

'Photos can do that.'

'Yeah. Thing is, Jacky *loved* Harry. And—' he looked up towards the treetops and blinked— 'Harry loved Jacky. They were best mates.' He looked away and passed his forearm over his eyes.

'I know,' I managed to say. 'I don't get it either.'

Maurice composed himself and looked back at me. 'Do you think he done it?'

The question threw me for a moment. I shrugged my shoulders. 'Everyone said he did.'

Maurice nodded and shuffled towards the fire pit. He bent down and grabbed hold of one of the old chairs that had been kicked over and lay in the long grass. He lifted it up and set it upright next to the weed-entangled fire pit, then shoved his hands in his pockets.

'Yeah, everyone said he did. Well, I better go. See ya.'

'See ya,' I said.

I watched him saunter away, his back hunched like that of an old man, until he disappeared around the corner into Harry's drive.

What did Maurice mean, it didn't make sense? I knew Maurice had been the one to lead the band of vandals to rip up Harry's garden, smash in the windows and paint the vile words all over the weatherboards. He'd been angry and grief-stricken for so long and it had sent him down a road of drunkenness and unhappiness. So why was he here now? He'd asked me if I came here too, as if coming to Harry's house was something he did regularly.

I took from my pocket the mottled stone I'd picked up at the beach and frowned at it. Why today, of all days, had I come here and found Maurice? I went over to the steps where Maurice had been sitting, set the stone on the top step, and set off for home.

In my bedroom, I put the box of journals, and all the other boxes, back into the cupboard. I didn't want to unearth any more of my writings yet. I'd go through the suitcase under my bed instead, which contained only seasonal clothes I hardly ever wore. As I sorted through them, deciding which to keep and which to toss out, I kept thinking of Maurice. Did he have doubts about Harry's guilt now? Harry was in prison so he must be guilty. The alternative was too disturbing.

Mum poked her head into my room and said, 'How's it going?'

I held an old poncho in my hands. 'Did I really wear this?'

Mum laughed. 'Into the give-away box then.'

'Mum? Do you think we could go for a drive to Dot's tomorrow?'

'Good idea, you haven't seen each other for ages. I'll give Fiona a call.'

As Mum went to telephone Dot's mother, I thought about Dot and Minnie-May at primary school. How they'd been practically glued to each other. I had a burning urge to talk to Dot about those days. About when Minnie-May saw Harry and Jacky arguing in the woods.

Mum and I headed into Durrunby on Saturday for afternoon tea at Fiona's—me driving. Mum's presumption that I was missing Dot wasn't too far off the mark. I did miss her a bit. Attending different schools—Dot in Hobart and me in Crayfish Cove—had meant we rarely saw each other. Especially as she stayed in town many weekends to practise with her choir.

I pulled the Datsun into the expansive gravel drive, turned in a semi-circle and backed up to the house. (I was getting good at this.) Their house was a long, red-brick bungalow with lots of windows and a wrap-a-round verandah. Behind it lay sheep paddocks to the horizon.

Fiona came out to greet us wearing a large, flapping orange dress and a broad smile. She ushered us into the living room of the wood-pan-elled home that smelt of the baked muffins cooling on a cake rack. The room was open plan and modern with more windows looking out onto the verandah and the back paddocks.

Dot appeared with her face lit-up and she gave me a hug. She looked so lovely—pink cheeked and glossy haired, her dark curls piled on top of her head and secured with a scrunchie. She had a classic beauty I wished I'd recognised when I was a silly, self-centred nine-year-old. I cringed when I thought of how I'd treated her and her friend, Min-nie-May.

'Sit down, sit down,' Fiona gushed. 'I've made some muffins. Tea ... coffee ...?'

To her credit, Fiona asked me all about myself first but, the truth was, I had nothing much to tell. So we heard all about Dot's ac-complishments—her singing lessons and state-to-state tours with her choir, which included solo performances. I was glad for her, I really was, and I made a point of nodding and smiling and asking questions. But when we'd finished afternoon tea, and the adults began chatting about things of no interest to Dot and myself, we escaped to Dot's bedroom where I had the opportunity to ask my questions.

Dot's room was neat and pink. The only indication she'd left her childhood and entered the teenage years was a record player and a stack of vinyls on a side table. I wandered over and ran my hand over the lid of the turntable.

'Nice,' I said.

'I saved up for it.' Dot had a soft, sweet voice which belied the strong, melodic one she sang with.

I flicked through the vinyls. 'Joan Sutherland. Who's she?'

'Oh, she's amazing!'

'Singer?'

'Yes.'

'As good as Pat Benatar?'

Dot looked at me blankly.

'You know—' I sang a couple of lines of *Hit Me With Your Best Shot*, but her face remained blank.

I shrugged. 'Anyway, what have you been up to lately, besides touring the country? Seen any of your old Cove friends lately?'

'No, not really.' Dot sat on a chair at her desk, with her body turned towards me. I sat on the edge of her bed.

'Do you see Minnie-May much?' I asked.

'Not these days. I haven't seen her for ages.'

'You were pretty good friends once, weren't you?'

'Yes, I guess. At school, anyway.'

'Oh, I thought you saw each other outside of school. Like in the holidays and that.'

'She wasn't really allowed out. I went to her house once but it was boring. All we did was play Scrabble with her aunt and uncle. Why are you asking about her?'

'I was thinking about her lately. Remember back when Jacky Hix died?'

Dot's face fell. 'That was horrible.'

'Remember how she told the police she'd seen Harry and Jacky in the woods?'

'Oh, that.' Dot turned away and fiddled with a sheet of paper on her desk.

'Did she say anything to you about it?'

The back of Dot's neck turned pink. 'Well … not much.'

'She did say something, though?'

'Um, it was a long time ago. Why do you want to know?'

'Like I said, I've been thinking about her. Do you think you could try and remember what she said?'

Dot turned to me, the remains of a blush on her face. 'Why?' A shadow passed behind her eyes that could have been irritation or fear.

'I was talking to Maurice and he reckons there are some things that don't add up. You know—about Jacky.'

'Oh.' Tiny sweat drops had gathered on Dot's upper lip. She pressed the back of her hand to her mouth to wipe them away.

'Dot?'

'I really can't say.'

'Why not?'

'I promised.'

'Dot—'

'I can't break a promise.'

'But what if it's important? What if—' I huffed in exasperation and shook my head.

Dot clasped her hands together in her lap and said, 'Well, I suppose it won't matter. It was a long time ago.'

I leaned forward, nodding encouragingly. 'You're right, it was. It won't matter now if you tell.'

Dot glanced at me, then down at her clasped hands. 'Well, she told me she didn't really see Harry in the woods.'

I stared at her.

Dot looked up again and flinched. 'What's the matter? Your face has gone white.'

I managed a strangled, 'Dot.'

'What?'

My hands flew to my cheeks and pressed. My heart raced. 'I don't understand. Why would she say she'd seen them if it wasn't true?'

'Someone told her to say it. Someone forced her. She was sorry about it, but she didn't have a choice.'

'Who forced her?'

'I don't know, she didn't say.'

'But why didn't you tell someone?'

'I couldn't. She made me promise. I crossed my heart and hoped to *die*.'

I searched Dot's face for any glimmer of understanding of the magnitude of what she'd just told me. But there was nothing in that sweet, innocent face but puzzlement.

'Anyway,' she said, 'it doesn't matter because they caught him, didn't they? He's in prison.'

'Dot,' I said quietly.

Dot raised her eyebrows and blinked. 'What?'

'Dot, what if it wasn't Harry?'

## 21

## Operation Donut

On the way home from Dot's, I drove with what felt like a brick in my stomach. Twice Mum yelped, 'Look out!'—first when I absent-mindedly veered too far to the side of the road and again as I almost turned in front of an oncoming car. She breathed a sigh of relief the moment I pulled into the drive.

'Dad can take you next time,' she said as she picked at the sticky-tape holding my L-plate to the windscreen and peeled it off.

I grabbed my shoulder bag from the back seat, said I was going for a walk and headed straight to the public phone box outside the general store. I found the Hix family's number in the phone book, dropped a twenty-cent piece into the coin slot and dialled. When Maurice himself answered, I said, 'Maurice, this is Lily. I need to talk to you.'

I filled him in briefly on what Dot had told me about Minnie-May and, after a few seconds of silence, he let out a burst of expletives. 'You've got to be kidding! What were they thinking?'

'I know. What should we do?'

Maurice quietened his voice to an almost whisper. 'I don't know. We have to tell someone.'

'Like who?'

'The police?' He sighed. 'Ugh, they'll say Harry Fernley was found guilty, end of story. But what if he didn't do it?'

'There would have been other evidence besides that, though,' I said.

'Yeah, true. They wouldn't throw someone in prison just from what a kid said they saw, would they?'

'No. Well, I don't suppose so.'

'Look, I'll call Miranda and we'll meet up, yeah? How about I pick you up at one tomorrow outside the chip shop? I'll try and get Jonathan too.'

When I arrived home, I went straight to my room and opened my cupboard containing all the boxes of journals. There were thousands of words in those boxes. Was there something in there somewhere? Information the police had missed? Evidence pointing away from Harry and towards someone else?

I closed the cupboard doors. No, he'd been found guilty by a jury. There had been enough evidence to convict him, though what that was I had little idea. No one had told us children much at the time.

The evening was mild and Dad announced Saturday-Snag-Night—a ritual involving him barbecuing sausages on the fire pit and us sitting around together in the dark, dripping sausage fat and tomato sauce on ourselves before toasting marshmallows for dessert. It was silly, messy and fun.

As we waited for the sausages to cook, Dad jumped up to turn on the tape deck and said, 'How about some Elvis?'

We groaned, but happily joined in singing *Blue Suede Shoes* as Dad took Mum's hand and swung her around the lawn.

'Mum's happy,' Maudie said.

I watched Mum spinning around, her golden hair flying about her face and glinting in the firelight. Dad pulled her in close to him and they grinned at each other, like everything in their world was perfect.

'She sure is,' I said.

My mind flung itself back to the day Dad told us that Harry had been charged—the hard edge to his words, dark storm of his face, my mother's distress. The way they didn't connect properly for ages after. How could I risk that happening again?

Dad dipped Mum as if he was Fred Astaire and she was Ginger Rogers. He held her there with his strong arms and gazed into her face.

'Have I ever told you you're the most beautiful woman in Crayfish Cove?' he said.

I knew I didn't want anything to change.

I sat with Maurice, Miranda and Jonathan at a corner table in the bakery in Durrunby, sharing a plate of party pies. Maurice had picked us up early that Sunday afternoon in his Holden Kingswood and blasted our ears with Led Zeppelin songs for the fifteen minute drive from Crayfish Cove. Now, I leaned on one elbow with my cheek propped on my fist, sipping a Coke Spider and relishing the quiet of the almost-deserted shop.

To anyone else, we would appear as four friends relaxing over lunch. But there was an almost palpable tension in the air. Maurice's face was haggard and I doubted he'd had much sleep the night before. As he took a bite of a sauce-smothered pie, Miranda laid her arm behind his chair and rubbed his back. Jonathan held a mug of coffee with both hands, his elbows on the table, staring out the window.

Jonathan turned to me and said, 'What do you think we should do, Lily?'

Three sets of eyes turned to me and I shook my head. I had no idea. For all I knew, Harry was guilty and we were dredging everything up for no good reason. What if I'd done the wrong thing by telling Maurice what Dot had said, and hurt him all over again?

'You know Dot better than anyone,' Jonathan said. 'Is she telling the truth?'

I pictured Dot's sweet face with her innocent eyes. 'Yes. She doesn't lie.'

'It's new evidence, then,' Maurice said.

Jonathan frowned. 'Maybe, but not necessarily. We should try to look at it from as many angles as possible.'

'What are you thinking?' I asked.

'What if Harry and Jacky really were seen arguing in the woods, but by someone else? And what if that person, for whatever reason, shouldn't have been there, so they made Minnie-May say it was her that saw them?'

'In that case, the evidence would be the same, just from a different source,' I said.

Miranda had been sitting with her head to one side as she listened. 'I can't see it, though,' she said.

'No,' I said. 'It's not likely, but it is possible.'

I leaned down to pull a notebook and biro from the bag I'd propped against my chair. I set it on the table and sat with the pen poised in my hand. 'We should take notes.'

Jonathan placed his finger on the notebook. 'How about we make two lists here. Things we know pointing to Harry being guilty, and things that could be evidence for him not being guilty.'

I drew a line down the centre of the page and wrote the headings *Guilty* and *Not Guilty* at the top of each section. 'The first thing we should write under 'not guilty' is that Minnie-May didn't see Harry and Jacky in the woods,' I said.

'Let's stick to the facts, though,' Jonathan said. 'Minnie-May *said* she didn't see them in the woods. It's not necessarily true.'

'Good point,' I said as I wrote. 'You sure you want to be a doctor? You could make a good detective.'

I made the first note under the second heading, reading aloud as I wrote:

**NOT GUILTY**
**- According to Dot, Minnie-May said someone forced her to lie about seeing H and J in the woods**

Maurice swallowed the last piece of his pie and leaned back in his chair, wiping his fingers on a paper serviette. 'We have to find out who forced her.'

'Agreed,' Jonathan said. 'Let's list what we know. Under the first heading, better put that Harry was found guilty by a jury. We also know he tried to strangle Kylie's uncle when they were at school.'

Miranda leaned forward. 'We don't know that for sure.'

'Yeah, we do,' I said. 'Mum remembers it. We should list it.'

The others agreed and I added those points to the list.

Miranda smiled grimly. 'I know you all knew Harry longer than me, but I saw the bond Jacky had with him. Maurice too, but especially Jacky. They were so close. That's why it never made sense to me. I could never picture it.'

'Apparently, Harry always said he was innocent,' I said.

Jonathan set his empty mug down and turned it round and round on the table, his eyebrows pulled into a frown. 'Do any of you still have the newspaper articles?' We answered in the negative. 'It's hard to remember the case. I think our parents kept a lot from us. We should try and get hold of them.'

Maurice sat up straight and said, 'My Aunt Jo would help us.'

'She's the one who ate the witchetty grub, right?' I said.

The tension eased a little and we found ourselves chuckling.

'She works as a librarian in Hobart. She might have the articles. If not, she can find them through the library.'

'Perfect,' Jonathan said. 'You give your aunt a ring. The sooner we have those, the better.'

Maurice's countenance lifted. 'Yeah, I can do that.'

'Will she be alright about it?' I said.

'She'd want to be involved. I don't want to bring it all up with Mum and Dad in case it doesn't go anywhere. They've been through enough. But Aunt Jo's different. She'll want to know what's going on and she'll want to help. She won't tell Mum and Dad if we don't need to.'

'I guess no one's written to Harry?' Miranda said. We stared at her. 'No, of course you wouldn't have,' she said, her cheeks reddening. 'I just thought—I don't know—if he is innocent...' She pulled the straw half-way out of her milkshake and fiddled with it, her eyes averted from ours. 'He's been there for three years.'

The back of my neck prickled. No one spoke for a moment.

Jonathan pushed his mug aside and clasped his hands on top of the table. 'Well, we'd best work fast. Whether Minnie-May was telling the truth or not, we need to tell someone what she said to Dot. Can anyone remember the name of the detective who was in charge?'

'That was the big bloke with the grey hair, yeah?' Maurice said.

'Bullard,' I said. 'He kept forgetting my name and calling me Laura, so I made a point of remembering his.'

'We could tell Constable Munnings,' Miranda said.

Maurice snorted. 'He'll tell our parents and that'll be the end of it.'

'Also,' said Jonathan, 'we don't want him asking the wrong people questions. If that sighting really was a lie, there could still be a murderer out there. We don't want to alert them. No, we need proper detectives on the case.'

There was a tinkle as the bakery door opened and a family with young children entered.

Maurice quietened his voice. 'Jonathan's right. We should be careful who we tell. If it was someone else who' —he hesitated— 'killed Jacky, we don't want him knowing we're looking for him.'

'Or her,' I said.

Maurice shook his head. 'Probably a man. I remember something about the killer having big hands. They could tell that by the strangle marks on Jacky's neck.'

I shuddered. 'I guess I should put that on the first list. Harry does have large hands.'

Maurice looked about the room as if to make sure no one could hear, and leaned in. 'We need an operation code name.'

Jonathan rolled his eyes. 'You've been watching too many cop shows.'

'No, Maurice's right,' Miranda said. 'We should be careful. If there is a murderer at large we don't want him suspicious. As long as he has his guard down, we have a better chance of finding him.'

'Alright, what's the code name?' I asked.

A little kid who'd come into the bakery with the family yelled out, 'Donut, donut!'

Maurice grinned wryly. 'Operation Donut,' he said, and we all laughed.

I turned the notebook around and pushed it towards the centre of the table. 'Anything else to add?'

The others scanned the two lists:

**GUILTY:**

**- Found guilty by a jury**

**- Tried to strangle Kylie's uncle when they were at school**

**- Killer had large hands — Harry has large hands**

**NOT GUILTY:**

**- According to Dot, Minnie-May said someone forced her to lie about seeing H and J in the woods**

**- Strong bond / friendship between H and J**

**- Harry maintained his innocence**

'That's a good start,' Jonathan said.

'Do you think they'll reopen the case?' Miranda asked.

Jonathan shook his head sadly. 'Not without new evidence, and we don't actually have any. Not without talking to Minnie-May, anyway. Lily, do you think you could talk to her?'

'Uh—'

'You'd have to be careful about what you said. Don't let on you've been talking to us. You don't have to if you don't want to, but she might open up to you.'

I pulled a face. 'I've never been close to her, but I'll see what I can do.'

We agreed to meet at my place the following Saturday evening, as Mum and Dad were going out and Maudie would be staying with Nan. Hopefully, we would have the newspaper articles by then.

We sat for a while longer, almost silent, as we finished the pies and ran our fingers over the plate to pick up the last crumbs. Maurice pulled a packet of Benson and Hedges out of his pocket and offered it round—more from politeness as the rest of us were non-smokers—and lit one. He took a long drag, leaned back and blew the smoke towards the ceiling. I closed the notebook and put it back in my bag.

We made small talk for a while, about Maurice's job at the sawmill and Jonathan's dislike of boarding in the city. When we ran out of conversation, we piled back into Maurice's car to head back to Crayfish Cove.

All the way back, we retreated silently into our own thoughts. I stared out of the side window and barely noticed the landscape rushing past. If someone *had* forced Minnie-May to lie, why had she told Dot and made Dot promise not to tell? Was it an attention-seeking ploy? Some people told lies to impress their friends. That didn't make sense, though. There wasn't anything impressive about her story.

I would keep pondering. There had to be logic in there somewhere.

'Mum says I need to take you driving.' Dad stood in the lounge room later in the afternoon, dangling the car keys in one hand.

I rolled my eyes. 'She can't handle me, then?'

Dad chuckled. 'Come on, there's time to drive out to Durrunby and back.'

'I've just been there.'

'You weren't driving though, were you?'

I happily reattached my L-plates to the front and back windows and hopped into the car with Dad beside me. Every opportunity to drive was a step closer to getting my full licence. Dad winced as I grated the gears and hit the curb backing out of the driveway. But, once I was out on the road, I was fine and Dad relaxed. I drove slowly and steadily to the end of town and took the turnoff to Durrunby.

'Was that Maurice Hix's car I saw earlier, dropping you off?'

'Yep,' I answered.

'Bit of a catch-up?'

'I had lunch at the bakery with Maurice, Miranda and Jonathan.'

'That's nice. I don't think you've seen them for a while, have you?'

'No. We kind of lost touch a bit.'

I saw Dad nodding his head from the corner of my eye. 'Slow down, there's a dog. That Jonathan's a nice kid.'

'Jonathan's eighteen.'

'Yeees...?'

'Well, he's not a kid.'

Dad chuckled. 'Alright, a nice young man then.'

I huffed. 'He's not that. He's a *guy*.'

'A what? A guy?'

'Yes.'

'Uh—alright. So, did he call and ask you out?'

'Ugh.' I turned briefly to Dad to pull a face at him. 'He's a friend.'

Dad put up his hands in mock surrender. 'Okay, okay. Just being a dad.'

'It was my idea, anyway. I thought it'd be good to catch up with them. I haven't seen them much since—well—for a while.'

'Ah, yep. Gotcha.'

Dad wound down his window, leaned his elbow on the edge and waved to various people as we drove between the two towns. 'There's young Bill,' he said, waving to a man on a tractor as we passed Blackford's dairy farm. 'He'll take over from his father. Got the farm blood. So, what did you find to talk about, seeing as you haven't seen each other for ages?'

'Not much.' I clicked on the indicator and turned the corner into the main street of Durrunby.

'G'day Trace!' Dad waved out the window to a middle-aged woman getting into her car outside the hairdresser. 'Drop back a cog and pull in at the servo, I'll buy you a Paddle Pop.'

I geared down and pulled the car smoothly into a parking space next to the service station.

'So,' he said as I switched off the engine, 'did the old murder case come up at all?'

'What?' I gave Dad a look which I hoped resembled irritated bewilderment. 'Why would it?'

'I was talking to Ron—Maurice's dad—this morning. He said he heard Maurice talking furtively on the phone to someone about Harry Fernley. I thought you kids might have been discussing it.'

'Furtively?' I blew air from my mouth, making a 'pffft' sound. 'We talked about Maurice's job and Jonathan's crappy boarding arrangements, if you must know.'

Dad again put up his hands in mock surrender. 'Sorry. I'll get you that Paddle Pop.'

I smiled sweetly and said, 'I'd rather a Hazelnut Roll.'

When Dad returned with the ice creams, he handed me mine and said, 'Do you know how much those things cost?'

'No?' I turned a wide-eyed, mock-innocent face to him and he burst out laughing.

We finished our ice creams and I reversed gracefully out of the parking space without hitting the curb. Dad flicked on the radio, leaned back and whistled along to Joey Scarbury singing *Believe It Or Not* as I drove. It was nicer than driving with Mum, who would grab her seat every few minutes.

'Can you take me driving every time?' I said, and Dad laughed again.

I tried to concentrate hard on the road, but my mind kept wandering. What would Ron Hix have heard from Maurice's side of our phone conversation yesterday? Not much, the call had been very brief. All the same, he had picked up that we were talking about Harry and the murder case. Then he'd passed that revelation along to my dad and who knows how many other people. I sighed inwardly. How were we ever going to keep our investigations from the ever-alert ears of the Crayfish Cove bush telegraph?

## 22

## An apology and a shortcut

I KEPT AN EYE out for Minnie-May at school during the week. We had no classes together and Kylie was with me at break times, so there was little opportunity to speak to her privately. What would I say anyway? *Minnie-May, I heard you lied to the police.* Obviously not. *Where were you on the afternoon Jacky died?* Too direct. I wished I'd asked the others to help me come up with an opening line.

'You're quiet,' Kylie said. She and I sat on a bench seat in the quadrangle, eating our lunch and watching a group of kids playing four-square on the concrete.

'Am I?' I forced my thoughts back to Kylie and the present.

'What's up?'

'Just a bit tired.'

It was only a half-lie. I'd lain awake for ages the night before, trying to figure out how to instigate a conversation about murder with someone I rarely spoke to. And how to do it without sounding like I was accusing her of being a liar. Was Minnie-May a liar? Maybe she really had seen Harry and Jacky arguing in the woods. But how could she when, according to everyone, she never went anywhere without Mr or Mrs Hammond? And yet, I had seen her by herself in the mist amongst the trees on Murphy's Lane.

Kylie clicked her fingers in front of my face. 'Snap out of it.'

One of the kids playing four-square missed the basketball and it bounced in our direction. Kylie put up her hands and slammed it back just in time to prevent it hitting her head.

'Darn,' she said, looking at her squashed fishpaste sandwich. 'Oh well, didn't want it anyway.'

'I just remembered,' I said, lifting a piece of greaseproof paper in my lunch box. I took out two individual apple pies and handed one to Kylie.

'Oh, I love your mum!' She closed her eyes as she took a bite. 'Mmm, so good.'

I munched on my own pie while watching a group of younger kids walking up from the oval towards the quadrangle. Minnie-May was amongst them, arm-in-arm with Sharn Skinner, a thin girl with a flat face whose family was rumoured to smoke pot together every evening.

'What do you think of Minnie-May?' I asked Kylie.

'Dunno, I don't see her much. Except at church. She's still a bit weird.'

I watched as Sharn yelled out to someone, slipped her arm out of Minnie-May's and jogged away towards a huddle of boys. Minnie-May stopped and watched after her for a few seconds before continuing on with the others.

'I wonder if the Hammonds know she's hanging out with Sharn,' I said.

'Doubt it. They'd do something about it, I reckon.'

'I wouldn't have picked those two for friends. Still, I guess Sharn's a bit weird too.'

Kylie leaned back against the wall of the building, stretching out her legs and gazing into the distance. 'Everyone's weird. Haven't you noticed?'

Kylie was home with a sore throat on Thursday and I had my chance to speak to Minnie-May at school. I was heading back from the toilet block to join some friends when I turned a corner and spotted her seated in the quadrangle by herself, reading a book. I stopped and doubled back, hiding myself behind the building. Here was a perfect opportunity. Minnie-May by herself and no one around to witness the conversation. But I still hadn't come up with the right opening line. I didn't even have a reason to sit down next to her.

I leaned against the brick wall for a moment, thinking. I could sit down, say hello, ask after her family—that sort of thing—and hope the conversation flowed naturally. I walked back around the corner and headed towards her.

Inspiration struck when I accidentally kicked a stone and sent it spinning across the quadrangle. As Minnie-May looked up, I feigned a limp and grimaced. 'Hi,' I said, as I sat down and pulled off my school shoe. I turned it upside down and shook it. 'I think I got a rock in my shoe.'

Minnie-May regarded me with an expressionless face.

'How've you been? I don't see you much,' I said, as I rubbed the bottom of my foot.

'Alright.'

'Sharn not here today?'

'No, she's got a cold.'

'Oh, Kylie too. Must be going round.'

Minnie-May nodded and her lips turned slightly up into a smile. I'd forgotten her smile, soft and vulnerable, that I'd only seen a handful of times in all the years I'd known her. Dot had been the only one who could really bring a smile to Minnie-May's face. Or was it that Dot was the only one who tried? Had the rest of us even bothered? A sliver of shame wriggled up from somewhere inside me.

We'd had fun together at the sleepover at Dot's place that time, when Minnie-May's aunt was sick—playing cricket, exploring, watching the baby lambs. But since that weekend, not only had I not bothered to be kind to Minnie-May, but I'd gone out of my way to hurt her. I had a flashback of Minnie-May's face collapsing in pain and melting into a line of school uniforms—the day I'd kicked her in the shins. The animal grunt that had followed me through the years.

My heart hit the wall of my chest again. There it was—the opening line—clear, perfectly formed and ready to be spoken.

'Minnie-May?' I took a deep breath. 'I need to apologise to you.'

She turned a puzzled face to me. 'What for?'

'Remember the day back when you were in grade six, when you were standing in line at the classroom door and I came up and kicked you?'

Minnie-May's eyes widened and she gave me a small nod.

'It was a horrible thing to do and I never apologised. I should have. It's been on my mind for a long time. So, I'm sorry.'

'It's alright.' Minnie-May looked down at her lap and fiddled with her book.

I rubbed my foot as I talked. 'I was so angry and scared back then, because of what had happened. Jacky being killed. Remember?'

I glanced at Minnie-May and saw her shoulders tense.

'Harry was a good friend of mine, you see, and I couldn't believe he'd do something so terrible. When I heard what you'd said to the police, I still thought it couldn't be true. So, I took my anger out on you and

I shouldn't have. That wasn't fair. You were just doing what you had to.'

I leaned back against the classroom wall with my shoe in my lap, twisting the lace around my finger. 'You saw Jacky and Harry arguing in the woods and you knew you had to tell the truth. I would have done the same. It's really important to tell the truth, isn't it? So the right person gets punished.'

I leaned forward to put my shoe back on and took my time tying the lace. I waited for Minnie-May to speak but she was silent. Once my shoelace was tied, there was no reason for me to stay, but I did. My heart was beating so quickly I felt light-headed. I turned to Minnie-May and we locked eyes. Her face took on a shuttered look and something unsteady moved in the darkness behind her eyes. She blinked and the soft, expressionless face returned.

'Yes,' she said as she stood up. She clutched her book to her chest, said, 'Well, see you,' and walked away. I watched her cross the quadrangle and slip through a door into the high-school block. I closed my eyes and waited for my heart to settle down to its regular rhythm.

Had I hurt Minnie-May all over again? What had she meant when she stood up and said, 'yes'? Yes, it's important to tell the truth? Yes, the right person should be punished? Or was she telling me that, yes, she had seen Jacky and Harry in the woods?

I stood and wandered down to the oval where my friends waited, sprawled out on the grass, telling their own teenage secrets.

On Saturday, by the time I found out Nan had a cold and Maudie wouldn't be going there for a sleepover, Maurice, Miranda and

Jonathan were on their way to our place. Supposedly to eat hot chips and watch movies while Mum and Dad went out for tea.

I relayed the message to my friends at the door about Maudie being home, accompanied by eye rolling and dramatic hand gestures.

'That's alright, there's plenty of chips for everyone,' Maurice said, holding up a paper-wrapped bundle.

Jonathan whispered, 'Maybe Maudie can help us.'

'She can't keep a secret,' I hissed.

Mum ushered my friends into the lounge room, asked about the videos we'd chosen and told us she'd left dessert in the fridge.

'What is it?' I asked.

'Some donuts from the bakery. I heard you telling Jonathan on the phone you were having donuts tonight but you forgot to buy any.' She looked surprised when we all glanced at each other and giggled.

Mum and Dad left and Maudie joined us. We laid out the chips and Fanta on the coffee table, turned the lights down and put on a video. When we'd finished the chips, I said I felt like a cup of tea and disappeared into the kitchen, jerking my head at Jonathan as I went so he would follow me. He crept in after me, then Maurice. I could hear Miranda talking to Maudie about the movie to keep her in the lounge room.

'Sorry, I didn't know Maudie was going to be here,' I whispered.

'Don't worry about it.' Maurice slapped a large yellow envelope down on the table. 'Copies of the articles from the *Mercury*. Aunt Jo's a trooper. She thinks she found everything. There's not a lot, but it's all there.'

'How was she about it?' I asked.

'Really upset, actually.'

'That we're doing this?'

'No, that the wrong person might have been put away for Jacky's murder.'

I glanced at the kitchen door. 'Let's have a quick look.' We sat at the table, huddled together, and Maurice pulled out a handful of paper sheets. Jonathan and I took some each while Maurice put the kettle on. I scanned some of the briefest articles first:

**Homicide detectives are investigating the murder last night of an eleven-year-old boy in the Crayfish Cove area. The boy died by strangulation.**

**...**

**The investigation into the murder of 11-year-old Jack Hix in the Crayfish Cove area continues. Detective Sergeant Frank Bullard is appealing for anyone with information to come forward.**

**...**

**The chief of the Hobart homicide squad charged a man at 2pm today with the murder of a young boy. The man will appear in the Magistrate's Court tomorrow morning.**

**The body of Jack August Hix was found under a bush in thick scrub by a local search team in Crayfish Cove on 1st April. He had been strangled.**

**...**

**Guilty of Murder**
**HOBART: Mr Harold David Fernley (33), was sentenced yesterday to life imprisonment for the murder of Master Jack August Hix (11), at Crayfish Cove on April 1st 1978.**

**Jack Hix's body was found strangled in bushland near Madding Hill.**

**A jury of six men and six women, after two hours deliberation, found Mr Fernley guilty.**

'If only someone else had seen something,' Jonathan said. 'Besides Minnie-May I mean, who might not have seen anything after all.'

'What about Molly?' I said. 'Sometimes she stands at that gate of hers all day. And I bet no one asked her at the time.'

'Nah, she couldn't have seen anything,' Maurice said. 'Jacky didn't get that far.'

Miranda appeared at the kitchen door. 'Uh, how's the tea coming along?'

'Whoops.' I jumped up and clattered cups around on the kitchen bench.

'It was two deliveries Jacky had on the day, wasn't it?' Jonathan asked.

'Yep, that's right,' answered Maurice. 'Arthur Gilchrist, then the manse.'

'And we know he didn't get to Arthur's.'

'Nuh, the police turned his place over from top to bottom and didn't find a thing.'

'So, assuming Jacky didn't reach Arthur's, he couldn't have reached the Hammond's either,' said Jonathan.

'That's not necessarily true,' said a voice from behind us. We all swung round to find Maudie standing at the kitchen door.

'Maudie—' I dropped a teaspoon on the bench with a clatter. 'Let's go watch the movie, guys. I've got my cup of tea.' My voice rose in pitch. 'Maudie, would you like a drink?'

'Why are you talking about Jacky Hix?' she asked.

Miranda smiled and walked towards her. 'It came up in conversation. Let's go back to the movie.'

'What are they?' Maudie pointed and stepped up to the table. 'They're about Jacky, aren't they?'

Maurice pushed all the news articles together and shoved them into the manilla envelope. 'Yeah, they are. I've been having another look at them. Remembering my little brother, you know?'

Maudie nodded. 'You're trying to figure something out. I'm good with problems. I could help.'

'It's okay,' I said. 'Don't worry about it. Let's—'

Maudie clicked her tongue. 'Why can't I help? You're always telling me how smart I am. Everyone says, *you're so clever Maudie... how smart you are Maudie,* but they don't ask for my help. I'm employed in a position where I solve problems every day. So why won't you let me help you with your problem?'

Jonathan stood. 'You're right, Maudie. Here, have a seat.' He pulled out a chair and held it for her. 'We could use your help.'

'Jonathan?' I tried out my what-do-you-think-you're-doing look and Jonathan gave me a quick nod in return. 'Come on, everyone,' he said. 'Operation Donut.'

As we arranged ourselves around the table, he leaned in towards my sister and said, 'What's happened is this: Maurice was thinking about his brother and he found himself worrying that Harry Fernley might not have been the person who killed him. He told us about his concerns and we agreed to help him go through everything again. Just in case mistakes were made.'

'Mistakes by the police?'

'Yes.'

I said, 'If Mum and Dad know we're doing this, though, they might not be happy about it.'

'I won't tell them, but I won't lie.' Maudie said.

'We'd never ask you to lie.'

'Okay.'

'Maudie, when you said, "not necessarily" before, what did you mean?' Jonathan asked.

'You said Mr Gilchrist's house is closer to Murphy's Lane than the church.'

'Yes?'

'It's only closer if you go along the road. Not if you take the shortcut to the manse. Nan and I go that way on Sundays.'

All four of us sat there staring at Maudie. She looked from face to face and, when we said nothing, stood up and left the room.

Maurice said, 'Where's she going?' and started to rise.

'Wait,' I said, 'she's doing something.'

Maudie came back into the kitchen carrying a notebook. She sat down and opened it to a page of writing and figures. 'I measured the distances with my measuring wheel. There's a track off the road behind the eucalypts that goes down to the back of the manse. Nan and I walk that way. It's 280.4 metres from Nan's place.'

'I know the one,' Maurice said. 'Jacky used to ride his bike down there. It's got a good slope.'

Maudie continued. 'But the road turns away from the church for a while before it turns back, which makes the distance along the road longer. Nan and I go the road way if it's been raining because the track gets slippery. From Nan's place to the church along the road, the distance is 431 metres.'

'Had it been raining, can anyone remember?' Jonathan asked.

'I don't remember any rain that day,' I said.

'If Jacky walked along the road,' Maudie explained, 'he would have had to cross the road to Mr Gilchrist's, cross back again and follow the street until he reached the church. Then he would have had to double back and cross the road a third time to go home. It would be more logical for him to have taken the short cut.' She looked at each of us and raised her eyebrows in expectation of a response.

'Maudie, you're a genius!' I said.

'I know.' She closed her notebook. 'Is there anything else I can help you with?'

We laughed.

'Wow, thanks so much, Maudie,' Jonathan said. 'So Jacky could have begun his round with his first stop being the manse. I guess someone should talk to Molly. She might have seen something after all.'

'I can do that,' I said. 'We've got three weeks off school now, so we should keep meeting up. I'll try and get Molly on a good day, when she knows who I am.'

Maudie stood, clutching her notebook to her chest. 'I'll measure up both routes and all the distances between each starting point and destination, and record them. We should be as accurate as possible. I assume you'll take the findings to the police?'

'We sure will,' Maurice said.

'Good, I'd like to help the police.'

We decided we needed hot drinks and I reboiled the kettle. On the way into the lounge with teas and Milos, Maudie stopped and turned back to face us.

'Just one thing,' she said. 'What is Operation Donut?'

23

# The teacher

Molly wasn't at the Sunday service the next day. I inquired after her and was told by Betty Crouch that she was bedridden with a bad cold. This did not bode well for our investigation.

On Monday, I went for a couple of walks to take a break from helping Mum with the spring clean. I checked the Crouch residence each time, but Molly wasn't standing at her front fence. I returned home to finish helping Mum scrub out the kitchen cupboards.

'I can finish this if you have things to do,' Mum said as she wrung out a cloth.

'It's alright,' I said. 'There's nothing much happening today.'

'Well, make sure you have plenty of fun while the school holidays last. Before you know it, you'll have finished school, be all grown up and slogging away at a job somewhere wondering where your youth went.'

I pulled a face at her. 'That was big, Mum. Are you alright?'

She laughed. 'Perfectly. It's been nice seeing you spend some time with your friends. That Jonathan's a lovely boy.'

'Don't you start.'

'I just meant—'

'Yes, he's a good friend.'

'Dad said Maurice has been talking about the murder case again.'

'Oh, really?' I turned away and began to place the cups one by one back into the clean cupboard.

'I hope he isn't getting depressed again. He's done really well to get back on his feet.'

'Yeah, he seems to like his job at the sawmill.'

'That's good. It wouldn't do to bring all that back up, about the murder. I doubt his mother could bear it.'

I closed the cupboard door and turned back to her. 'No. But what if...'

'What if...?' She raised her eyebrows and I recognised the look on her face. She always did have a way of drawing information out of me.

'Nothing.' I smiled. 'I'm going to sort out some more stuff in my room. Want me to make a pot of tea first?'

I took my tea into my bedroom and set it on the bedside table. Time to do some more digging. There was a period of time, after Harry was charged with Jacky's murder, when I had forced myself to write only mundane things in my journals—what I had for breakfast, what time I arrived at school, lists of subjects and teachers and homework, after school activities. What might I have written, innocently at the time, that may shed some light on the murder?

The fact was, if Harry was innocent, someone else was guilty. But who? I didn't remember there being any strangers around at the time—wrong time of year for seasonal workers. There may have been a few apple pickers, but most of the orchards were closer to Durrunby than Crayfish Cove, and the workers tended to stay and shop in Durrunby.

I pulled out two journals from my cupboard from around that period, sat on my bed and opened the first. I'd already been through it, of course, but not thoroughly. Last time, I had been looking for something obvious, thinking it would leap out at me. But what if the truth was hidden in my everyday words? To find it, I should read every sentence slowly and meticulously and ponder it. Deep reflection, our English teacher called it.

> **Weet-Bix for breakfast. I'm sick of Weet-Bix. Mum won't buy Froot Loops because they have too much sugar.**

Not much to deeply reflect on there.

> **Got to school at 8:52. Today we had:**
> **English with Mrs Foggarty**
> **Sport with Mr Allenby**
> **Maths with Mr Gilchrist**

Perhaps I should think about the teachers I'd listed. Mrs Foggarty lived in Crayfish Cove. Her husband was a fisherman. I couldn't imagine either of them hurting Jacky, or having any reason to. But that was the problem—as much as we'd tried, none of us could think of anyone in the community who could have had something against Jacky. There was no possible reason for a person to strangle him. Unless it was a serial killer.

Apparently, serial killers killed for no reason but the thrill of it. If Jacky was murdered by someone for the thrill of it, you'd expect them to kill again. However, they hadn't killed anyone in the last three years. At least not in Crayfish Cove. That didn't mean they hadn't done it elsewhere though. How could we find out about other seemingly unprovoked murders? Perhaps Maurice's aunt could help.

Mr Allenby—the sports teacher. Everyone liked him, but that didn't mean he was innocent. Sometimes the nicest people turned out to be murderers (according to *Cop Shop*). Mr Allenby lived in Durrunby so was unlikely to have been in Crayfish Cove on that day. And anyway, he only taught the high school students. He probably didn't even know Jacky.

I mentally crossed the Foggartys and Mr Allenby off the suspect list.

Mr Gilchrist—our Maths teacher. Also well liked, he was known as a kind and gentle man, as well as a good teacher. But did I see him that way because he taught Maudie and I needed him to be? He had an eccentric appearance—tall and beanpole thin, long grey moustache, always wearing a bow tie. And everything he did was with a flourish, as if he was an actor on a stage. Actors played parts—pretended to be someone they were not. Did we really know who Arthur Gilchrist was?

I kept reading.

**We played Truth, Dare or Promise at lunch time.**
**TRUTH: Debbie let Marcus kiss her behind the toilet block (I knew it!)**
**PROMISE: Kylie promised to lend Tina her new curling wand.**
**DARE: Tina dared me to go up to Minnie-May and start sucking my thumb. I told her she was mean and I wouldn't do it but she said I had to. I don't know if I want to play this game anymore.**

Poor Minnie-May. As I recalled, I didn't follow through with the dare, and Kylie and I stopped playing the game after that.

Here was more about Mr Gilchrist:

> **Toast and Marmite for breakfast.**
> **Got to school at 8:48.**
> **Maths was first lesson but Mr Gilchrist was late. We waited for ten minutes. We saw him through the window running across the oval. He was holding his briefcase in one hand and the end of his scarf in the other. He looked so funny!**

Mr Gilchrist lived a few minutes from the school. On the rare occasion I was early to school, I'd see him walking along the road towards the front gates. For him to be running across the oval meant he must have taken a short cut from the back of his place. His yard backed onto the outermost edge of the school oval.

I lay back against my pillow and pictured Mr Gilchrist's house. It stood about halfway between the school and the turnoff to Murphy's Lane. On the day Jacky died, he hadn't made it to Arthur Gilchrist's place to deliver his vegetables. Or so the police thought. They'd searched Arthur's house thoroughly, Maurice said. But what if Mr Gilchrist had met Jacky outside the house? He could have taken Jacky around the back where the whole place was surrounded by trees.

Mr Gilchrist had come to our house once to tutor Maudie. I'd been sick at home so Mum couldn't take Maudie to the school. He'd looked funny hunched over our kitchen table with his long legs stuffed between the chair legs. I remember him pulling a paper sheet from his jacket and making a show of peeling off a gold star with his long fingers and sticking it inside Maudie's workbook. My sister had given him such a beautiful smile, I'd envied him the luxury of receiving it.

I closed my eyes and re-pictured the scene. Yes, Mr Gilchrist's fingers were indeed very long.

It was time to have another chat with the others.

'A serial killer?' Maurice stared at me.

'Well, I've wracked my brains and I can't think of anyone with a motive,' I said.

We four had met for lunch, this time at the small park in Crayfish Cove opposite the general store. We'd found a seat away from the road, behind some bushes, where we wouldn't be disturbed.

'I guess I can ask Aunt Jo if she knows about any unsolved murders over the past three years. I can't think of any.'

'Me neither,' said Jonathan. 'But people do go missing, don't they? There are probably bodies out there, buried all over the place, that no one even knows about.'

Miranda drew in a quick breath. 'Ugh, what a horrible thought!'

'Molly's still sick so I haven't been able to talk to her yet,' I said as I pulled the pastry top away from my meat pie to let the steam out. 'She might not even remember the day.'

'All the same, it's worth a try,' Jonathan said. 'If we could just pin down Jacky's movements.'

'I've been wondering about Mr Gilchrist,' I said.

'What about him?' Maurice asked, before taking a bite of his sauce-smothered meat pie.

'Remember about the murderer having large hands? Mr Gilchrist does have very long fingers.'

Miranda frowned. 'My dad has long fingers. I hope you're not going to accuse him next.'

'I'm not accusing anyone. Think about it though. Jacky had a delivery for Mr Gilchrist that day. We still don't know whether he went to the manse first, but what if he didn't? What if he did go to Mr Gilchrist's house?'

'The police searched his house though,' Maurice said.

'I know. But Jacky might not have gone inside. What if Mr Gilchrist called him round the back? There's nothing behind his house but trees and the school oval. No one would have seen what happened there.'

'Crikey!' Maurice said. 'I never thought...'

Miranda shook her head. 'He's so nice though.'

'So everyone says,' I said. 'But what do we really know about him?'

We nibbled at our lunches for a few minutes, not saying anything. Maudie loved Mr Gilchrist so I didn't want him to be the murderer. At the same time, if he was, I wanted him well away from my sister.

Jonathan finished the last mouthful of his pie and screwed up the paper bag. 'Have any of you been to Arthur Gilchrist's house?' he asked.

None of us had.

'Anyone up for a visit?'

I gaped at him. 'Visit Mr Gilchrist? Are you serious?'

Jonathan shrugged. 'Maybe not visit him. We could take a walk along the school oval and have a bit of a look at the rear of his place.'

'I have to go back to work,' Maurice said.

'I can't go either. Dad wants me to help in the shop,' Miranda said.

Jonathan looked at me and raised his eyebrows.

'Oh, alright.' I wasn't sure this was a good idea, but the niggling thought that Jacky could have set out for Arthur Gilchrist's that day wouldn't go away.

'Let us know if you find anything," Maurice said, rising from his seat.

We brushed the pie crumbs off ourselves and disposed of our rubbish. Jonathan and I said our goodbyes and headed up the main road together.

'Are we really doing this?' I said.

Jonathan thrust his hands in the pockets of his jacket. His hair flopped over one eye as he grinned sideways at me. 'Gives me an excuse to hang out with you for a bit longer.'

There weren't many people about—a few teenagers huddled outside the chip shop with cans of soft drink, a couple of dog walkers. Jonathan and I slipped through a side entrance into the school grounds and wandered between the primary block buildings. It felt a bit eerie seeing the vacant seats, the quiet quadrangle, nothing moving but us and a few starlings pecking at the ground. As we came upon the primary playground area, Jonathan inclined his head towards the equipment.

'Come on. I'll push you on the roundabout.'

I laughed. 'I thought we were on a mission.'

'We can make a detour. I haven't been on this thing for years!'

I sat on the edge of the roundabout, gripping the hand-hold as Jonathan grabbed onto the side of the large, metal wheel and ran. It made a high-pitched squeal as it spun round and round. Jonathan jumped on beside me and we clung on tight as it spun, our bodies straining against the centrifugal force.

'I forgot how much fun this is,' I said as the roundabout slowed.

Jonathan puffed. 'Me too. There's nothing like this at college. It's all climbing ropes and gym equipment.'

We jumped off the wheel together, stood for a moment to wait for the dizziness to pass, and resumed our walk towards the oval.

'Are you looking forward to uni next year?' I asked.

Jonathan took a big breath and let it out slowly. 'Yeah. It's a bit scary, but it'll be good. How about you—excited for college?'

'I guess.'

The thought of boarding in the city and going to a new school was terrifying in a way. But, like Jonathan, I was looking forward to the new adventure.

'Don't worry, you'll love it,' he said.

'So, what about when you've finished studying? Do you want to be a city doctor or a country doctor?'

'Hmm.' Jonathan looked up into the sky, and back at me. 'That might depend on a few things.'

I glanced at him and caught an earnest expression on his face. Before I could think about what it meant, he turned away and pointed across the oval. 'There it is.'

The red roof of Arthur Gilchrist's cottage jutted over the tops of a crop of trees. Beneath that, a snippet of picket fence. We followed the perimeter of the oval, past a cricket pitch and a long-jump sand pit, until we were a few metres from Arthur's place. This end of the oval was bounded by a few clumps of bushes before merging with a neighbouring field.

'Now what?' I said.

Jonathan crept up to the fence and made a show of studying it closely. He came back to me and said, 'No spy holes.'

'We could sneak a look over the fence,' I said.

'Off you go then.'

'I was thinking you, actually.'

Jonathan shrugged one shoulder and said, 'Okay.' He turned and headed towards the house.

'I was joking!' I hissed behind him.

He looked over his shoulder, grinned and kept going.

'Jonathan!'

He edged up to the wooden fence that backed the house and I slipped up beside him. Together, we peered over the top, me standing on my tippy-toes. It was just as well Arthur wasn't in his back yard. We would have looked a sight—two heads and two sets of eyes spying over his back fence.

The yard was immaculate—perfectly mowed lawn, ornate bird bath, low garden beds on all sides with shrubs and pruned rose bushes, neat and weed free. A small, covered verandah jutted out from the back of the weatherboard house, with a wooden outdoor setting and pots of geraniums.

'What a lovely place,' I whispered.

'Now we know what Mr Gilchrist does when he's not teaching Maths.'

'To think, he lives here all on his own.' A man alone, tending to his garden. A bit like Harry, though Harry was more a vegetable man. Arthur was evidently an ornamental gardener.

'Shh, what's that?' Jonathan whispered.

We stood still and cocked our heads. A deep voice, singing in a baritone, sounded from somewhere in the distance. We moved away from the fence and peered out past the perimeter of the oval. Arthur Gilchrist was striding across the field next door, waving one hand in the air and singing. We strained to discern the words ... honour, valour, something about night?

He rounded a crop of bushes and headed towards us, gazing into the sky. Now we could hear the words of his song:

'...by chivalry and gallantry, by bravest heart and true, a lady's hand is sought and won by deeds of derring-do. Of derring-do, of derring—'

He stopped short when he saw us. His face, showing no sign of embarrassment, broke into a delighted smile and he walked towards us. 'Good afternoon Mr Abbott and Miss Craig. And what brings you two out this fine day?'

We said hello and Jonathan and Arthur shook hands. We mumbled something about going for a walk. I hoped he hadn't realised we'd been spying over his fence.

'Ah, perfect day for a walk. If you're going as far as Cook Lane, don't miss the banksia. It's looking magnificent.'

'Alright, thanks,' Jonathan said.

'But before you continue on your way, you should take refreshment. Would you care for some lemonade?'

'Well...' Jonathan glanced at me.

'Sure,' I said. 'That'd be nice.'

Wasn't this what we wanted—to have a good look around Mr Gilchrist's place? Check out how Jacky might have been abducted and killed here? I felt almost guilty as we followed Arthur through the gate into his back yard.

He invited us into the house and we sat in the kitchen while he added ice cubes to glasses and filled them with lemonade. The kitchen was as neat as his back yard—coloured cannisters in a row on the bench, patterned cups hanging from hooks underneath an overhead cupboard. Even a vase of fresh flowers in the centre of the table. It wasn't how I envisioned the kitchen of a man who lived alone.

'Do you have any plans for the holidays?' Arthur asked.

'Not really,' I said.

'Enjoying a break from all that homework, no doubt? How's Maudie enjoying her work?'

'She loves it,' I said.

Mr Gilchrist smiled warmly as he opened a packet of Scotch Fingers. 'I thought she would. I'm glad to hear it.'

Arthur invited us to take the drinks out onto the verandah. We set our glasses, the lemonade bottle and the biscuits on the wooden table and sat down.

We chatted comfortably for a while about school, college, our future career plans. He seemed genuinely interested. How could I entertain the idea that this gentle man was capable of hurting anyone, let alone a child? I had to keep an open mind though. We couldn't afford to trust anyone until the truth was uncovered. Seemingly good people hid secrets and did terrible things. We knew this just by watching the six o'clock news.

'Your garden is nice,' I said as he poured me a second drink.

'Thank you. I have a penchant for flowers.'

'It's very neat,' Jonathan added.

Arthur nodded. 'Nature is imbued with order, symmetry, pre-dictability. I like to try and replicate that harmony in my own garden. It fosters a sense of calm, don't you think?'

We probably stared blankly at him.

He smiled at me. 'Your sister understands it. She's a great believer in the power of symmetry.'

'Is she?'

'Oh yes. Let me show you something.' He went inside and came out holding a pressed fern frond. He offered it to me, placing it carefully on my outstretched hand.

'Maudie gave me that as a gift. It was a thank you for teaching her about patterns and predictability in nature.'

I studied the frond, the symmetry of its pattern of leaves, wide at the bottom and tapering to a point at the top. And each leaf made of similar shaped segments, each also tapering to a point. Patterns within patterns.

I looked up to find Arthur grinning at me.

'Maudie craves patterns,' he said. 'She says they make her feel safe—knowing that everything is interconnected and follows a pre-dictable course.'

'Really?' I did not know this about my sister. How could this man know more about my own sister than I did? I handed the frond back to Mr Gilchrist and he set it gently on the table.

'Humans are the wild card, of course,' he said. 'We're the unpre-dictable ones. Take you two, for example.'

'Us?'

He nodded. 'A deviation from a usual pattern. I've never seen either of you here at the back of the oval before. It must mean something is afoot.'

Jonathan and I met each other's eyes briefly.

'It's none of my business, of course. Young things will do as young things will.'

Jonathan said, 'Oh no, we're not—er—'

'Something else, then.' Arthur smiled. 'I had the feeling as I rounded the bend that it's something to do with me. However, neither of you have been brave enough to reveal what that something is.'

'We were just going for a walk,' I said.

His look of kind disbelief me made me blush.

Jonathan sighed. 'We're doing some research.'

'Oh, yes?'

'Into Jacky Hix's death.'

I shot Jonathan a look. Why had he divulged that information? Wasn't Arthur Gilchrist one of our suspects? And yet, I understood why Jonathan had opened up to Mr Gilchrist. There was something about the man which made you want to confide in him.

'I see.' Arthur nodded slowly. He looked to the ceiling for a moment, then back at us. 'And yet, I don't see.'

'Some doubts have come up about the original case, Mr Gilchrist.'

I clicked my tongue at Jonathan. 'We're not supposed to tell anyone.' I turned to Arthur and said, 'The police are—well, they will be involved.'

'Ah, serious business then. I take it you're doing a bit of investigating yourselves?'

'Yes,' Jonathan said. 'We've been walking around town trying to get a sense of where Jacky might have gone.'

'Hence, I find you outside my back fence?'

'Uh—'

Arthur nodded. 'It's alright. I understand how you'd want to get a sense of my place. If you're intent on investigating, you should do it properly. Everyone's a suspect until proven otherwise, isn't that right?'

Jonathan's cheeks turned pink and I guessed mine probably did too.

'I'll tell you what I know. Jacky Hix was on his way to bring me some vegetables. Something happened to him before he could get here. I have no idea where or how it happened because I didn't see him.'

Jonathan adjusted his position nervously in the seat. 'I believe you, Mr Gilchrist. All the same, we'd like to try and figure out Jacky's movements on the day, if possible. If you didn't see Jacky, did you see anyone or anything out of the ordinary?'

'It's a good question and exactly what I've been saying—look for aberrations in the ordinary course of things. There was something odd. I told the police, of course. However, I'm not sure what they did with it.'

We leaned forward expectantly.

'I was taken up with my own concerns that day—garden beds that needed weeding, amongst other things. But I did see two people. One was Wayne Bottle pedalling down the road on his bicycle. He did that quite regularly, so I thought nothing of it. The unpredictable incident was the appearance of the Hammonds' niece, Minnie-May.'

'You saw Minnie-May?'

'Only for the briefest moment. I was attending to my camellias in the front garden. But yes, I did see a flash of her red head as she passed my house.'

'So she really did go walking that day?' I said.

Arthur stroked his moustache and stared off into the distance. 'It did strike me as odd at the time. I'd never seen her out walking alone before. And being as far up the road as my place—well, that seemed particularly out of character.'

He leaned back and looked at each of us in turn. 'Perhaps that was one aberration I should have thought more about. You never know when something will prove to be important.'

We thanked Mr Gilchrist, helped him take the glasses and biscuit plate back to the kitchen and he let us out through the front door. As he walked us to the gate, he pointed out his garden beds and gave us a mini flower growing lesson.

'I'm sorry,' Jonathan said to me as we walked towards Cook Lane together, having promised Mr Gilchrist we'd check out the banksias.

'What for?'

'Spilling the beans. I couldn't seem to help myself.'

'Me neither. There's something about him, isn't there? He just draws stuff out of you.'

'Yeah, he's so...'

'Nice?'

Jonathan nodded. 'Like everyone says. But sometimes people only look nice. It doesn't mean they are.'

I sighed. 'I know. How are we supposed to tell?'

We agreed to drop the subject of murder for a while and simply enjoy the walk. And we discovered the banksias to be every bit worth the effort, as Arthur had assured us they would be.

## 24

## What Molly saw

On Wednesday afternoon, as I rounded the corner opposite the church, there was Molly. She stood at her post by her front gate, waving at some kids crossing the road and calling out their names. I hurried up to her, puffing.

'Hello Lily, are you in a hurry?' she said.

'I heard you haven't been well, Molly.'

'Nah, had a bit of a cold. I'm better now.'

'That's good. I'm glad.'

'Look at the sun shinin', ain't it lovely? Harriet's in her garden.' I followed her gaze across the road to the church garden where the minister's wife squatted, a brown scarf tied around her head, pulling at weeds. It was so nice to see Molly happy and relaxed. I dreaded bringing up Jacky and the subject of murder, but it had to be now, while she was lucid.

'Molly?'

'Yes, sweetie? Oh, wait there...' She fumbled about with her dress, found a pocket and slipped her hand inside. She brought out a cellophane packet and handed it to me. 'Here you go.'

'Thank you,' I said as I took a peppermint and popped it in my mouth. 'Mmm, remember how Jacky used to love peppermints?'

Molly's smile slipped slightly and I almost regretted the question. 'Yeah, me Jacky loved his peppermints.'

I quickly crunched the sweet between my teeth and swallowed. 'Listen, Molly. I need to ask you a question.'

Molly shuffled her feet and pushed the bottom set of her false teeth out and in again. I wasn't sure if she'd understood what I'd said, but her green eyes looked straight into mine and she said, 'You want to ask me about Jacky.'

'Yes, I do.'

Molly nodded.

'Molly, Maurice has been looking into his death and I'm helping him. Can you remember if you saw Jacky on the day he disappeared?'

'Uh-huh, I seen him.'

'On that day?'

'On the day he went missing.'

'Where?'

'There.' Molly pointed across the road.

'At the church?'

She nodded.

'Can you please tell me about it, Molly.'

'He went in.'

'Into the church?'

She shook her head.

'The manse?'

'Nah, the shed.'

'He went into the church shed?'

Molly nodded. 'He had some bags.'

'What did they look like?'

'Grocery bags, you know the ones.'

'How many, do you think?'

'A couple.'

'Do you know what was in them?'

'Silverbeet.' Molly nodded once. 'Silverbeet was sticking up out of them. He was taking silverbeet to the Hammonds. Must've come from Harry's.'

'What happened, what did you see?'

'He knocked on the door. At the manse, you know?'

I nodded.

'But no one answered, so he went to the shed. Must've gone to see if they was in there. He opened the door and went in.'

'Well done, Molly, for remembering. Now listen, this is really important. Can you remember what happened next?'

Molly's lips quivered.

'Did he leave the vegetables there? What happened when he came out? Did you see where he went next?'

A low whimper emanated from her lips.

'I'm sorry, I know this is upsetting.' I touched the top of her arm gently with my hand. 'But it's really important.'

Molly's face crumpled. 'He never come out.'

'Sorry?'

'He never come out.' She made a choking sound from her throat and looked to the ground. 'Never come out.'

'Are you saying—?'

Suddenly, Molly began to wail, over and over, 'Never come out—never come out—never come out!' until Amos Crouch rushed out of the house, shot an angry look at me, and coaxed her back inside.

I ran home, grabbed the phone book in the hall and flicked through until I found the number of the sawmill where Maurice worked. I dialled, asked for Maurice and waited.

Mum called from the kitchen, 'Is that you, Lily?'

'Yes, Mum. I'll be there in a tick.'

Finally, I heard Maurice's voice. 'Hello?'

'Maurice, it's Lily,' I hissed. 'Operation Donut. Urgent!'

I piled my peas into a mound on my plate and watched them topple and roll. If Jacky went into the shed that day, what happened after that? How did he end up at Madding Hill? Was Molly talking about the day of the murder or did she mix it up with another day?

A pea rolled under a piece of silverbeet. I lifted the silverbeet—*come out little pea*—and draped it over the pea mound. Silverbeet in grocery bags. Silverbeet and lettuce poking up out of the tops of the bags. She must have been talking about the right day.

Dad cleared his throat and raised his eyebrows pointedly at me. 'Lily, eat your tea or set your plate aside, please.'

I poked a forkful of vegetables into my mouth. They were cold. I resisted the urge to spit them out.

'Something on your mind?' Mum asked.

'Nah, I'm not really hungry. Might go for a walk after tea.'

'Where to?'

I shrugged my shoulders. 'Around the block to get some exercise.'

'Can I come?' Maudie said. There was a glint in my sister's eye.

'Sure,' I said.

We slipped out the gate as dusk fell. We'd wrapped ourselves up in our woollens but the evening was mild.

'Where are we going?' Maudie asked.

'The phone box. Maurice is ringing his aunt at seven and I'm going to talk to her.'

'You lied to Mum.'

'Not really, I do need some exercise. We can go for a walk first, it's only a quarter to.'

'I liked Harry,' Maudie said as we strolled along the footpath.

'Yeah? What did you like about him?' An echo from the past—Harry asking me a similar question about Maudie.

'He helped me with my gumnut collection.'

'When?'

'The first time Mum took me to his place, remember? When he made us tea in the billy can. He helped me find gumnuts.'

Another memory—Maudie wandering about Harry's place, picking things up from the ground. I'd assumed she was inspecting twigs or leaf litter. I'd forgotten about her gumnut collection. All the gumnuts had to be the same size. She used them as Maths counters because she liked their smell.

'He helped me find the last thirty-three to make my collection up to one hundred.'

Something else to add to the list of good things Harry did.

We took a stroll around the park before seating ourselves on a bench in view of the telephone box. All was now dark. The store and Amos' mechanic shop were locked up for the night. Only the light in the phone box shone out eerily into the blackness around it.

'Is there anything else you liked about Harry?' I asked.

'His eyes.'

'Really?' I turned to my sister who had always struggled to make eye contact with people.

She nodded. 'I could tell by his eyes he was a good person.'

Dot had said something similar once. *Sometimes you just know.*

Energy bounded up from deep inside me. We were on the right track. We were doing the right thing. Hang on Harry, we're coming.

'Thanks Maudie,' I said. And before she could move out of my way, I leaned over and pecked her cheek.

I stood in the phone box with the handset to my ear as Maurice's Aunt Jo said, 'Oh my goodness, oh my goodness,' over and over. Maudie stood in the booth beside me. Maurice was outside with his head bowed, one hand covering his eyes. Miranda had her hand on his shoulder.

Jo was quiet for a moment. I heard her sniffing. 'Lily,' she said, and her voice was soft but firm. 'Maurice tells me you're a good writer. Do you think you could write everything down in a letter?'

'Um, yes.'

'Address the letter to Detective Sergeant Bullard. You'll find his name in the articles I sent you. Outline everything you and Maurice have explained to me, in point-form might be best. But address the envelope to me.' Her voice became more determined. 'I'm going to hand deliver it and insist on speaking with the detective. I'll make sure your voices are heard this time.'

Next, we phoned Jonathan and told him of the new developments. Before we parted company, Maurice surprised me by giving me a hug and whispering, 'Thank you, Lily,' into my neck.

As Maudie and I walked home, my sister said, 'I know you'll do a good job. You're a talented writer, Lily.'

That evening, I spent a couple of hours in my bedroom, meticulously writing and rewriting the letter until I was happy with it. I folded it neatly, placed it in an envelope and wrote the address Maurice had given me for his aunt on the front. I tucked the final draft of the letter into my journal and hid it beneath the bottom drawer of my bedside table. On the following morning, I would go for a walk and drop the letter into the post box. After which, there wasn't much more we could do but wait.

## 25

# A Letter

Dear Detective Sergeant Bullard,

We are writing to inform you of some new information regarding the murder of Jacky Hix in Crayfish Cove on 1<sup>st</sup> April 1978 for which Harry Fernley was charged and sentenced to prison.

We have new evidence showing that another person might have been responsible for Jacky's death.

1. During the investigation, Minnette-May Levers told police she saw Harry and Jacky arguing in the woods on the day Jacky died. She also told a friend that someone had forced her to lie about it and that she hadn't really seen them at all. Her friend didn't tell the police and only recently admitted this to me (Lily).

2. Jacky set out to deliver two bags of vegetables. It was assumed he would go to Arthur Gilchrist's house first, being the first stop along Main Street. We know he never arrived at Arthur's house. We have since discovered he liked to take a shortcut to the church through some bush. If he went that way, his first stop would be the church and his second stop would be Arthur's house.

3. Molly Crouch, who lives opposite the church, saw Jacky going into the shed of the church on the day he went missing. She said he was carrying a couple of bags of silverbeet and he went into the shed and didn't come back out again. No one saw him after that. Molly tried to tell people at the time that she'd seen Jacky, but no one listened.

4. If Jacky took the above route, then he and Harry would have parted company somewhere around Murphy's Lane and Jacky would have continued on his way to the church. Then Harry wouldn't have been the last person to see Jacky alive.

5. Harry always maintained his innocence.

At the time, no one asked us children about what Harry was like. We had information that would have been useful because we knew Harry better than anyone. Now we're all older, we would like to be given the chance to tell you what we know.

Yours faithfully,
Maurice Hix, Lily Craig, Miranda Lockhart and Jonathan Abbot.

On Friday evening, I was squished into the Main Street phone box again, this time with Maurice, Miranda and Jonathan.

'Talk really loud, Jo, so we can all hear,' Maurice said into the handset. He held it towards us and we leaned into it, our faces so close we could feel each other's breath. Jo's voice—sounding more energetic than the last time we'd spoken—shouted from the earpiece.

'Detective Bullard's *retired*!' she yelled. 'I was told I'd have to speak to Detective Sergeant Brown! So I said, *fine*, I'll speak to *him* then. They said he was out and he could be out *all day*, but I said that's alright, I'll *wait!* So I *waited.*'

'All day?' Jonathan said into the mouthpiece.

'*Yes!* I took the day off *sick*.' She giggled. 'The policewoman on the desk took *pity* on me and brought me a sandwich. She was nice but I think she thought I was a bit *strange*. Anyway, I saw Sergeant Brown finally, and he's very *concerned!* He's coming down to see you on Monday. Did you hear that? *Monday!*'

Jo relayed the information we would need about meeting Sergeant Brown and another detective on Monday and we tumbled out of the phone booth. Miranda put both hands on her cheeks and opened her eyes wide. 'It's really happening!'

Maurice threw his arms around her and appeared to be speechless.

'Well, I guess we'll have to tell our parents what we've been doing,' I said.

Jonathan said, 'I'm waiting until I hear what the detectives say.'

I thought about the evening my parents danced around the back yard to *Blue Suede Shoes*. Perhaps they didn't need to know about our investigations yet. Like Jonathan, I would wait and see what the detectives had to say first.

## 26

# Spying through a pair of binoculars

ON SATURDAY MORNING, MAUDIE and I went out with her measuring wheel and measured all the distances between points that Jacky could have taken on the day of his murder, and I wrote them down in my notebook. We concluded Maudie's initial conviction to be correct—it was far more time efficient for Jacky to have taken the shortcut to the manse, cross the road to Arthur Gilchrist's and continue on to his own home.

'Are you giving those to the police?' Maudie asked, indicating the notes I'd taken.

'Yes, we're seeing them on Monday.'

'What a pity I'll be at work.'

'They might want to talk to you anyway, Maudie. If they do they'll probably come to your work. Is it okay if we don't tell Mum and Dad yet?'

Maudie frowned. 'Why?'

'You know how people joke about the bush telegraph?'

'How news travels fast because of people gossiping?'

'Yes. If Harry's innocent, the real murderer is still out there somewhere. If they hear that the police are asking questions, they'll be on their guard and it might be harder to catch them. Do you understand what I'm saying?'

Maudie nodded. 'We have to be careful about who knows.'

'That's right.'

'Tell the police I'd like to help.'

I walked Maudie home and set off to find Kylie. I was feeling guilty about everything I was keeping secret from her, but I couldn't risk her mother finding out about our investigations. I remembered her hatred of Harry.

It was a sunshiny day so we bought ice creams and wandered down to the Hollow. I'd asked Kylie to bring her binoculars, with the notion that spying on the townsfolk from a distance might yield some vital clues to add to Operation Donut.

'I love the holidays,' Kylie sighed, setting her bag on the ground and settling herself against the rock wall. 'What will we do for the rest of them?'

I sat beside her and looked out over the bay. The water shimmered in the sunshine. Gulls cawed and circled the jetty.

'Anything we want,' I said, closing my eyes as a breeze wafted over us, carrying the briny scent of the sea.

'Why don't we ask Dot and Minnie-May to come out with us one day?" Kylie said. "I don't think we've done anything together since that time we stayed at Dot's, remember?'

I opened my eyes and regarded her as she licked up the last drips of her ice cream off the stick.

'Yeah, that was fun. How about we stop at the Hammonds later and ask Minnie-May.'

Would Minnie-May want to come? She might be uncomfortable with me after our conversation at school last week. I felt a bit regretful about it, especially as it hadn't yielded any new information.

Kylie pulled a bag of lollies from her backpack and handed them to me before rummaging for her binoculars. 'Good idea, this,' she said, taking off the lens covers and putting the binoculars to her eyes. 'Let's see what's going on around town.'

'Remember how we used to write down what we saw through them?' I said through a sticky caramel cobber.

'Especially the weird things we saw people doing.'

'What did we see that was weird?'

'Well, there was the day we saw Minnie-May running down the jetty and Mrs Hammond going after her.'

'Gosh, I forgot about that.' I made a mental note to check my journals for the entry, and for everything I wrote around the time of Jacky's murder.

'What about the black limousine that pulled up outside the shop that time?' Kylie said.

'Didn't we decide it must be a movie star?'

'Yeah, Mark Hamill, because we thought he was so dreamy!'

'Huh, why did we think he'd visit Crayfish Cove, though?'

Kylie giggled and handed me the binoculars. 'Here, you have a go. There's not much happening today.'

I looked across the bay, adjusting the focus as I scanned the wharf. The only movement was a dog zigzagging along the jetty with its nose to the ground and tail in the air. Further along, at the road end, a blue car pulled up and a stooped man in a bucket hat got out. I shifted my view up the bank and along the road. A few folk mingled outside the general store, a kid rode past on a bicycle and a white ute stopped at the petrol bowser outside Amos Crouch's auto-repair garage. Maudie would be in the garage now, working in Amos' office.

As I watched the building, there was a movement at the back of it. I kept the binoculars trained on the spot until a head appeared from behind the far corner of the building, then vanished again. A few seconds later the head reappeared and seemed to look around for a few moments, before the person's whole body emerged. It was Amos Crouch. He shuffled along the side of the building, hands in the pockets of his overalls, to the front of the shop, said something to the person filling their ute at the petrol pump and entered the garage through the front door.

'That was weird,' I said.

'What?'

'Amos Crouch acting strangely.'

'Oh, but he *is* strange.'

'You think?'

'Yep. I'm pretty sure he's alright though.'

'I hope you're right,' I said, 'because my sister's in there.'

Kylie held out her lolly bag to me and I put the binoculars away. When we'd munched through all the sweets, we went the beach way back into town and cut up through a bush track which joined the main road not far from Amos' shop.

As we passed the building, Kylie asked where I'd seen Amos through the binoculars. I pointed and Kylie said, 'Let's check it out.' She tip-toed up the side of the building and looked around in an exaggerated show of being sneaky.

'Don't be dumb, come back!' I hissed.

'Come on,' she hissed back.

There was no way I was going up there. Instead, I leaned on the side of the shop to wait for her. As she slunk along the edge of the building, Amos emerged from behind it and both of them yelped at the same time. Amos stared at Kylie, then at me. He hurried away from Kylie and frowned at me as he made his way to the front of the shop.

Kylie continued to the back of the building and poked her head around the corner.

'Anything behind there?' I called.

'No,' she said as she came back. 'Something must be going on though. Why was he there twice?'

I shrugged my shoulders. 'Let's go to the Hammond's. This place is freaking me out.'

The church garden was bursting with spring flowers. As we walked in through the driveway, a water spray burst into the air from behind a rhododendron bush. I saw Mrs Hammond's head behind the tiny droplets of water that rose and fell over the plants in an arc. The arc moved towards us and Mrs Hammond stepped out from the bushes, holding a hose. Her back was bent slightly as she stood there, looking straight ahead through the blooms. As she turned to face us, the water sprayed in front of her and her hair glinted in the sunlight. For a brief moment, I was seeing Mrs Hammond as if through a mist.

'What?' Kylie waved her hand in front of my face.

My mind had flown back to an image I'd carried about and puzzled over for three years. The day I'd walked up Murphy's Lane and saw a figure standing under the trees in the fog—a bent figure, red-gold hair, staring ahead. At the time, I was sure it was Minnie-May, but now...

'Nothing,' I said, and walked towards Mrs Hammond.

As we approached, she turned off the hose and waved. 'Hello girls, lovely day isn't it?'

'We were wondering if Minnie-May's in?' I asked.

'Yes. I'm not sure what she's up to.' Mrs Hammond set the hose on the ground.

'Could we see her?'

'Of course, one minute.' She gathered an armload of flowers and greenery she'd picked from the garden and headed towards the manse. We followed her through a neat hallway and into the kitchen where she set the flowers on the dining table. She indicated for us to sit and left the room, returning soon after with Minnie-May who edged into a seat, glancing shyly at us. We greeted each other and engaged in some general chit chat while Mrs Hammond poured glasses of lime cordial.

'What are your plans for the holidays?' I asked.

'Um...' Minnie-May lifted her eyes to the ceiling as if thinking.

'We're visiting family in Launceston next week, remember?' Mrs Hammond said.

'Oh, yeah. I forgot. I'm going to see my cousins.'

At this point, I thought Mrs Hammond might leave us to talk in the kitchen or offer us somewhere else to go. Instead, she set a large vase on the table and began to sort the flowers. The vase had a round, column-shaped bottom opening out into a wide rim, much like an up-side-down sunhat, designed for extravagant arrangements. I recognised it as the one that sat on the front platform in church on Sundays.

'I'm doing the flowers for tomorrow,' Mrs Hammond said. 'Flowers do cheer a place up, don't you think?'

Kylie agreed and added, 'We wondered if Minnie-May could come out with us and Dot one day in the holidays.'

Minnie-May's eyes opened a little wider and I saw the hint of a smile.

'That sounds nice.' Mrs Hammond took up a pair of scissors and snipped the end of a  tulip. 'We'll see when we arrive back from Launceston. So, how is your mother, Kylie? I wasn't able to visit this week.'

'Oh, she's alright.' Kylie frowned, perhaps at the sudden change of topic.

I smiled at Minnie-May. 'How're you finding grade nine?'

'It's good.'

'Do you have Mr Gilchrist for Maths?'

'Yes.' She really did smile this time. 'I like him, he's a good teacher.'

'He explains things really well, doesn't he?'

Kylie set her empty glass on the table and thanked Mrs Hammond for the drink. She leaned forward in her chair and I had the impression she was about to make a move to leave.

Quickly, I said, 'I haven't seen your room.' I stood and smiled sweetly at Mrs Hammond. 'Is it alright if Minnie-May shows us her bedroom?'

Minnie-May shot a glance at her aunt, who stood with a fern suspended in the air. Before she could answer, I took Minnie-May by the elbow and ushered her out of her seat and through the kitchen door with Kylie following.

Minnie-May led us through the hallway and into a small bedroom with a single bed and yellow bedspread. As Kylie came in behind us, she closed the door.

'Wow, I love your walls.' Kylie ran her hand over the striped wallpaper interspersed with posies of pink and blue flowers. 'Mine's boring green paint.'

'Thank you,' Minnie-May said as she sat on the edge of her bed.

Kylie flopped down beside her and I lowered myself to sit cross-legged on the carpeted floor.

'When are you going away?' I asked.

'Tomorrow. We'll be back next Saturday night.'

'We thought we might do something with you and Dot. Maybe have a picnic on the beach or something?'

Minnie-May grinned. 'Sounds like fun.'

'Remember when we stayed at Dot's that time?'

We reminisced for a while about that weekend—the cricket game we'd played in the paddock, the baby lambs, watching movies and eating pizza. Minnie-May's face opened up like a flower as we talked. I felt regret all over again about our conversation the week before at school when I had tried to make her admit to lying about Harry and Jacky.

'We'll wait until you come back and we'll organise something, okay?' I said. 'The four of us will do something fun.'

Minnie-May's face appeared so hopeful, I wished we could whisk her away then and there. But why not? What was stopping us taking off straight away? As I opened my mouth to ask if she wanted to go and buy chips or something, Mrs Hammond knocked, opened the door and looked in.

'I need your help to get the church ready, dear,' she said.

Minnie-May's expression dulled. She stood up, I scrambled to my feet and we followed her aunt into the hall. Mrs Hammond had set the vase, filled with fresh flowers, on the hall table by the front door. As she picked it up, Minnie-May opened the door for her and we filed outside.

'Thank you for your visit, girls,' Mrs Hammond said. 'Do give my regards to your parents.'

We said our goodbyes and trundled off. I turned to wave to Minnie-May and she gave me a wave back, before hurrying ahead to open the door of the church for her aunt.

Before I turned away, I glanced at the vase. Mrs Hammond carried it with her hands wrapped around the top of the column where it began to open out into the brim. I couldn't help but notice that, for a woman, Mrs Hammond had the largest hands I'd ever seen.

# 27

# Detectives in the park

On Monday at midday, I sat at a picnic table at Durrunby Park with Maurice, Miranda and Jonathan, a diminishing pile of hot chips between us. The sun was warm and the park dotted with golden pools of daffodils.

'I'm so nervous,' I said. My insides had been churning all morning.

'Me too,' said Jonathan. 'Did you bring the info for the police.'

I pulled my notebook from my bag and slapped it on the table. 'I added some more notes. Maudie and I measured the distances between Harry's and Mr Gilchrist's and the manse, via the road and the short-cut.'

'Well done,' Jonathan said.

'Also, Kylie and I saw Amos Crouch acting suspiciously yesterday. He was sneaking around as if he was up to something, so I wrote that down too.'

Jonathan laughed. 'He's a nervous character. I think he's alright, though.'

'That's what Kylie said, but we should consider him anyway.'

'As a suspect?'

'Well, we're light on suspects, aren't we?'

'Anyway, keep your eyes peeled,' Maurice said, looking about. 'They'll be the only ones in suits, we'll spot them a mile off.'

Maurice's Aunt Jo had insisted the police officers meet us in Durrunby, away from the prying eyes of the Crayfish Cove folk. So here we were, sitting in a park looking out for strangers. As it was the school holidays and Durrunby was a tourist town, there were plenty of those.

'While we're waiting,' said Jonathan, 'have a think about who has access to the church shed.'

'Everyone,' Maurice said, flatly.

Miranda counted off on her fingers. 'The Hammonds... Amos and Betty are always doing stuff in there... whoever's on the roster on Sunday morning...'

'Arthur Gilchrist,' I added. 'He keeps the Sunday School stuff in the cupboards. Is it locked during the week, do we know?' No one did.

'We may as well add that to the notes, anyway.' I opened my notebook and wrote the heading, *Access to Shed,* and started adding the names beneath it.

'If it's not kept locked, anyone could have been in there that day,' Miranda said.

'Although,' I said, 'I don't think they would have been waiting for Jacky specifically. How would they know he'd go there?'

'He did deliver there regularly,' said Jonathan. 'And there was the arrangement they had, that if no one answered at the manse, he'd leave the delivery in the shed.'

'So it must be kept unlocked,' Miranda said. 'Someone might have seen him going along the road and knew he'd go to the Hammonds. They could have been waiting for him in the shed.'

'But who would do that?' I said. 'Who could possibly have a reason to hurt Jacky?'

'Wayne Bottle?' Maurice said.

'He was a bully back then,' said Jonathan, 'but I don't see him as a murderer. Write him down anyway, just in case. What's he up to these days?'

'He was doing some bricklaying,' Maurice said. 'But I don't know if he still is.'

'Look!' Jonathan moved his eyes to the left, raising his eyebrows. We followed his gaze to two men in grey suits striding across the grass and heading in our direction. We all sat up straight in preparation for the meeting. But as the men neared us, they veered away towards the carpark.

Maurice slouched back down and pointed to my notebook. 'I was thinking, we should write a list of people with big hands.'

'Gosh, which of the men doesn't?' Miranda said.

I wrote another heading, *Large Hands,* and began a list. 'I'll add Mr Gilchrist to that, because of his long fingers. And did you know Mrs Hammond's hands are enormous?'

'Really?' Jonathan said. 'You don't think...?'

'We have to keep an open mind.'

We were so engrossed in our discussion, we didn't see the police officers until they'd walked right up to our table. I thought they were a couple who'd come to ask for directions or something.

'Hello, are you Maurice Hix and friends?' asked a round-faced man in fawn-coloured pants and a polo shirt.

Maurice appeared taken aback. 'Er, yes.'

The man held out his hand to shake Maurice's. 'Detective Sergeant Brown. And this,' he said, indicating the woman by his side, 'is Detective Constable Floris.'

We tried to stand but were thwarted by the bench-type seat being too close to the table edge.

'That's alright,' Sergeant Brown said, 'there are some better seats over here.'

We collected up our near-empty chip paper and followed them to some benches set together under a tree like three sides of a square. We arranged ourselves on two of them while the detectives sat on the other. The woman was not what I would have expected a female detective to look like. She was dark-haired and young—she didn't look much older than us, though I guessed she must be—and wore a skirt and blouse with a blue woollen jumper draped across her shoulders. She crossed her legs and smiled, her cheeks dimpling. We introduced ourselves and Constable Floris wrote our names and addresses in a notebook.

Sergeant Brown said, 'I must apologise for being late. We encountered cows.' The wry way he said the word 'cows' made us all grin. 'Thank you all for your letter. It was very coherent. We've had a look through the original case notes—'

'Will the case be reopened?' Maurice said, cutting him off.

'It's too soon to say. You've brought up some interesting points, though. Now, we have some questions for you.' He took a sheet of paper from his briefcase and I saw it was the letter I'd written. My ease disappeared and I clasped my hands together to stop them trembling.

Detective Sergeant Brown looked at each of us. 'You were all friends of Harry Fernley's.'

We murmured our agreement. He nodded thoughtfully and said, 'I understand that you would like to believe your friend wasn't guilty.'

Maurice shot to his feet, his face a sudden blaze of red. 'Hang on. If Harry did kill my brother, I don't care if the—I don't care if he rots in prison. I hope he does. I've hated him for three years.'

Sergeant Brown appeared unfazed by Maurice's outburst.

Maurice folded his arms across his chest. 'But the things we've heard lately seem to point to him being innocent, and that bothers me. What if he *is* innocent? We can't let him stay in prison, can we?'

'We agree there, Mr Hix,' the sergeant said. 'Please have a seat.'

'It's Maurice. Mr Hix is me dad.' Maurice slumped back down on the seat.

The female detective smiled and leaned towards him. 'Maurice? As we assured your aunt, we will be investigating thoroughly. If Harry Fernley is innocent and someone else is responsible for Jacky's death, we intend to find that person. New evidence may mean Harry can appeal and have a retrial.'

My stomach felt queasy as I thought about Harry having to go through another trial. At least we'd be there this time. I would insist on going.

Sergeant Brown said, 'Who is Minnette-May Levers' friend who said she had lied at the time?'

'Dot,' I said. 'She lives here in Durrunby. She's very sweet and didn't think a thing about keeping the secret. I don't think she realises what she did. She was only twelve at the time.'

Constable Floris asked for her full name and address and added it to her notebook.

I said, 'Is that why Harry was sent to prison, because of what Minnie-May said?'

'All the evidence was taken into consideration,' the sergeant said.

I thought about my visit to Minnie-May's home with Kylie. How her aunt had stayed in the kitchen with us. 'Was Minnie-May with her aunt and uncle when she was questioned?' I asked.

'I can check that,' Sergeant Brown said. 'She lives with them, yes?'

I nodded. 'Her mother was Mrs Hammond's sister, so when her parents died the Hammonds took her in. Are you going to question her again?' My determination was giving me confidence.

'Yes, we will.'

'You should get her alone. It'll be hard because they're always with her. But I really think you should talk to her alone. She's fifteen, you can do that, can't you?'

'Noted.' Sergeant Brown nodded to the constable who wrote something down.

'Oh, and they're away on holidays this week. They're coming back Saturday night.'

'Lily, do you have an idea who may have asked her to lie?'

I shook my head and squeezed my hands together in my lap.

The sergeant referred back to my letter. 'Tell us about Molly Crouch who says she saw Jacky going into the church shed. We'll speak to her, of course.'

We four looked at each other and the detectives caught our expressions. I had a sinking feeling in my stomach. Sergeant Brown raised his eyebrows. 'Is there something we should know?'

Jonathan sighed. 'She has dementia.'

'But she has good days,' I said. 'And I spoke to her on one of her good days when she remembers everything.' I heard the panic in my own voice.

Constable Floris smiled at me. 'Lily, do you think Molly would talk to you and me together?'

'Yes—maybe—I think so. I saw her that day, you know. The day Jacky— I was on my way back from Harry's. She waved to me but I didn't stop to talk. I wish I had.'

'How did she seem?' Constable Floris asked.

'Happy. She was smiling.'

Constable Floris wrote something down.

'It's going to be all around town, you being here,' Jonathan said. 'What happens if the murderer's still out there and he hears about it? It'll put him on guard.'

The sergeant nodded. 'Some discretion is needed. Keep things to yourselves for the time being. Although, it might make things easier if you can tell your parents.'

We spoke for a bit longer. I tore from my notebook the pages of notes we'd made and gave them to the officers. They gave us their cards and told us where they were staying. As we all stood up, I glimpsed a familiar car pulling into the carpark.

'Um, if you're doing interviews today, you might want to start with Dot,' I said.

'Why's that?' asked the sergeant.

I pointed to the carpark. 'Because there she is, with her mother. The white Toyota.'

After a hasty goodbye, the police officers hurried across the carpark. They stopped Fiona and Dot as they were walking towards the bakery.

'Ooh, how's this going to go?' Miranda said.

We watched as Sergeant Brown said something to Dot's mother, who nodded. He spoke again and Fiona gasped—we heard it from where we stood under the tree. Her eyes opened wide and she slapped her hand to her mouth. And next to her, Dot's face bloomed a sudden beetroot red.

'Well!' said Maurice. 'We just opened a bloody big can of worms.'

I sat on my bed, flicking through my journals and diaries. There were a number of entries in the earlier ones about our spying adventures at the Hollow. They started in 1976 when Kylie received a pair of binoculars for her eleventh birthday. The first time we'd seen Minnie-May through them was when she'd gone into the general store with her aunt and uncle and come out eating an ice cream. The next entry about her was written in the same year:

**Our spyings from the Hollow...**
**Minnie-May running down the jetty and Mrs Hammond going after her. She grabbed her hand and they walked back to the car.**

Where was the car? I couldn't remember now if it was parked at the beginning of the jetty, up on the road or at the shop. How far had she run, I wondered? And had it been a game, or something else?

In these boxes of journals, the whole story of my friendship with Harry had been written. Was there anything here that revealed someone else's guilt—something missed by the police?

I flipped through all of the books until I came to the entries around the time of the murder, when my emotions were in a terrible tangle. I'd written of my grief over Jacky's death and, almost immediately after, my distress about Harry's arrest, followed by disbelief and anger over Minnie-May's claim that she'd seen them arguing.

**I kicked Minnie-May as hard as I could. She deserves it for saying she saw Harry arguing with Jacky in the woods. She's a big fat LIAR and I hate her!!!**

Why was I so sure at the time that she'd lied? After all, I had started to believe in Harry's guilt myself soon enough, when all the talk about him circulated around Crayfish Cove. When he was arrested, people had called him all sorts of things—strange, a hermit, unnatural, violent, a predator. All the adults had called him a murderer. So, for three years I'd believed he was.

I looked for Minnie-May's name throughout my journals but found nothing more of significance. Was there anything here that might illuminate someone else's guilt? I searched my writings through the afternoon, but found nothing.

When I heard Maudie come home from work I went into the hall to greet her. As she came through the front door, she set her briefcase down, took off her shoes and arranged them neatly by the door next to our untidy shoe pile.

'Is Mum home?' she asked.

'She's at the shops. Can I ask you a question?'

'I have to change my clothes first.' She disappeared into her bedroom to change out of her work skirt and blouse.

I waited in the kitchen until she came in to make herself a cup of tea. When she sat down at the table with her drink, I asked, 'Maudie, is Amos a good boss?'

'Yes.' Maudie turned her cup in its saucer and looped her finger through the handle.

'Is he nice to you? Do you feel comfortable with him?'

'He is nice and I feel comfortable.'

'I saw him the other day coming out from the back of the garage building. He looked like he was sneaking out and didn't want anyone to see him.'

'He does that all the time.' She took a sip of her tea.

'Oh, why?'

'He smokes behind the garage. Betty doesn't like him smoking.'

'But Betty wouldn't see him smoking *in* the garage.'

'She comes in a lot so he goes behind the building where she won't see him.'

'Okay, thanks Maudie.'

'Why do you want to know that?'

'I was—um—' I fiddled with my hair as I tried to think of an answer.

'Is this about the murder case?'

I nodded.

'You saw Amos looking sneaky so you thought he might be the murderer.'

I grinned at Maudie. 'I really was grasping at straws, wasn't I?'

To think, I'd written Amos' name down as a possible suspect in the notes I gave the police. I felt myself blushing. I must have been desperate to jump at Amos Crouch as a suspect.

Was that what had happened to Harry? The folk of Crayfish Cove needed someone to blame, and quickly? As far as anyone knew, Harry was the last person to see Jacky alive. Had that been an unfortunate grasping at straws too?

The phone rang. I left Maudie in the kitchen and went into the hall to answer it.

'Lily!' The voice at the other end was puffing as if out of breath. 'Lily, it's Fiona. This is your mum's shopping day, right? Is she still out?' Dot's mother sounded frightened.

'Yes,' I answered.

'Oh, good. Listen, the police have been talking to Dot.'

'I know.'

'They said you wrote them a letter. It's alright, they explained every-thing. I simply can't believe it! Have you spoken to your parents yet?'

'No.'

'They didn't think you had. Do you think you should?'

'Um, I don't know.'

'Look, I'm not going to spread it around town or anything, but I do want to discuss it with your mum.'

'Oh.' My heart sank.

'I'm coming over to visit her tomorrow. You really should tell them.'

I hesitated.

'Please Lily?'

I sighed. 'Alright.'

'Good girl. I can't believe it. If it's true...oh, I can't believe it. Look, I might see you tomorrow.'

I went back to the kitchen, sat at the table with Maudie and waited for Mum to come home.

## 28

# Childhood revisited

Dad and Mum sat together on the couch staring at me. Maudie was on one lounge chair with her legs crossed and I'd curled myself in the other with my knees up, making myself as small as possible. I'd waited until Dad had come home from work to tell both Mum and Dad at once.

'I've been helping the police too,' Maudie said. 'I measured all the routes Jacky could have walked to find the one he most likely took.'

'Why on earth didn't you tell us?' Mum said.

Dad stood up and paced the room, coming back to my chair to glare at me. 'Whose idea was this again?'

'I don't know, all of us,' I said. 'Maurice and Miranda had been talking. I happened to bump into Maurice. He didn't say he thought Harry was innocent, he was just talking about it and it put a doubt in my mind. That's why I asked Dot what I did.'

Dad put his hand to his forehead and shook his head. 'Lily.'

'You should have told us,' Mum said.

'It had to be kept secret,' Maudie said. 'So the real murderer doesn't find out the police are investigating.'

'What makes you think we couldn't be discreet?' Mum said.

I hung my head and fiddled with the cuff of my jeans.

Dad grabbed his jacket from the end of the couch. 'Where are these detectives staying?' I told him and he took off out the door.

'Am I in trouble?' I asked.

'No, of course not.' Mum leaned back in her seat and sighed. 'It's a lot to take in, that's all. So Minnie-May really said someone had forced her to lie? Who would do that?'

'The killer, I guess,' I said.

She shook her head and closed her eyes. 'This is going to turn the town upside down. Again.'

Maudie cooked us her favourite meal of fish fingers and mashed potato and we were about to sit down to eat when we heard the car drive in. Dad came into the kitchen and right up to me, put his arms around me and said, 'I'm sorry, love. You did the right thing.'

Mum's hand flew to her neck. 'There's really doubt?'

'There is. So let's keep it to ourselves and let the police do their job.'

Detective Constable Floris called for me the following morning to request my presence while questioning Molly Crouch.

'You'll take care of her, won't you?' Mum said.

'We certainly will.' Constable Floris flashed her dimpled smile at Mum, which seemed to put her at ease.

'If anyone asks, I'm Maria Floris, a family friend,' she said to me as we walked down the main road together. 'There's an elderly woman standing at the gate of the address you gave us. I presume that's Molly.'

'That'll be her,' I said.

Sure enough, as we turned the corner near the church, there was Molly leaning on the gate in her usual position, looking out at the world. As we approached, she lifted her hand in a wave, but there was a hollowness of expression that made my heart sink.

'Hello, Molly,' I said as we stopped at the fence.

Molly gripped the top of the metal gate with both hands and squinted at us. 'Hello, dear.'

'It's me—Lily. This is my friend, Maria.'

'Hello, Mrs Crouch,' Constable Floris said. 'It's nice to meet you.'

'Ah, yes.' Molly smiled uncertainly.

'Molly, do you remember when I asked you about the day Jacky went missing?' I said.

'Jacky me boy. How is he?'

'Remember how you saw him going into the shed with the bags of vegetables?'

'Oh, he takes the veggies round.'

'Mrs Crouch—Molly—I'm a police officer and I'm investigating Jacky's death. Lily said you might know something. Do you know anything about the day Jacky died?'

Molly stared, her lips quivering. 'No, not Jacky. He's me boy.'

'Did you see him on the day he died, going into the church shed?'

'There's the shed, over there.' Molly pointed across the road. She fumbled about with her dress until she found her pocket. 'No peppermints today, sorry.'

Constable Floris smiled. 'It's alright. It was nice to meet you, Molly. Have a nice day.'

'Nice day. Lovely.' Molly waved as we departed.

'Sorry,' I said, as we headed back towards my house.

'It's fine, I'll try and question her again.' She smiled at me. 'On a good day.'

'She does have them,' I assured her. 'She's like you and me on a good day.'

The detective turned to look about her. 'This is a lovely town. I can imagine settling down somewhere like this.'

'Somewhere like this without a murderer in it, you mean.'

'Yes,' she said, wrapping her arms around her body. 'Without that.'

'It's awful.' Jonathan stared at Harry's cottage, his hands in his pockets.

'I know. What will the police think?' I stepped up beside him and regarded the smashed windows, the foul words painted across the weatherboards, the devastated garden.

'If Harry's innocent, we'll need to fix the place up.'

Maurice's Kingswood rattled around the corner and pulled up beside us. He and Miranda emerged and Maurice glanced up at the house and cringed.

'Don't worry,' Jonathan said, 'the police don't need to know who did this.'

'What makes you think it was me?' Maurice said drily.

The detectives wandered in on foot shortly afterwards and turned equally dismayed eyes to the devastation of Harry's cottage. They said nothing about it, however.

'Thanks for meeting us here,' Sergeant Brown said. 'I'd like us to do something a bit different. Come for a wander about and tell Constable Floris and myself about Harry. Anything you like that comes to mind. We want to form a picture of him.'

'No one asked us before,' I said.

'That was an oversight.' He turned around and pointed at the fire pit. 'You could start by telling us about this.'

'Billy tea!' Miranda and Maurice said in unison. We laughed and all of our faces lit up at once. The detectives watched us.

'Harry used to make it for us,' Jonathan said. 'He'd spin the billy can without a lid and not spill any, and we couldn't figure out how he did it.'

'No other tea ever tasted as good,' I said.

'Remember the sing-a-longs?' Maurice said. 'Harry played our favourite songs on his guitar. Jacky loved that.'

'Oh yeah, the kookaburra song,' Jonathan said. 'Jacky did a good kookaburra impersonation, remember?'

'Jacky loved the garden.' Maurice looked to the broken fence and the tangle of weeds and his shoulders slumped. 'That was me,' he said quietly. 'I shouldn't have done that because it was Jacky's garden too.'

I blinked back the tears welling at the back of my eyes. 'He built us a treehouse,' I said. 'Want to see?'

We led the police officers past the shed and the fruit trees to the big pine at the back of the block. A few of the boards had been ripped out and thrown to the ground, but the rest of it was up there, mostly hidden by branches.

'You can't really see it, but it's there,' Jonathan said. 'It used to have a ladder.'

'Someone snitched it,' Maurice said.

'There was a tyre swing too,' Miranda said. 'We loved it. We loved all of it.'

We showed the detectives around the whole block, talking about the things Harry would do to entertain us. We told them how he fixed Curly's billy cart, how he gave away vegetables to families who couldn't afford to buy them at the shop, how he was always free to talk to and to listen. How he'd always tried to help.

'He was very kind,' Jonathan said.

The detectives walked with us, watched us and said little. We didn't know at the time how our stories could help the investigation, but, as they were leaving, Sergeant Brown nodded to us and said, 'Thank you, all of you. You've been most helpful.'

As they were about to leave, the sergeant turned back and said, 'One more thing,' and I wondered if all detectives learned that technique from watching *Columbo.* 'There was evidence that Harry and Jacky went somewhere else together when they left the house. Lily, you showed Constable Munnings the place.'

'In the bush, by the fallen log,' I said.

'You said he'd taken you there once. Why?'

I thought of the day Harry told me about seeing the Tassie tiger. How he'd kept the secret because he couldn't bear people to track it down and cage it. But the reason he'd taken me there wasn't about the tiger—it was about Maudie.

'I was worried about my sister. He took me there because it was a nice place to go and talk.'

'Can you tell us more about it?'

'There was someone who would try and bully Maudie, call her names.' I blinked, realisation dawning. 'Actually, it was Wayne Bottle. That makes sense.'

'What does?'

'Wayne used to bully Jacky too. That's why Jacky was upset, because he didn't want to see Wayne. It makes sense that Harry would take Jacky there and talk to him about it.'

Constable Floris retrieved her notebook and scribbled something down.

I continued. 'We sat and talked for a while and afterwards, I felt much better about Maudie. Harry had a way of helping you see things more clearly. Like Jonathan said, he was kind.'

Sergeant Brown narrowed his eyes. 'At the site, there was evidence of a struggle.' As he spoke, he watched our faces. 'Scuffed earth, fibres caught on the log matching those of Jacky's and Harry's clothing. All centred in the one spot, near the fallen log.'

I was shocked for a moment, but Maurice grinned. 'They probably wrestled,' he said.

'Tell us more about that.'

'Play fighting. They did it all the time. If you knew my brother... Jacky couldn't keep still. He had all this bottled up energy that needed to be used somehow. Harry helped him with that. They wrestled a lot. It made Jacky feel better.'

'Do you think that would have been a logical thing for them to do on that particular day?' Sergeant Brown asked.

'For sure. Jacky was agitated. Harry would have talked to him, wrestled with him, then sent him on his way nice and calm. Harry could always tell when Jacky needed a scuffle.'

'Thank you. We'll be in touch,' Sergeant Brown said. They turned away and this time, kept going.

I felt sick in my stomach. 'Maurice, they would have treated that site as a crime scene.'

Maurice's grin vanished and he swore. 'You're right. Why couldn't those other cops have questioned us properly? I'm beginning to think the whole thing was botched.'

Maurice had to go back to work so he and Miranda left soon after.

As Jonathan and I walked up Harry's drive, Jonathan stuffed his hands in his pockets and said, 'What are you doing now?'

'Um, nothing planned. Well, except helping Mum with the spring clean but that can wait. Why?'

'Want to grab a milkshake and go for a walk down to the park?'

'Sure. I'd like that.'

It was nice to spend some time away from the others and all the talk of Jacky and Harry and crime scenes and investigations. We ambled around the park together, sat on a bench and talked of many things. And neither of us said a word about murder.

We didn't see the detectives again for a few days. Later in the week, they sent word they were returning to Hobart and would be back on the weekend. I met Miranda, Maurice and Jonathan for lunch at the chip shop one day, even though Mum had again become paranoid about me going out because of a possible killer lurking about.

We sat at a table by the window. Some kids were playing pinball and the constant rattle and ping of the machine was a good mask for our conversation.

'Aunt Jo's hanging out to come down and see us,' Maurice said. 'But she doesn't feel like she can, what with this going on and Mum and Dad being in the dark about it.'

'That's awkward,' Jonathan said.

'Yeah, can't wait till they catch the sod so we can go back to normal.'

'Didn't we say that last time?' I said.

'Look.' Miranda inclined her head towards the window.

A stocky, blonde-haired young man wearing a tank top and tattoos up his well-muscled arms was walking towards the shop. Wayne Bottle. He pulled open the door, walked through the plastic fly-strips and made his way to the counter. A short time later, carrying a can of Coke, he headed back towards the door and turned to look at our table on the way. He exited the shop, stopped outside and opened his can, glancing back at the window where we sat.

'Don't look now, he's coming back,' I said quietly.

Sure enough, Wayne poked his head back through the door and looked directly at us.

'Hix,' he said, and jerked his head as an invitation for Maurice to follow him.

Maurice raised his eyebrows at us, stood and followed Wayne outside. We watched them through the window. They exchanged some words, Maurice nodded and pointed at us, and the pair of them came back into the shop. Maurice pulled out a chair from another table, set it next to us and they both sat down.

'Wayne here was questioned by our friends a couple of days ago. I said it was alright to talk in front of us four.'

We greeted each other and Wayne took a long swig of his Coke. He wiped his mouth with the back of his hand and said, 'So they got the wrong bloke, aye?'

'It's looking that way,' Maurice said.

Wayne swore and said, 'Poor Harry.'

'Do you know Harry?' I asked.

'I knew 'im a bit. Thought he was a good bloke.'

'What did they ask you?' Maurice said. 'Were they after more information?'

Wayne snorted and set his can on the table with a thump. 'That's the thing, right? Them other cops—three years ago weren't it?—they asked if I'd seen that chick, Minnie-whatsit. I said, yeah I'd seen her. They asked where and I told them how she was walking down the road. They asked what time and what direction and that.'

We nodded, leaning in and listening carefully. Wayne embellished his vocabulary with so many expletives, it was difficult to understand his actual point.

'Then the big one says in his poncy voice, "That'll be all, you may go." Never asked nothin' else so I figured it was all they needed. So I didn't tell 'em the other stuff.'

Wayne called the police officers a derogatory name, picked up his can and took another swig.

We glanced at each other and Maurice asked, 'What other stuff?'

'About that chick. It was weird, man.'

'What do you mean?'

'She looked like she'd seen a ghost. She was walking with her arms around herself like this, like she was feeling sick or something. Then, get this—she stops and goes up the side of the road a bit, near the bushes, and chucks.'

'What?'

'I ain't kidding, she really hurled it, man. Anyway, she got goin' after that. But they never asked me about that, did they?'

'Did you tell the police about it the other day?' Maurice asked.

'Oh yeah. They asked me all sorts of stuff so I told 'em everything I could think of. They even gave me their card in case I think of anything else. And they said thank you, which is more than I got from that other git. I was very helpful, they said. Ain't that nice?' He puffed out his chest and grinned.

'That puts a new spin on things,' Jonathan said.

'What, then?' Wayne said.

'Not sure, but we'll have to try and figure it out.'

'So, you lot are playing detective, aye?'

'Something like that,' Maurice said.

'Well, mate, I hope they catch 'im. Your brother was a good little fella, man. I know I was a jerk back then.'

He stood up, scraping his chair on the floor, and reached out a hand to Maurice. Maurice stood, they shook hands, and we said our goodbyes.

When Wayne left, Miranda giggled and slapped her hand over her mouth. 'Sorry, but he's so funny.'

'Bit of a character,' Maurice agreed. 'So, what do we think? It sounds like Minnie-May saw more than just two people arguing.'

'Unless she really was just sick,' Jonathan said.

'You'd think if she was sick, she wouldn't have gone for a walk in the first place. I reckon she saw something else.'

'But what?' I asked.

'A dead body?' Miranda said. 'That's all I can think of that might make her vomit.'

Jonathan shook his head. 'Jacky's body was found near Madding Hill. She couldn't have walked that far and back.'

'Well, something spooked her really bad,' Maurice said.

Even with all our imaginations combined, we couldn't figure it out.

# 29

# The most important things

I'd CLEANED MY BEDROOM from top to bottom and discarded a great many things—old ornaments, clothes, school books, toys—but I saved my boxes of journals. There was history in there. Stories from many years of my childhood, and not just my adventures with Harry.

It was Friday afternoon. I made myself a hot chocolate and settled down on my bed to flick through some of the books again. I'd written very little around the time of the murder, but the day itself was etched into my synapses, deep and painful still. I could close my eyes and see Jacky's face as clearly as if I was back there—his hand reaching out to the door, his face turned back towards us. His eyes pointedly locking with Harry's and his words, *you know why.* Harry knew why he wouldn't go to Gerda Hoffman's—because Wayne Bottle might be there. The boy who had bullied Jacky because of his learning difficulties.

I saw Harry's face and its expression of fury. Yes, for that brief second he had been angry. But not at Jacky—I knew that now. It was never about Jacky. I believed the moment had triggered a memory for Harry—one of being bullied and humiliated at school by Kylie's uncle. What had the boy called him? Maybe *dumbhead* or *idiot.* Hurtful words. Words that had riled Harry up so much, he'd grabbed the boy by the neck.

I opened a later journal—one from the latter half of 1978. Once Harry was found guilty, I wrote about friends, school, weekend family jaunts and anything else except Harry. I remember trying desperately not to think about him—averting my eyes from his gate when I walked to Nan's, bursting into chatter about some silly thing whenever his face popped into my head uninvited. Had I really processed my grief properly?—unlikely.

I found an entry from a weekend I spent with Kylie, no doubt organised by both sets of parents to distract me.

**I went with Kylie's family to Bicheno for the weekend and we stayed in a motel. We were near a beach but it was too cold to swim so we went for walks on the beach and played in the sand dunes. I asked Mum and Dad if they can take us there sometime because Maudie would love it.**

**Kylie's mum kept asking me if I was having fun. She bought me and Kylie a necklace each made out of shells.**

Kylie's mother's repeated queries about my enjoyment must have been particularly pointed, for me to have recorded them in my journal. I remember it as being a pleasant holiday, but no-where in the entry had I written that I was having fun. Perhaps it was too soon after Harry's trial for me to relax properly.

I remember Kylie being relieved that Harry was out of my life. We spent more time together on the weekends—playing table-tennis, walking on the beach, learning to roller skate. Always avoiding the topic of Harry.

Maudie would come into my room sometimes and ask about him. Now I wondered if she'd sensed something wasn't right.

I flicked through the journal to the entries made in the following year. 1979—coloured Levis, mood rings, dancing in the lounge room to Racey's *Lay Your Love on Me,* Kylie's brief lunchtime romance with Adam Flower.

**Adam tried to kiss Kylie on the monkey bars but he missed her lips and got her ear and she fell off and sprained her ankle.**

A term of ballroom dancing lessons and the end-of-year community dance at the school hall.

**The dance was so much fun. Jonathan came. He's been learning to dance at his school too and he did the Pride of Erin waltz with me. He's pretty good at it.**

I'd written 'so much fun,' a good indication that I was moving on from my grief and was genuinely enjoying life. Jonathan had helped. Good, solid Jonathan with his sensitive nature and lovely manners.

I found a whole page drawing of my mother wearing an apron and a pair of wings, holding a spray bottle in one hand and a cloth in the other. Underneath I'd written:

**Mum said - If I have to clean another window I'm going to grow a pair of wings and fly away.**

My fourteen-year-old self had taken that comment and turned it into something funny and sweet. This week, Mum had finished spring-cleaning the whole house and though Maudie and I had helped, Mum had done most of the work. She seemed happy enough, though there were times in the past when I'd worried. Like in the days after Harry was charged with murder and my parents' relationship was strained for a while. I remembered finding Mum outside one evening, lying on a blanket next to the crackling fire pit and listening to Bob Dylan's *Hurricane* in the dark. I'd sensed a melancholy surrounding her that I hadn't understood at the time.

I put the journal down and went to find her, discovering her in the bathroom, wiping down the vanity.

'There, I think we've finished,' she said, putting the spray bottle in the cupboard under the bathroom sink.

'Don't you get tired of it?' I asked.

Mum straightened up and we met each other's eyes in the mirror. 'Why would you ask that?'

'I found a picture I drew of you back in grade eight. You've got a spray bottle in your hand and a pair of wings and you're saying if you have to clean another window you're going to fly away.'

Mum laughed. 'Did I really say that? I'm sure I was joking.' She put her arm around my shoulders and I watched her reflection as she turned and kissed me on the cheek.

'Let's make a cuppa,' she said.

We settled ourselves in the lounge room with our tea. Mum leaned back on the couch and stretched her legs out to rest her feet on the edge of the coffee table. Her golden hair, that she wore these days in a shoulder-length wolf cut, had streaks of grey at the temples.

'Did you ever wish you'd done something else?' I asked.

'What do you mean?'

'I know you like your job at the school and you'll be a teacher soon. But do you ever wish you'd done it when you were younger, and had kids later?'

She smiled serenely. 'Of course not. I wanted to do the most important things first.'

'Do you think having kids is more important than having a career?'

'No, not at all. What I mean is, I did what was most important for me. When it's your turn to make those decisions, you should do what's right for you.'

'So, what if I want to be a writer and not have kids at all?'

'Then I will be very proud of you.'

'And if I want to have kids first, like you?'

'Then I will be very proud of you.'

I laughed.

Mum took a sip of her tea and gazed out the window. 'I couldn't have done things any other way. When I realised I was in love with your dad, all I wanted was to marry him and have you two. Now that you're both older and can take care of yourselves, I'm ready to do some other things. And I have more time to do them now, which is nice.'

We heard the front door open and the sound of Maudie taking off her shoes and going into her room. Without speaking, we stood up and went into the kitchen to join Maudie in her routine. Having changed her clothes, she came into the kitchen, greeted us and made herself a cup of tea.

Once seated at the table, she said, 'I talked to the police officers today.'

'Oh, they're back already?' I said.

'While I was walking home, they stopped and got out of their car. Detective Constable Floris thanked me for taking all the measurements.' She took a sip of her tea. 'She said they'll be at church on Sunday and we're to pretend we don't know them. It's sort of like lying but it's not, because it's police business.'

Mum sighed. 'I wish it was all over.'

'They said they're closer to the truth,' Maudie said.

'Really?' Mum wrapped her arms around herself. 'But what is the truth, I wonder?'

'I guess we'll soon find out,' I said.

Once more, I sat under a tree at Durrunby Park with Jonathan, Maurice, Miranda and the two police officers. It was Saturday and though the grass was damp from a morning drizzle, the clouds had since scudded away. The sky was bright blue and open with promise—like a herald of something good.

Maurice was particularly perky this morning, after a conversation with his aunt the night before. 'They're close,' he'd said to us before the detectives arrived. 'They've been putting together a picture. Just a few loose ends to tie up, Aunt Jo said.'

'Do they know who the murderer is?' I asked.

'I dunno. Maybe they'll tell us today.'

Now we sat expectantly as Sergeant Brown leafed through his notebook. He wore jeans and a T-shirt today, as if he was an ordinary bloke at the park with his teenage kids.

'Lily, your friend Minnie-May said she's returning home with her family tonight?'

'Yes,' I said.

'Constable Floris is going to try and talk to her by herself at the church service. We thought you might help us?'

Constable Floris said, 'She may be more likely to talk to me if you're there.'

'I can try.'

Maurice sprang from his seat and thrust his hands in his pockets. 'So, do you know who done it? You'd tell us if you knew, right?'

'Trust us, Maurice,' Sergeant Brown said. 'We know what this means to you, but you'll have to be patient a bit longer.'

Maurice plonked back down on the edge of the bench seat, put his elbows on his knees and leaned his head in his hands.

'Assuming Molly Crouch did see what she told Lily, after some further enquiries we've come up with a likely scenario. However, we don't have all the pieces yet. And a cohesive statement from Molly would be helpful.'

I sighed. 'Getting her on a good day is the challenge.'

'We'll keep trying,' Constable Floris said.

Jonathan had been sitting quietly all this time with a thoughtful look on his face. He cleared his throat, drew his body up straight and said, 'You've spoken to Harry, haven't you?'

Everyone turned to look at him. The detectives remained silent.

Jonathan nodded. 'Harry knows exactly when he last saw Jacky and likely the time Jacky started walking towards the church. So you've taken Harry's story and put it together with Molly's and found they corroborate each other.'

I looked at the other faces around me, at the hope springing up in all of them.

'And,' Jonathan continued, 'those stories line up with everything else you've gathered from us and elsewhere. Am I right?'

Sergeant Brown took a deep breath and let it out slowly, I assumed to give himself time to think. 'We still don't know who the culprit is, assuming it wasn't Harry.'

'You have a good idea though.'

I clasped my hands in my lap, turned to Sergeant Brown and said, 'How was he? How was Harry?'

The detective smiled grimly. 'He's optimistic. I'm sorry, that's all I can say.'

When the detectives had left, we talked for a while longer.

'If Jacky really did go into the shed that day,' Jonathan said, 'how did he get from the shed to Madding Hill?'

'Well, he didn't walk,' Maurice said.

Jonathan stroked his chin with his hand as if deep in thought. 'Someone had to have taken him. The real question—well, two questions—who was it, and was Jacky alive or dead at the time?'

Miranda gasped. 'You mean, someone killed him in the shed?'

Maurice jumped up from his seat, strode a few metres away and stood there with his back to us.

Miranda looked up to the sky and blinked. 'Remember how Harry used to play all our favourite songs on his guitar?' She lowered her eyes and looked at each of us in turn. 'And once he knew your favourite song, he never forgot.'

After a few moments, Maurice turned around and walked back to us.

'I've got a feeling about tomorrow,' he said.

'Me too,' said Jonathan. 'We'd better make sure we're all there.'

'Mind you,' Maurice added with a crooked grin, 'I haven't been to church for a while. You realise the roof might cave in?'

## 30

# A hand that does great damage

WE SAT IN A row at the back of the church auditorium—me in the corner, then Jonathan, Maurice and Miranda. For once, I was glad Kylie was away with her family. We'd spied the police officers on our way in, dressed casually and chatting with some of the regulars.

As we waited for the service to begin, I studied the backs of Minnie-May and Mrs Hammond, seated together in the front row next to the organ. From behind, they could have been copies of each other—two heads of fine, strawberry blonde hair, both dressed in grey. Both had rounded shoulders and a slight slouch, as if an invisible hand leaned on their backs. Minnie-May's small, white hand appeared and rubbed at the back of her neck. She turned slightly, as if sensing my eyes on her.

The service played out like any other. Amos Crouch gave a communion message and appeared to have trouble standing still as he spoke. He shifted from foot to foot, repositioned a glass of water, adjusted the cloth of the communion table with one hand and fiddled with his hair. At the conclusion of the message, he told a joke and everyone laughed. I caught Mr Hammond shaking his head.

Arthur Gilchrist, in a purple checked bow tie, led us in a song, twirling his hands in the air as if conducting an orchestra. Then we sat down to listen to Mr Hammond expounding the virtues of walking the narrow path. Jonathan's arm was touching mine and having a strange effect on my concentration. I gave up on trying to understand the sermon and scanned the congregation instead. Was there a sinister presence here, somewhere? Someone who knew exactly what happened to Jacky Hix three years ago?

Molly Crouch, on an aisle seat, was tapping her foot and nodding. Where were Molly's thoughts this morning? Was she listening to the sermon? Was she contemplating the wisdom of the narrow path or had her mind wandered elsewhere, combing the streets of the past? Did she think of Jacky often? Of all the local children, Jacky had been her favourite.

A word pulled me back to the preacher at the podium. The word 'righteousness' hung in the air and I remembered an earlier time and a similar message. Kylie had almost wet herself laughing that morning, when Mr Hammond had called from the front, *what about you!*, his face round and red with bursting capillaries and his hands gripping the sides of the pulpit, as they were doing now. In a quiet voice, he'd inquired of the audience, *Can you count yourself among the righteous?*

At the time, I hadn't understood the message. Kylie and I had been trying not to laugh at the expression on Mr Hammond's face. The word *righteous* had stuck in my head, though. I'd asked Harry about it and he'd explained how it didn't mean being perfect and that no one was really righteous. I studied Mr Hammond now, his back straight, his clear, grey eyes scanning the congregation. Did he believe himself to be righteous? I shifted my gaze to the row I was sitting in. From my vantage point at the side wall, I could see the whole line of faces from my side of the auditorium to the opposite wall. One long row of noses, all pointing to the front and the pulpit.

Later, I hung about in the foyer, surreptitiously keeping an eye on the detectives and waiting for an indication that they needed my help. Jonathan started up an animated conversation with the local doctor while Maurice and Miranda went to make a drink. Mum and Dad had disappeared into the tea-room and Nan was helping Maudie put the hymn books away.

I watched the detectives mingling and chatting as if they were a couple down from Hobart for the weekend. I even heard someone say 'your wife' to Sergeant Brown and he didn't correct them, so I realised that must be their cover. It was quite exciting, knowing there were undercover police in our midst which most of the congregation had no idea about. But nerve-wracking too.

As the crowd shuffled about, I spied Minnie-May leaning against a wall. She stood with her mouth slightly open, looking at something I couldn't see because of all the people. I contemplated whether to ask her to come outside and talk. I could give a wink or a raised eyebrow to Constable Floris on the way past so she'd follow us out. Or I could simply go and stand next to Minnie-May and say hello—it would be a start.

As the crowd shifted, I saw that she was watching a group of girls giggling in a corner, some of whom I recognised as being from her class at school. One of them grabbed another's elbow and the whole group began weaving their way through the crowd, heading towards the door to the carpark.

Minnie-May's expression was wistful as she watched them. As they passed by her, one of them turned their head, said something and gestured for her to follow. Minnie-May's face illuminated in a smile and she stepped forward to go with them. I moved too, quietly following behind, feeling an urge to make sure she managed to join the group.

The girls slipped through the milling bodies with Minnie-May behind them, and me behind her. She caught up with the girls as they reached the door and she was about to step outside.

The rest happened so quickly, I had to replay it afterwards in my head to convince myself of what I'd seen. There she was with her foot on the threshold, her hand reaching out to the girl in front of her, a new energy and purpose in her expression. At that moment, Mr Hammond entered the foyer through the door of the tea-room, stepped up beside her and wrapped his hand around her head. In one smooth action, he turned her head with his hand and Minnie-May's body moved with it, until she was facing the opposite direction. She showed no surprise. Instead of stopping, she kept walking the way she was now facing, back into the foyer. The girls went one way and Minnie-May the other. She didn't even flinch, but walked straight over to her aunt and stood beside her. Mrs Hammond glanced briefly at her before turning back to Glenda Hill to continue their conversation, while Minnie-May stood next to the two women, staring vacantly.

Mr Hammond, meanwhile, had stopped to talk to a group of men, his face a picture of affability.

Jonathan drew up beside me, frowning. 'You look like you've seen a ghost.'

I was shaking slightly. 'Not a ghost, but—' I shook my head— 'something.'

'What?'

I looked over to where Mrs Hammond and Glenda stood, but Minnie-May wasn't there. 'Did you see where Minnie-May went?'

'No, I haven't seen her,' Jonathan said. 'Listen, I need to help Dad with something but I'll be right back. Don't go away.'

Where could Minnie-May have gone? I looked around the foyer. People were beginning to head outside to the carpark so I followed a chatting group to the door and looked outside. The girls Minnie-May had tried to follow were grouped together in a huddle by the wall of the building, admiring each other's painted fingernails and talking in high-pitched voices. No sign of Minnie-May.

She wasn't in the tea-room either. I slipped back through the crowd and approached the serving hatch to the kitchen. 'Mrs Crouch, have you seen Minnie-May?' I called.

'No, I don't think so, love,' Betty said, and went back to drying the cups.

I glanced through the open door of the store room but it was empty. Then I looked into the auditorium. At the back row, the two detectives were seated with Molly. Constable Floris was talking to her in a low voice and nodding. I quietly snuck through the door and stood still, straining my ears to hear.

'So, he didn't come out of the shed after that?'

'No, no.' Molly shook her head. 'Jacky never come back out.'

'Did anyone else come out of the shed after Jacky went in?'

'Oh yes. They came out and locked the door. They never lock the door, you know. But they did that time. Poor Jacky. They locked him in the shed.'

'Molly, who came out? Who locked the door?'

Someone touched my arm and I turned. It was Miranda. I put my finger to my lips and slipped noiselessly back into the foyer. I quietly closed the door to the auditorium to give Molly and the detectives some privacy.

'Molly's talking to the police,' I whispered. 'She's remembering!'

'Oh, that's so good!'

Jonathan hurried up to us and said, 'Lily, I saw Minnie-May go into the ladies' toilets.'

'Thanks. I think there's something wrong with her, Jonathan. Don't go without me.'

I left them and headed for the bathroom, pictures of Minnie-May filling my head as I went. Her perpetually bowed head, the way she'd sucked her thumb right through primary school, her soft, downy cheeks that resembled peaches. The day she ran along the jetty—was she trying to run away? Going to her house was boring, Dot had said. *All we did was play Scrabble with her aunt and uncle.*

The crowd in the foyer was thinning. Mr Hammond stood at the door to shake the hands of congregants as they departed. I was about to head up the hallway when Mum and Dad came up beside me.

'We're off,' Mum said. 'Nan's gone already with Maudie.'

'Okay, I'll catch you up,' I said.

I continued up the hall and peered into the ladies' bathroom, but saw no one. I was about to leave, thinking I'd missed her, when I heard something and went in. All the toilet stall doors showed 'vacant,' but opposite these was a shower stall and from there, I heard sniffing. I knocked and pushed the door a little way.

'Minnie-May, is that you?'

When there was no answer, I poked my head inside and found her. She leaned with her back to the wall and her head bent. She looked up at me and I was shocked by her expression. For a moment, I saw Harry's bewildered eyes looking out from the back window of the police car.

'Are you alright?' Stupid question, she was obviously not alright.

Minnie-May looked away and didn't speak.

'I saw you out there with the other girls before. They're in the carpark, admiring each other's fingernails.' I smiled, but she didn't look at me. 'You could go out there and join them if you wanted.' I didn't know if they were still there, but I needed to somehow elicit a response from Minnie-May.

She swung her head to look at me, narrowed her eyes and said, 'I don't care.'

'Sure you do,' I said gently. 'They're nice girls. Wouldn't you like to spend some time with them, have a bit of fun?'

Minnie-May looked back down at the floor.

Dot's voice came back to me again— *She wasn't really allowed out.*

'But you're not allowed to, are you?' I said.  It was a stab in the dark, I knew, but the response from Minnie-May convinced me I was on the right track. Her bottom lip quivered.

'You don't see Dot much anymore, do you? You two used to be really good friends.'

Minnie-May shook her head.

'Remember, we're going to do something together soon, the four of us. I'll arrange it with Dot.'

A pained expression crossed Minnie-May's face. Despair. Like a broken flower, bent at the stem, her face like bruised petals. I felt an overwhelming sadness rise up in my belly.

'Minnie-May,' I said softly. 'Do you need help?'

The face she turned to me was fearful. 'No!' She pushed past me through the shower door and stumbled towards the exit.

'Minnie-May, please.' I put out my hand and touched her arm. 'What's going on?'

She stopped and turned to me. She opened her mouth to say something, but changed her mind and hurried out the door.

I stayed there, a ball of something black and sinister rising inside me. Something was wrong and I had a sense it was connected with Harry.

I exited the bathroom and made my way back to the foyer. People were clearing up. I caught a glimpse of Arthur Gilchrist in the auditorium, picking something up from the floor. I looked around for the detectives but couldn't see them. Betty and her helpers were clattering crockery in the kitchen. People were gathered in groups here and there, in conversation. Jonathan's father was amongst them, but I couldn't see Jonathan. I stepped outside into the carpark. Except for a few cars, it was deserted.

Jonathan would be here somewhere. I'd wait for him in the sunshine, clear my head a bit. As I stood there, soaking up the warmth, I heard someone clearing their throat. Looking down the side of the building, I saw that the door of the shed was ajar. The thought of the shed gave me the creeps. What had happened in there?

The person cleared their throat again and I recognised the sound as coming from Mr Hammond. The vision of him wrapping his hand around Minnie-May's head loomed in my mind, along with Minnie-May's face—haunted, resigned.

My insides bubbled with anger. How dare he be so cruel? I approached the shed with no actual purpose in mind, just a growing anger and a determination to set something right. I looked inside. There was the sofa with a crocheted rug draped across the back, a desk pushed up against the wall, rows of shelves lining the walls. Then I saw movement as my eyes adjusted to the dimness of the room.

Mr Hammond was bending down, his back to me, putting something away on a low shelf at the far side of the shed. Boxes of communion cups perhaps, or books?—I wasn't sure. I went further inside and stood, watching him.

He straightened himself, turned around and saw me.

'Hello Lily. Can I help you?' His eyes took in all of me, travelling from my head to my toes, and returning to my face.

I found myself at a loss for words. Why had I entered the shed? I should have brought Jonathan with me.

'Is there something I can do for you?' He tilted his head slightly and raised his eyebrows.

'It's Minnie-May,' I said.

His expression altered for a moment, so briefly I almost missed it, after which he smiled and said, 'Oh? What about her?'

I floundered. I shouldn't have come in here. I thought of Minnie-May's face in the bathroom, her haunted eyes.

'I—she's—' My heart was pounding so quickly it made me breathless. I took a deep breath, let it out slowly, and said, decisively, 'It's not right.'

He froze for a moment before turning away to straighten something on the shelf. Was there something tight and unnatural in his movements? He turned back to me with a smile on his face that didn't match the rigidity in his body.

'What are you saying, child? Is something the matter with my niece?'

'It's not right,' I said again, still floundering for the right words to say.

The expression was back—a hardness behind his eyes like a glint of steel. Then in a mere moment, his face had relaxed into an expression of tenderness.

'What do you mean?' he asked.

I was confused. I doubted myself. Had I really seen what I thought I'd seen on his face? Maybe there was something else going on in Minnie-May's life. She'd been hanging around with Sharn Skinner at school, whose family took drugs. Maybe the Hammonds were only trying to protect her.

But I'd seen his hand around her head.

I willed my legs to move, wanting to turn around and escape out into the sunlight. Mr Hammond licked his lips and moved towards me, at the same time shifting his eyes about the room as if he was looking for something. I couldn't say why I felt scared. Minnie-May had looked scared when I asked her if something was wrong. When I asked if she needed help.

My palms were sweating, and my breathing had turned shallow. The air of the shed was thick and suffocating. Mr Hammond moved towards me. His face had flamed, broken capillaries standing out red against his cheeks.

I should leave, but I wanted to tell him what I thought first. The anger inside me was building again. 'Poor Minnie-May,' I said as I backed towards the door.

He moved past the couch, reached down to straighten the blanket there and took something small and bright from the seat and enclosed it in his hand—the large hand that had gripped his niece's head and turned it away from her friends.

As he closed in on me, I felt anger emanating from him. But I was angry too. So angry.

'I saw you. How could you do that to her?'

His face was before my face, contorted in fury, his nostrils flaring. He lunged and his hands gripped my throat.

I stumbled backwards and cried out. I was falling and choking, grabbing at his hands, tearing at his fingers. Pain seared my back as I was crushed to the floor and pinned there. My breath was gone. My throat hurt. Still I hit out and clawed and choked, until the world began to dim.

A scream ripped the air. There was a crash and the grip on my throat lessened. Voices shouted. Mr Hammond was pulled off me. I saw Amos and Arthur, gripping Mr Hammond's arms, their faces contorted in horror. My hands went to my throat. Oh, how it hurt. And there was Minnie-May, frozen, her mouth open as if in a scream.

I gasped for air and gentle arms wrapped around me. It was Jonathan, holding me and saying over and over, 'It's alright, you're alright, I've got you.'

Then, a deep, authoritative voice rang out of the chaos.

'I'm Detective Sergeant Brown. Walter Hammond, I'm arresting you on suspicion of the murder of Jacky Hix...'

Everyone gasped.

Finally, I caught my breath and Jonathan helped me stand up. Still holding my throat, I looked around. Minnie-May was sobbing onto the shoulder of her aunt who appeared dazed. Arthur and Amos, dishevelled, were brushing themselves off. People crowded around me, their eyes like saucers. Maurice's voice rang out with colourful expletives while Miranda rubbed my back. I gathered from the commotion that someone had sprinted off to find Constable Munnings.

The voices swirled about me— 'What does he mean?'... 'murder of Jacky Hix?'... 'Walter Hammond?'... 'That can't be right.' —and I was led outside into the sunlight where I sucked clean air into my lungs. Jonathan stood beside me with his arm around my shoulders.

Constable Floris came up beside me, breathless. 'Are you alright, Lily?'

'He tried to strangle me,' I croaked, incredulous.

'The doctor's been called. He'll check you over, and we'll take photos of your injuries. Jonathan, stay with Lily. I'll be back.'

She took charge of the crowd which quickly found itself being ushered towards the church building. A siren sounded and everyone turned as one to see Constable Munnings pull into the carpark, leap out and open the back door of the police car. He rushed into the shed. A few seconds later, Sergeant Brown led Mr Hammond out in handcuffs, in front of everyone, and put him in the back of the car. The crowd watched, stunned, as both police officers drove away with Mr Hammond in the back.

'Where will they take him?' I croaked, holding my neck.

'To the police station for the moment, I guess,' Jonathan said. 'What happened? No, don't talk. Tell me later.' He squeezed my shoulder and I felt incredibly grateful for his presence.

As proof of the effectiveness of the Crayfish Cove bush telegraph, our Datsun screamed into the carpark and Mum and Dad leapt from the car, calling, 'Lily! Are you alright?' They rushed up either side of me, inadvertently shoving Jonathan aside. Once they were convinced I was fully alive and in no danger, Dad's face clouded over and he looked towards the shed. 'Where is the—'

I grabbed his arm and pulled him with me towards the door of the building. 'They've taken him away,' I rasped. 'Come on, we have to give statements.'

Sergeant Brown had closed the shed door but as we passed it, I glimpsed a small, bright thing on the ground, flattened and dirty as if it had been dragged there by a scuffle of feet. It was the thing Mr Hammond had picked up and held in his hand—one of Minnie-May's rainbow-coloured hair ties.

Inside the church building, Betty switched the urn back on and set out the tea things. Constable Floris gathered everybody in the auditorium where she attempted to sort out who had useful information about the incident. I was sent into the Sunday School room with Mum and Dad to wait for Sergeant Brown to return. Jonathan gave my hand a squeeze before we left. As we exited the auditorium, I saw Minnie-May sitting in the corner of a pew with her aunt, their heads touching.

The rest of the afternoon went by in a blur. My throat hurt and every time I thought about Mr Hammond, my body shook. Mum and Dad stayed with me in the Sunday School room while I was checked over by the doctor and photographs of my neck were taken. Sergeant Brown took my statement.

'Lily, try to recount as accurately as possible everything that led up to you going into the shed. Then the actual incident, particularly what was said between you. Can you do that?'

My hands shook in my lap. Dad put his hand over mine and squeezed.

'Take your time,' Sergeant Brown said kindly. 'There's no hurry.'

I took a few deep breaths. I thought of Harry in prison. He'd been in there for three whole years and I knew in my heart he should never have been sent there. This was important.

I squared my shoulders and looked directly into Detective Sergeant Brown's eyes.

'It started with Minnie-May,' I croaked. 'She was following a group of friends...'

# 31

# Fixing up Harry's place

THE TRUTH WAS THERE in my journals all along. The truth of Harry's innocence, that is. All I had to do was believe what I had written. There was not one entry, in all those hundreds of pages, that hinted at Harry being anything other than what he was. A good man.

Oh, how he must have grieved for Jacky! Grieved in prison all by himself with everyone believing he had murdered his friend. I tried not to think about it too much as I couldn't bear the thought.

'Would you like to become a detective, Lily?' Sergeant Brown said as he reached for another one of Mum's shortbread biscuits. 'I think you'd make a good one.'

'No, I'm going to be a writer,' I said. I sat on the couch with Mum and Maudie, holding the shell Harry had given me for my tenth birthday tightly in my hands.

Constable Floris sat in the other armchair opposite the sergeant and Dad had pulled up a kitchen chair.

'Well, I wish you all the best. Let me know if you change your mind,' Sergeant Brown said with a wink.

Dad leaned forward with his elbows on his knees and his hands clasped. 'What's the news?'

Sergeant Brown spoke. 'Walter Hammond has made a full confession to the murder of Jacky Hix. His niece, Minnette-May, was a witness to the murder.'

My stomach flipped. 'Poor Minnie-May! But why? Why did he kill Jacky?'

'And why would he hurt Lily?' Mum asked.

The detectives glanced at each other. Constable Floris set her cup on the saucer. 'We can't tell you that just yet.'

'What about Harry? When's he coming home?' I asked.

'Soon,' said Sergeant Brown. 'But first some comfortable arrangements will be made for his accommodation for a short time to allow some, er, changes to be made to his property.'

Dad slapped his hand to his forehead. 'Good grief, Harry's place is a mess!'

'Amos Crouch is going to organise a clean-up,' Sergeant Brown said.

'We can all help with that,' Mum said. 'Tell us the rest, please, Sergeant.'

The sergeant continued. 'Walter Hammond strangled Jacky in the church shed. He locked his body in the shed and later, in a quiet part of the afternoon, put it into the boot of his car. He took his niece with him to Madding Hill where he hid the body. On the way back, he dropped Minnie-May off closer to town to walk the rest of the way home. That was so people would see her and corroborate the story he instructed her to tell—that she'd been walking in the woods and had seen Harry Fernley and Jacky arguing.'

Mum slapped her hands to her cheeks. 'That poor child!'

'That's why she was sick in the bushes,' I said.

'How do you know that?' Sergeant Brown asked.

'We talked to Wayne Bottle.'

'Your friend, Molly, was helpful, Lily,' Constable Floris said. 'She saw Jacky go into the shed with the vegetables, then saw Walter Hammond come out with Minnie-May and lock the door. Molly knew Jacky was still in there.'

'That's what she was so distressed about,' I said. 'She tried to tell us back then. She kept saying 'never come out' and everyone thought she didn't want to come out of her house, but she was talking about Jacky.'

'Don't blame yourself, though,' Constable Floris said. 'No one is at fault here but the offender.'

I thought of how Jonathan had said a similar thing to me outside the church, just before we were ushered inside to give statements. He had his arm around me and I'd leaned in to him and said something about regret and how we hadn't seen the truth when we should have.

'Only one person's to blame,' he'd said, squeezing my shoulder. 'Don't blame yourself for someone else's evil.'

When I was told what else had happened that day, it took some time for it to sink in as it was nothing I could have imagined. Mum's way of explaining it was, 'He was hurting her, Lily. And Jacky walked in on it. Do you understand?'

I was sixteen and thought I knew everything, but my brain wouldn't grasp the meaning of her words at first. I guess all of Crayfish Cove lost some of its innocence that year.

Mum said, 'It makes you realise how you saw things, but you didn't know what it was you were seeing. Poor little cowed thing.'

Over the next while, the pieces of the puzzle slipped into place and Crayfish Cove again had to work through the tragedy.

When I'd confronted Mr Hammond in the shed about his treatment of Minnie-May, he thought I knew more than I did and, in a sudden fit of rage (or perhaps fear), had attempted to silence me.

'What makes a person like that?' I asked Dad. But Dad, who had an answer for almost everything, shook his head in angry bewilderment.

I wondered again why Minnie-May had told Dot about her lie, then asked Dot not to tell. I could only assume it was her way of throwing out a lifeline. Had she hoped Dot *would* tell someone? But rescue hadn't come because Dot had kept her mouth shut.

Regret over the day I kicked her in the shins and called her a liar filled me anew. I remembered the way she'd grunted and melted into the line of students, absorbing the pain, accepting the abuse like she must have given in to all the other abuses. Shame boiled inside me. When I called her a liar, she must have thought Dot had told me about her lie. Did she believe that I would tell someone then? Did she wait hopefully, thinking she was about to be rescued?

I was particularly ashamed of what I'd said on the weekend Kylie and I had spent with Dot and Minnie-May at Dot's house. When we'd played the silly game of Truth, Dare or Promise. Minnie-May had asked whether it was okay to tell a secret, and I was so adamant in my reply—*you should never, ever tell a secret.* Maybe she was trying to gather the courage to tell someone about what was happening to her. And I had thoughtlessly shut her down. How I wished I'd known what I was seeing. If only we'd been able to rescue her. If we had, Jacky and Harry would have been saved too.

There was a rumble of engines and two trucks pulled into Harry's yard, one carrying building materials and the other, a load of gravel. Jonathan, Maurice, Miranda and I were cleaning up the garden—rebuilding the garden beds, refilling and digging them over. We'd been first on the scene early in the morning and people had been turning up ever since in trucks and cars that were parked all the way down Murphy's Lane. Even Kylie was expected later in the morning, having accepted that Harry was not the monster her mother would have her believe.

Harry's place was packed with people sawing, hammering, shouting, putting windows in, cleaning gutters, even painting the roof. Some had taken days off work to see the job done before Harry came home.

Amos Crouch had brought the team together. As told by my father, what happened at the local pub was this: Dad went in there to find Amos just as Amos stood up at the bar and whistled. Everyone quietened down and Amos said, 'Listen up. We're gonna fix up Harry Fernley's place. Who's in?'

A few hands shot up and voices called out, 'Count me in.'

'Thought he could use some plumbing, Brian,' Amos said to my dad. And Dad said, 'Reckon I could do that.'

Amos kept standing at the bar and as each person came into the pub, he said the same thing, 'We're gonna fix up Harry Fernley's place,' and each man would nod, say something like—*yeah, I got some fence posts not doin' nuthin ... I've got paint leftover... does he need his roof fixing?...* Before they knew it, virtually the whole town was on board. Some headed out to Harry's that evening to assess the damage and what was needed. A collection was taken up and used to purchase new glass with enough left over for a good second-hand lounge suite to replace the one that had been slashed.

Now, here we all were. Mum was in the house with a hoard of other people, clearing up the mess and scrubbing down the walls ready for a fresh coat of paint. Harry's old lounge suite had already been taken away. Once the walls were painted, we'd be moving the new furniture in. Betty had made a dozen meals and put them in the freezer, and I heard there were a ton of cakes and biscuits being baked in various kitchens around town as well. Even the children were helping, although I think a lot of them had discovered the treehouse and had gone off to play.

Maurice looked up from the garden bed he was turning over. 'Aunt Jo's coming down soon. She's that proud of everyone.'

'I can't wait to meet her,' I said.

There was a hush and Miranda said, 'Look.'

Walking down the driveway, hand-in-hand, were Mr and Mrs Hix. Everyone stopped working and watched them. Faces appeared at the door, looking out. Maurice dropped his trowel and headed out the garden gate. People were going over to them, shaking Mr Hix's hand and welcoming them. Maurice stooped down to give his mother a hug, and his father gave him a friendly clap on the back.

Mr Hix stood straight and tall, looked out at all the neighbours gathered, and said, 'We've come to lend a hand.'

The party livened up even more after that. Some of the children returned from the treehouse and took up cloths and scrubbing brushes. Sarah Pevensie was sweeping the front steps and her brother, Bobby, sat on a chair near the fire pit, working intently at something on his lap. I set my spade down and went over to lean on the newly-repaired garden fence to take a closer look. He was sanding one half of the little wooden shelf that had been ripped off Harry's kitchen wall and broken. The other half lay on a chair beside him and I wondered how he was going to put the two halves together.

Jonathan came up beside me. 'Just look at us,' he said, and I followed his gaze to the activity going on around us—building, digging, cleaning, fixing, shouting, laughing.

Someone called out, 'How about some music.' Someone else started to sing *Tie a Yellow Ribbon Round the Ole Oak Tree* and we all joined in. Betty, in her apron and a scarf around her head, danced down the steps with her mop and Arthur Gilchrist appeared from somewhere and twirled around the fire pit. Everyone was dancing or clapping or cheering or being silly.

And in that moment, I was so proud of everyone, I thought for a minute I might cry.

In my book, *Folklore and Fairytales,* is the story of the emperor who paid an exorbitant sum of money to a couple of crooks posing as tailors, to spin him clothes they said were so fine that only the most intelligent people could see them. Too embarrassed to admit he could not see the clothes, the emperor wore them in his grand parade. He was, of course, naked, but his servants and all the people pretended to be able to see his clothes so no one would think them stupid. 'Look how grand the emperor looks in his fine clothes!' they cheered.

A child in the crowd called out, 'The emperor has no clothes on!' Another child laughed and said, 'He has nothing on at all!' And everyone realised the truth, that the emperor was naked.

I thought of Harry. Just like the townsfolk in the story, I'd believed what I'd been told—the murmurs, the slurs, the stories of Harry's violence that had flown like birds through the winds of the bush telegraph. Rumours of what he'd done, how he'd done it, where and when. If only I had been like the children in the story who trusted their own judgment, who had opened the minds of the adults around them with the truth. I should have believed my own story—the one written over years in my many journals—showing a man who would not have done that terrible thing. Instead, I soaked up the slurs and the gossip with the rest of them and allowed it to mar my story. I had accepted that Harry had taken Jacky by the throat and strangled him. How ashamed I felt now!

I heard Harry's voice echoing from my memories. The day Jacky had tried to dig a hole to China, and Harry said, *Jacky knows he can't because he tried.* He'd taught us to find things out for ourselves. He'd said to me once how some people preferred to sit still with their ears open and their brains switched off. If I hadn't switched off my brain, maybe he wouldn't have been put away for three years.

Yet, I was only a child. What could I have said to Sergeant Bullard, who kept calling me Laura, that would have made him listen? Policemen only listened to young children in storybooks. Real children were manoeuvred by the adults around them, some more than others—I thought of Mr Hammond's hand around Minnie-May's head.

In retrospect, we could see how we children had held the answers, but no one had asked us the right questions. What was Harry like?—I could have told them Harry chopped up the wood he'd been saving to build a verandah and burnt it, so I would have the birthday party I longed for. That he helped Dot to find her voice. That he nailed his best ladder to a tree so every child would have access to the treehouse. I could have said how he was the only person I knew who could look past the outside of a person and see the best inside them, and bring it out.

That's what I could have told them. But I was only twelve, and what power does a twelve-year-old have against a crowd hurling insults and screaming, 'Crucify him, crucify him!'

# 32

# Dear man

SPRING HAD TAKEN HOLD and the world felt new as I walked along Main Street. The church garden was filled with colour and the wattle trees along the road were waving their golden arms. In Murphy's Lane, I stopped at Harry's gate and rested my hand on the newly painted gate post.

For a moment, I turned around to look back across the lane at the poplars and thought of the figure I'd seen there in the mist. I was sure now that it had been Mrs Hammond. But why had she stood there, watching Harry's gate? Did she have an idea something was not right about Jacky Hix's death? We would probably never know. Mrs Hammond and Minnie-May had moved away to be with family. I hadn't seen Minnie-May since the day her uncle was arrested. She had been the one who found us and screamed and most likely saved my life. I hoped I would see her again.

Harry's driveway, overlaid with new gravel, wove before me, between the eucalypts. I gathered my courage and left the gate, my boots crunching as I followed the drive past the oak tree and around the corner into Harry's place.

There it all was—the repaired garden fence, his little cottage pristine with new paint, ute, shed, lean-to stacked under with firewood. And of course, the fire pit with the circle of chairs, ever-ready for visitors.

Inside, we had painted the walls and piled handmade cushions on the new lounge suite. I'd reframed the story I'd written for him and set it back by the fireplace. Bobby Pevensie had beautifully sanded the two halves of Harry's wave-shaped shelf, glued them together and reattached it to the kitchen wall. I set Harry's photograph of his parents back where it belonged. Bobby had hung the shelf slightly crooked, but no one said a word about it, just clapped him on the back and said, 'Good job, Bobby.'

I stood at the corner near the oak tree, looking at Harry's place—and at Harry. There he was, outside of course. I could count on one hand the times I'd visited and found him indoors. He wasn't working this time, though. He stood with his back to me, hands on his hips, leaning back and gazing up, apparently into the trees, or perhaps up into the hills. The familiarity of his stance brought waves of emotion rippling through my body. I tried to control my breathing and hold myself together.

Harry's hair was still dark and curly, though shorter than I remembered. It lifted a little in the wind as I watched, and I had a flash of the first time I saw him, striding down Murphy's Lane with his rucksack and fishing rod.

Dear man.

Perhaps he felt my eyes on him. Perhaps the fondness emanating from my gaze touched him. He turned and saw me, and his face was puzzlement.

'Lily? Is that you?'

I walked slowly towards him, both hands in the one wide front pocket of my windcheater. I wanted to say hello but struggled to open my mouth.

'You've grown, you're—' Harry appeared to be struggling too. 'Well, you're all grown up.'

I giggled a bit and nodded. I stopped walking and we stood, staring at each other.

Harry moved his hands awkwardly and said, 'Well, how about I make us a cuppa?'

I followed him into the cottage and leaned on the door frame as he pottered about at the kitchen end, boiling the kettle and finding the cups and teapot. He kept glancing up at me and I saw that his face was different. There were lines where I didn't remember them being and his skin had paled. His eyes too—something dark had grown behind them. He didn't look the same. I couldn't see *my* Harry.

He moved awkwardly, as if uncomfortable in my presence. A chasm lay between us and there appeared to be no bridge. Nothing to connect us. I was floundering. Harry had been in prison for three years. All because of me. I could have saved him.

My body would not hold me up. I pulled out a chair and sat down, rested my elbows on the little table and held my face in my hands. I must keep myself together. He's home now. He's alright.

But the vision of Harry behind a wall of bars persisted. He was stirring the milk into the tea, now tapping the spoon on the side of the cup, the sound like a bell ringing out from the past—Harry handing out cups of milky tea to a group of children.

Harry looked up and met my eyes and it was too much. I gulped, the tears spilled, my body betrayed me.

'Hey, Lily.' Harry rushed over and sat beside me. 'Lily.'

It all heaved out of me in great, wracking sobs. Harry put his arms around me and I felt like a child again. There was the smell of him—woodsmoke and earth—a scent so familiar it brought fresh tears that poured like a fountain and wouldn't stop. He held me until I had cried out all the tears my body could produce.

And the gap between us closed like that—Snap.

I looked into his face and saw again the blue eyes I knew, behind which I knew was goodness.

'I'm sorry,' I whispered.

'What for?'

'For not saving you.'

Harry shook his head. 'Don't ever blame yourself. You got me out, Lily. Thank you.'

Fresh tears prickled my eyes, but I blinked and kept them in. 'It was a combined effort.'

He smiled and stood. 'I want to hear about it. Tell me over tea. What would you like with it? We have a choice of about half a dozen kinds of cake and several sorts of biscuits.'

'Yeah, the ladies went a bit overboard.'

We settled on Anzac biscuits and took them to the other end of the living room. Harry sat in one of the new armchairs and I curled up on the couch.

'What was it like—in prison?' I asked.

Harry took a deep breath and looked to the ceiling as he let it out. 'What can I say?'

'You don't have to tell me. I wish we'd worked it out sooner.' I could hear the bitterness in my own voice. 'Actually, we shouldn't ever have believed what people said in the first place.'

Harry shook his head. 'It's alright. Nothing's wasted. You know that, don't you?'

'What do you mean?'

'Well, I got to do a job while I was in there. Something that needed doing.'

'What job?'

'A bloke in prison. I won't mention his name, but he had three fingers missing and a scar from his forehead to his neck. Thanks to me, he now knows how to grow potatoes.'

I pulled a face. 'Potatoes?'

'Gardening is a good healer for some people. So, tell me how you worked it out.'

'We put everything together like a puzzle. Even Maudie helped. In fact, she's the one who figured out Jacky had taken the shortcut to the church.'

'I must thank Maudie.'

'She'd like that. She's working for Amos Crouch, did you know? Doing his books.'

'I'll bet Amos' books are spot on, then.'

'Oh yeah, he's getting more than he pays her for. I suspected him for a minute, you know.'

'Amos?' Harry laughed. 'Poor fellow.'

'Yeah, he got a bit spooked when he caught me and Kylie following him.'

Harry sat his tea down on the hearth, leaned in towards me with his arms on his knees and his hands clasped. He smiled, his blue eyes crinkling up, and there he was—*my* Harry.

'Tell me everything,' he said.

I started from the beginning, the day I came across Maurice at the cottage. I told him the whole story. I didn't dwell too long on the state of his property from the vandalism, but I did describe in detail the week the community came together and fixed everything up.

'Sorry about your lounge suite,' I said. 'I know it belonged to your parents.'

'That old thing needed replacing. Too many mice had lived in it over the years.'

'Gross!'

'Oh well, they needed a place.'

'How about your shelf? Bobby tried really hard to get it right.'

Harry looked towards the kitchen where the little, lop-sided shelf sat above the sink, and smiled. 'That,' he said, 'is a work of art.'

After our tea, we went for a walk down past the shed and the fruit trees. The big old pine was there, the tyre swing rehung with new rope. The walls of the treehouse could be seen above the recently returned ladder. And someone—one of the Pevensies I was sure—had hung a garland of flowers from one of the branches. They were wilting but still colourful.

'All ready for the kids to come,' I said. Perhaps I had a premonition of my own children adventuring at Uncle Harry's place in the future.

'Who knows?' Harry said.

I looked at him and saw uncertainty flicker across his face. 'I was talking to Nora Pevensie the other day,' I said. 'There are more little Pevensies grown up just enough to be wanting a treehouse.'

Harry smiled. 'Good to know.'

'And, with the place being so quiet for the past couple of years, you might even get a visit from a Tassie tiger.'

'That'd be something.'

'Did you hear about the sightings up at Mole Creek?'

We ambled back to the cottage, talking of tigers, finally at complete ease with each other. I even linked my arm in his and felt the old thrill of having such a grown-up as Harry Fernley for a friend.

We stopped and looked up at the house. It was like a fresh face that had had a flannel taken to it. Its windows sparkled like eyes given new life. The team had done a magnificent job of bringing it back, even making it better.

'They didn't get your verandah built, though,' I said, regretfully. 'I did tell them you were planning one.'

Harry grinned and shook his head. 'That was Dad's dream. To be honest, I don't need a verandah. Look at what the birch tree's done in the last three years.'

The wind-battered birch had taken off. The new branch that had grown from the bend had shot up and thickened into a strong trunk from which myriad branches sprouted and climbed above the roofline.

'There'll be plenty of shade under that tree in summer, once it bushes up again,' Harry said. 'In fact—' He grabbed hold of two of the chrome chairs by the fire pit, one in each hand, and dragged them to a space beside the birch tree. 'There. You and I can sit under here and watch the sunset.'

And that's what we did, me and Harry. We sat under the birch tree to watch the sun sink into the hills, and listen to the ravens yarning.

# 33

# New beginnings

I STEPPED UP ONTO the stage and set my papers on the podium. My heart did cartwheels as I looked out at the congregation and tried to catch my breath. Arthur Gilchrist appeared beside me—dressed in a pink shirt and bow tie—and handed me the microphone with a flourish. I gripped it in my shaky hands, lifted it to my lips and spoke.

'My friend, Harry, loves children. He collects them like some people collect shells or...' —I turned to Arthur— 'fancy bow ties.' A few people laughed. 'Perhaps "collect" isn't the right word, but he does seem to always have a collection around him.

'Children have a sense for people. They gravitate to Harry because they trust him. Because, you see, Harry has a gift. He sees past the outside of people and into their insides, and brings out the best in them. He reached inside my friend Dot, and brought out her confidence. Now she sings all over the country. He helps children to reach inside themselves and find their capacity to create things—like treehouses and billy carts and whatever else their imaginations can come up with. He told me I was a leader and encouraged me to lead with my words. He taught his friend, Jacky, how to help God grow things. He taught us about respect and trust. He taught us to believe in ourselves and to always look for the beauty in each other.

'He also taught us how to whistle like the birds. Harry loves birds and how all their different voices add to the richness of the forest. Kind of like people and our different voices. He once likened himself to the raven—one who did his best to sing but without a tuneful voice.'

I paused to gaze out at all the different faces looking back at me.

'But I've since learned, there's more to a song than just the melody. And I think Harry's life is one of the most beautiful songs I've ever heard.'

There was a round of applause as I set the microphone on the podium, picked up my papers and stepped down from the platform. I glimpsed Betty Crouch in the front row dabbing her eyes with a handkerchief.

Twelve-year-old Aileen Pevensie came up next and sang *This Little Light of Mine* to a guitar played by one of her brothers. Amos Crouch had enthusiastically agreed to speak but had then forgotten about it, so told jokes instead. We were still figuring out how the Sunday service was going to run, but so far, everyone was having riotous fun with talent springing from unexpected sources.

Jonathan came up to me in the tea-room later, grinning. 'Gosh, Lily, that was amazing.'

'Oh, thanks,' I said. Little bird wings fluttered behind my rib cage.

'You're such a good writer. Maybe you could write the whole story one day?'

'What do you mean?'

'Harry's story.'

Something sparked inside me. I think it was that moment when I knew I was going to do just that. Write Harry's story the way we, the children, knew it.

'Are you going to Harry's after this?' Jonathan asked.

'Yes,' I said.

'Great, I'll meet you there. Maybe we could go for a walk later. Along the beach or something?'

'Orright.' I felt my cheeks heating up.

For some incomprehensible reason, I lifted myself up on my tip-py-toes and dropped back onto my heels. Which made the bird flap harder in my chest and my cheeks heat up even more. When I couldn't bear for Jonathan to witness my flaming face any longer, I took off.

One afternoon in November, Harry and I were out the front of his place stacking some second-hand bricks into a manageable pile. He was expanding the garden again and creating interesting spaces for his new direct-to-the-public enterprise. I wasn't surprised to hear Wayne Bottle had been helping him, and that Harry was teaching him how to grow potatoes.

'I got the lettuce and silverbeet in,' Harry said. 'Have to put the carrot seeds in next.'

'What are these for?' I shoved another brick into the pile.

'Thought I'd see if Bobby wants to design something nice to plant flowers in. Pretty the place up a bit. He's quite creative, you know.'

We moved onto another pile of bricks and Harry indicated the spot where he wanted them stacked.

'Have you heard from Minnie-May?' he asked.

'No. Mum's going to try and find out where they are. They might not want to be in touch, though.'

'No, you'd have to respect that.' Harry stretched his back, looked up into the trees and shook his head. 'I wish I'd known.'

'You don't know how many times I've said, "I wish." Anyway, you helped a lot of kids. You can only do so much.'

'True. Still.' He bent down to lift another brick.

'I did hear something,' I said. 'It's gossip.'

Harry laughed. 'Up to you.'

'Mum heard it from Betty. She reckoned something was hushed up in the church he was at before and he was sent down to us.'

Harry frowned. 'You probably shouldn't repeat that.'

'Why?'

'It's likely just a vicious rumour. Things like that, well, you wouldn't like to think it could actually happen, would you?'

Suddenly, Harry's eyes widened as his gaze shifted to something behind me. 'Hello, who's this?' he said.

I turned to see a woman literally tripping up the drive where Harry had created a veritable obstacle course with mounds of soil and pine bark, more bricks and an upturned wheelbarrow. The woman was incredibly pretty, and I think Harry noticed too because he just stood there, staring.

She was dressed in a long skirt and canvas jacket with a red scarf tied around her head from which curls of auburn hair had escaped. She carried a knitted bag.

The woman hitched up her skirt to clamber over a pile of planks, and approached us with her face turned towards Harry.

'I beg your pardon,' she said. 'I'm looking for Mr Harry Fernley. Are you Mr Fernley?'

'I'm Harry, yes. And this is my friend, Lily.'

'Lily! Oh, I'm *so* glad to meet you at last,' she said, dropping her bag and grabbing my hand. She vigorously pumped my hand, then Harry's. 'I just—well I had to come and, you know, say how glad I am that everything worked out. Well, it worked out in the end, didn't it? I'm *awfully* sorry it took so long, I really am.'

The woman's face contorted in an anxiety of emotion as she spoke, now a blaze of redness, now a paleness and profusion of freckles. 'It's just so lovely to meet you both!'

Harry's eyes blinked rapidly and the muscles of his face worked as if he wanted to say something, but couldn't figure out how to force the words out.

'Oh!' She threw her hands in the air. 'I almost forgot.'

She bent down and retrieved her knitted bag from the ground where she'd dropped it, rummaged around inside and drew out a package wrapped in brown paper.

'This is for you. I—um—I heard you like seed cake.' She thrust it towards Harry and turned her freckled face up to him. It was like seeing Jacky all over again.

Harry took the parcel, looked at it and broke into a grin. He looked up from the gift, his blue eyes squarely meeting her brown ones.

'I heard *you* like witchetty grubs,' he said.

There was a moment of silence, then Joanne Hix—Maurice and Jacky's aunt Jo—threw back her head and laughed.

'I believe I have a lot to thank you for,' Harry said.

'Oh, it was nothing' —she waved her hand in the air— 'well, it was *something...*'

Harry nodded gravely. 'It was something.'

'Well, I made that detective listen. I wouldn't go away until he did.'

'Did you really sit in the police station—'

'All day, yes. I wasn't going anywhere until he heard me. I had him twisted around my little finger in the end.'

Harry laughed. 'I bet you did.' He gazed at her admiringly for a few moments, then remembered himself. 'Uh, do you like tea? I'll put the billy on and we can have some of this cake.'

'I'd love to, yes.'

Jo turned to me and grabbed my hand as we followed Harry to the fire pit. He disappeared inside the cottage to find the billy tea box, and Jo said, 'I can't tell you how happy I am. I've heard a lot about Harry and Jacky's friendship and—' She stopped, blinked and gathered herself. 'I'm glad my nephew had such a good friend before he died.'

I gave her a hug and said, 'Thanks for everything you did.'

'Here we are, ladies.' Harry carried the box down the steps and set it by the fire pit. 'I'll show you how to make billy tea, Joanne.'

'Please, call me Jo. I've heard all about your billy tea, Harry.'

'Oh? And what else have you heard?'

I thought I noticed Harry's cheeks turning a little pink, but he put his head down before I could be sure.

We sat on the old chairs and watched as Harry went through the billy tea ritual. Jo clapped her hands as he expertly swung the billy can and sighed over the taste of the tea. She sat back, looked up into the trees and said, 'What a wonderful place.'

Harry followed her gaze into the eucalypts, took a sip of his tea and said, 'I like it.' A kookaburra chortled as if in agreement.

Harry leaned towards Jo and said, 'So, what did you tell the detective the first time you went to see him?'

Jo grinned. 'Well, the first thing I said was, "I have important information for you and you need to hear me out" and then...'

Harry and Jo had a lot to catch up on. As they chatted away comfortably with each other, I began to feel that my presence was superfluous and made moves to leave. Joanne gave me a tight hug and Harry jumped up and hugged me also.

'I'll be back tomorrow,' I said.

'Good-o,' Harry said. 'I've got plenty more work for you to do.'

I rolled my eyes. 'May as well take advantage of cheap teenage labour when you can.'

We laughed and I headed off, waving as I went. At the corner near the oak tree, I looked back to see Harry taking down the billy can while Jo sat back on the old chrome chair, gazing up at him and smiling.

Everything was as right as it could be at that moment. Somehow, I knew Harry would be safe with Jo. She didn't look like someone who'd make him live in a posh house, and I was pretty sure she'd like fishing and listening to the birds.

Anyway, I had to hurry home as Jon had asked me to the town dance and I still hadn't decided what to wear. As I thought about that, my heart fluttered. Deep breath.

And off I went on my new adventure, leaving Harry to his.

# Author's Note

For those who are curious about the Tasmanian town of Crayfish Cove, it is a fictional place. As is Durrunby, the tourist town close by.

However, I have loosely based the topography of Crayfish Cove on the town where I was raised. Nubeena is a fishing and farming community on the Tasman Peninsula, named for an Aboriginal word meaning 'crayfish', which is how I came up with the name for Crayfish Cove. The cove in the story resembles Parsons Bay with its sandstone cliffs that look like honeycomb and its view of the local jetty, where I have pleasant memories of rambling as a child.

Despite the above similarities, the people and events of Crayfish Cove are fictional. Any resemblance of characters to real persons, living or dead, is entirely coincidental.

# Acknowledgements

This is the part where I get to thank the people who have helped to bring this book into existence. I express my heartfelt gratitude to:

Iola Goulton from Christian Editing Services from whom I've learnt so much about the novel writing craft, not least of all that fourteen points of view don't make a good story.

Lynne Lloyd from Lloyd-Moss Editing for identifying my bad habits and helping me make this book a far better read than it would have been.

Jennifer Magno for creating the gorgeous cover and title pages for this second edition of *When All The Birds Sing*. I can't stop gazing at it and wondering what that bird with the beady eye is *thinking!*

My online writing group – Barb, Dienece, Donna, Kel, Steph and Sue – for encouragement, knowledge sharing, feedback, photos and laughs. You are my people!

Janet Tiitinen for your honest critique about what works and what doesn't. Every writer needs a friend like you.

Rose Ising for your brilliant proofreading skills. You're like a super-vacuum cleaner that picks up all the last bits of fluff.

Paul Vlachos for your clarification around police ranks and procedures. (You saved me from modelling my police force on a British crime series). Any remaining errors in the book are entirely mine.

My parents, Carol and Eric, for casting your minds back to the seventies and answering my many questions. Special thanks for 'Gossamer Invisible Net' which revived my own memories of Mum dressed up for the evening in a bouffant and sequined minidress.

My brother and sister-in-law, Darren and Leanne, for believing in me. Keep asking me how it's going. (It helps.)

My biggest thanks always to my husband, Doug, for being my rock. I love you to bits. Thanks also for answering all my gardening and plant questions. (Any remaining errors are mine.)

And, of course, thanks to everyone who reads my book. I hope you enjoy my other Crayfish Cove stories.

# Book club questions / topics for discussion

1. Do you have a favourite character from the story? Who is it and what do you like about them?

2. How is your knowledge of the seventies? Could you relate to any of the references to the era (eg. rotary-dial telephones, doors being left unlocked, simple childhood pastimes.)

3. Did you grow up in a similarly close knit community? What was the same or different?

4. The story touches on the heavy issue of institutional abuse. If everyone in the group is comfortable to do so, discuss what factors you think contributed to the occurrence of abuse in the story.

5. Lily speaks to her church congregation about people being like birds. What is your interpretation of the title of the book?

6. Why do you think the children were not taken seriously during the first police investigation?

7. Discuss Harry and Lily's relationship. Would you have been similarly drawn to Harry? Why or why not?

8. As you were reading, what were your thoughts about Harry's character? Did you believe he was a good person or not?

9. Did your ideas regarding the culprit change as you read through the story?

10. What do you make of Harry's comment: 'I reckon I can hear God better out here.' ?

# About the author

Suzie Peace Pybus lives on a little fruit and vegetable farm in southern Tasmania with her husband and springer spaniel, Pepper.

Her first manuscript won the Omega Writers CALEB Award for unpublished fiction in 2022, which she later recrafted and published as *Paint the Walls Red*. Her debut novel, *When All the Birds Sing,* was a finalist in the 2025 ACFW Carol Awards.

Join her newsletter at: suziepeacepybus.com